My Dakota Boys

Carol Benzel-Schmidt

Prov. 3:5,6

By Carol Benzel-Schmidt

PublishAmerica
Baltimore

© 2009 by Carol Benzel-Schmidt.
All rights reserved. No part of this book may be reproduced, stored in a retrieval system or transmitted in any form or by any means without the prior written permission of the publishers, except by a reviewer who may quote brief passages in a review to be printed in a newspaper, magazine or journal.

First printing

All characters in this book are fictitious, and any resemblance to real persons, living or dead, is coincidental.

PublishAmerica has allowed this work to remain exactly as the author intended, verbatim, without editorial input.

Hardcover 978-1-61582-276-8
Softcover 1-60836-776-2
PAperback 978-1-4512-5905-6
PUBLISHED BY PUBLISHAMERICA, LLLP
www.publishamerica.com
Baltimore

Printed in the United States of America

Dedication

To Shirley M. I could not have chosen a more kindred spirit than you for our friendship journey through life. From the time we were toddlers, on to school, marriage, children, grandchildren and even through a move of a thousand miles, our hearts have never been separated. The post office has been kept in business with the hundreds, maybe thousands of hand-written letters that have flowed between us for more than 60 years. Thank you for being you—and for choosing me as your "BSF."

Acknowledgments

To Jackie, diligent proof-reader and "Queen" of errant quotation marks. To the Blue Heron Writers, for their unflagging support, critiques and encouragement—Miriam, Rhonda and Marc. To family and friends who have been waiting and urging me to write the sequel to my first book, "Dakota Breezes"—now you have the continuing saga of the DeFoe family.

Chapter 1

Robin Hudson stared down at the flat brown envelope in her flour-coated hands. The pleasant clink of silverware and low drone of conversation in the café faded away as a feeling of dread settled in the pit of her stomach.

"Robin?" Marietta's voice called her back to her surroundings, and Robin glanced up at the teenage waitress. "Do you have Andy's order ready?" The girl was giving her a quizzical look. And no wonder. This was the busiest time of day at the Sweet Schoppe, the only place to eat in Silverdale. This was not the time to get distracted.

"Coming up." She laid the envelope aside before rinsing her hands and serving up a plate of chicken-fried steak, complete with trimmings.

Questions about the packet bounced around silently in her head. It must be important or else her lawyer would not have sent it. The official-looking envelope had been dropped off by George Olson, a retired gentleman who picked up her mail from the post office along with his own mail. He used his daily stops at the Sweet Schoppe to justify his indulgence of her German delicacies, fresh out of the oven each morning.

Turning to push the steaming plate to the service window, Robin mustered up a smile for Andy Vayle, who owned the lumberyard/feed/hardware store kittykorner across the street from the café. He normally ate his noon meal at home, but today his wife Margie had taken a carload of senior citizens shopping in Rapid City. "Here you go!" Robin gave him a smile that she hoped looked normal as she sat the plate on the serving pass-through.

He saluted her as Marietta took the plate to put in front of him. Seated next to him was Frank Schneider, the mechanic from Silverdale Auto Repair, who was already digging into his meatloaf dinner and kidding about being more special because he had been served first.

Robin glanced past the men to the crowded café and again felt a surge of gratitude for the warm, caring people of the town who patronized her cafe. They had rallied round like one big family when she'd lost her husband Randy two years ago.

None of them knew, however, that she was barely making ends meet, but at least those ends didn't wave at each other at month's end, due to the summer influx of visitors to the Badlands. However, the future was a big question mark. Her growing sons would soon need new shoes, but she put that aside for the time being—God had supplied her needs thus far and she would continue to trust Him.

As soon as there was a lull, Robin left Marietta to take care of customers and wiped her hands on a damp towel. Grabbing the envelope and picking up the lunch she'd packed for the boys, she slipped through the connecting door to the attached apartment at the rear of the café. Heading down the short hall to her private kitchen, she heard childish voices before she rounded the corner.

Her heart melted with love as her gaze fell on her sons, Jason and Jeremy. The companion she'd hired for them for the summer was Andy and Margie's eleven-year-old daughter, Laurie Vayle. The three were bent over colorful papers spread out on the yellow and chrome table that had stood in this kitchen for over fifty years. Laurie wasn't old enough to babysit by herself, but this "mother's helper" job had worked out well for both her and Robin. The young teen gained valuable babysitting experience, as well as having a summer job, and Robin was only a few steps away if needed.

"Look!" cried Jason, her older son of seven years. He held up a folded piece of paper. "We've been making organ gamies!" His little brother, five-year-old Jeremy nodded, holding up his creation. They both had auburn hair, and Randy's good looks were stamped on their features, along with his clear brown eyes. She thanked God that she had them as a reminder of her late husband.

"That's very creative!" she complimented the artists as she set the basket on the table.

"Whatcha got, Mommie?" Jason eyed the basket.

"How would you three like to go out on the lawn for a picnic?"

Both boys jumped up and down, cheering. Jason scraped his papers together. "You comin' too, Mommie?"

"No, honey, I'm going to read my mail, then I have to go back to the café. But you go ahead with Laurie."

"Aww, Mommie," Jeremy sighed, coming to hug her around her legs. Both boys were small for their ages but when they'd had their last inoculations, the doctor had assured her that they were healthy and not to worry. Jeremy laid his head on her thigh and rubbed his cheek against her jeans. Her heart squeezed and she leaned over to give him a hug. There just weren't enough hours in the day to spend the time with them that she'd like.

Laurie got up, tossing her long black braid over her shoulder and came around the table to take the basket. "Come on, guys." She took Jason's hand, cocking a dark eyebrow at Jeremy.

"Go with Laurie and Jason, honey," Robin cooed to him. "It's going to get really hot this afternoon, but right now, the picnic table is in the shade so you won't get sunburned while you eat. I have to read this mail now." She gave him a nudge and watched as he reluctantly followed the other two down the hallway towards the back door.

Her gaze lingered on them. Poor little tykes. Their memories of their father had dimmed to the point they seldom mentioned him. Even as she tried to be both mom and dad to them, she knew she should provide some type of male influence for them. It was times like this that she wished her parents had not retired to Florida. Her father would have been a steadying male figure for them, but then her conscience stabbed her—how could she deny her parents a relaxing retirement after working hard all their lives? Randy's parents too, had moved—Silverdale, South Dakota held too many memories of their only child, and they had never recovered from his death. They didn't completely ignore their grandchildren, but they'd pointedly distanced themselves and let it be known that they would see the children at their instigation. Perhaps it hurt too much for them to see the boys. She sighed. Most people thought the Hudsons would have lived their son's life vicariously through Jason and Jeremy. But most people would have been wrong.

She sank into a kitchen chair and opened the envelope. The words "bankrupt" leaped off the page and she could hardly believe her eyes as she scanned the legal papers.

The connecting door to the café squeaked open and shut, then her best friend, Dorine, poked her head around the doorjamb. "Okay if I come in?"

"You've never needed an invitation before!" Robin quipped, waving her friend in.

Dorine DeFoe, tanned and slender in a white sleeveless blouse, jeans and cowboy boots, plunked down in a chair. "I *asked*, smarty pants, because you're not usually back here during noon hour. What's up?" She eyed the manila envelope in Robin's hands.

The two women had been friends since kindergarten, though they were different in many ways. Dorine was a tall, dark brunette who lived on a ranch and loved horses. Robin was petite with curly reddish hair, lived in town and steered clear of horses. Dorine had gone away to college after high school, while Robin had married her long-time sweetheart the week after graduation. The two women remained the best of friends, sharing their love of the Lord as their strongest bond.

That bond was a lifeline for Robin during the dark days after Randy's accident. A freeway crash had taken her husband's life as he was driving his semi truck back from Texas. Dorine had been Robin's anchor during her grief, but gradually, Robin had regained her balance, her effervescent personality slowly bubbling back to the surface. Only those who knew her well could see the lingering shadows in her hazel eyes.

Now, she thrust the papers at Dorine. "Read for yourself. The trucking company that was supposed to pay compensation for Randy's accident is filing for bankruptcy."

"But it was court-ordered!" Dorine's dark brown eyes perused the legalese, a frown between her brows. Her long hair was French-braided and she absently twirled the curly end of the braid as she read. "They've been paying up to now…now this."

"My lawyer says we can go to court about it, but it will probably be tied up for years, and, we could still lose. In that case, I'd be liable for court expenses and you know that I'm barely making it now." Robin's troubled gaze slid to the small kitchen window where the prairies of South Dakota could be seen, with summer winds rippling the grass in undulating waves like a sea of green and gold.

She sighed. "Maybe my sisters were the smart ones to get out of Silverdale."

Dorine reached over and laid a hand on Robin's arm. "You know you don't mean that. You've always wanted to run the Sweet Schoppe for as long as I can remember."

"Yes, Randy and I had such great dreams. We thought that with his trucking jobs and the café, we could get enough money put aside to remodel this place and after awhile, he could stay home and help me run it." She gazed around the 1950's era kitchen. "His insurance barely stretched beyond the funeral and I even had to sell my old pickup just to keep up the insurance premiums on the café."

Dorine squeezed her arm. "I'm sorry, kiddo. I wish you'd let—"

"No!" Robins eyes flashed. "No," she repeated more quietly. "You're a good friend and I appreciate you sticking by me, but I can't take anything because I'd never be able to pay you back." She raised her chin and a stubborn expression slid over her face.

"I wouldn't want you to repay me," Dorine answered quietly.

Tears welled up in Robin's eyes at her friend's kindness. Dorine had inherited a sizeable ranch when her parents died, and she was now married to one of the DeFoe brothers, who owned the largest ranch east of the Badlands—she could have bought Robin out many times over, but Robin was determined to get through this on her own. So far she was keeping her head above water, by the grace of God. The state had recently opened a gravel pit nearby, and the extra business from the workers had eased her finances somewhat. But if an emergency came up, she was sunk.

She looked back at Dorine. "Thanks," she whispered. Using the edge of her apron, she dabbed a tear from the corner of her eye and stood up. "I better get back out there and help Marietta." She shuffled the business papers into a pile and stuck them into the napkin holder in the center of the table.

Dorine rose too and hugged her. "We'll be praying for you," she whispered.

"Where are those twins of yours?" Robin questioned as the two women moved back out to the café, and Dorine laughingly related her sons' latest escapades.

After closing the café later, Robin cleaned, sweeping and mopping. She probably should have Marietta stay to help, but she was stretching finances now to cover the girl's wages. Glancing over the dining room, she checked to see if tables were set for morning.

Late afternoon sunrays streamed in through the west windows, painting the north wall with burnished gold and dancing along the row of gleaming bakery cases. Overhead fans slowly turned above the crisp red-and-white checked cloths covering round tables, which were surrounded by mismatched chairs. Along the south wall was a row of out-dated wooden booths with worn red vinyl seats that matched the red stools at the counter stretching across the rear of the room. The old-fashioned soda fountain behind the counter had been put in by her German grandparents when they'd opened the Sweet Schoppe more than five decades ago. Robin's mother had run the café/bakery while Robin's dad worked for the telephone company in Kadoka. The Edwards' had raised their six daughters here before turning the café over to Robin and Randy eight years ago.

Robin sighed, drawing her fingers across the nicked but highly-polished wood countertop that had seen years of use. Seemed like she was doing a lot of sighing these days. How would her parents take it when she told them she was about to lose the café that they had poured their hearts into for years?

A cattle truck rumbled by outside, drawing Robin out of her musings. She flipped off the lights and opened the connecting door to walk into her private world.

After supper and cuddling time, she put the boys to bed and heard their prayers. Returning to the kitchen, she pulled out the café's account books. The television was on low volume in the living room down the hallway to keep her company, and she gave a wistful glance out the back door at the lawn and flowers that invited her to "come play in the dirt." She treasured the little garden sign that the antique storeowner, Mrs. Getty, had given her: "You're nearer God's heart in the garden, than anywhere else on earth."

However, her early rising at 4 a.m. precluded twilight gardening and she turned to the ledgers. Working silently, her head bent low over the accounts, a frown began then grew deeper the longer she worked. She slowly put the pen down.

There was no way around it. Figures didn't lie.

She was going to have to close the Sweet Schoppe if something miraculous didn't happen in the next few months.

Her throat burned with tears and her eyes brimmed. Oh, if only Randy were here! A salty tear slid down her cheek and she wiped it off with the back of her hand. Of course, if he were here, she wouldn't be in this financial quandary. She took a tissue and wiped her eyes. She'd always handled the business side but Randy was her supporter, her encourager, her helpmeet. His shoulder was a comforting place to share burdens. A sob shuttered through her before she drew a deep breath and straightened up.

Well, he *wasn't* here, even though she'd wished him back many times. She'd have to figure this out herself, just as she'd done everything else the past two years. She silently prayed, closing her eyes and letting God's peace flow over her. *Take it just one day at a time, don't borrow trouble for tomorrow.*

Finally, putting the books away, she got ready for bed. As she pulled pajamas out of the top bureau drawer in her bedroom, the framed pictures there caught her eye.

Her wedding picture with Randy showed two young people smiling joyfully into the camera and…was it just her, or did Randy look younger? She gently touched the glass over his face with her slim fingertips and it suddenly occurred to her that he'd be forever young. Caught in a timeless moment, he exuded a boyish exuberance that looked forward to a glowing future. A future that was cut short by a flaming accident.

She, however, was growing older and would continue to do so. A wave of loneliness swept over her but the gut-wrenching grief that usually followed had dulled with the passing of time. Was it because Randy was gradually slipping away from her?! *No!* She couldn't let that happen! She had to keep his memory alive, but was dismayed to realize the sound of his voice was fading from her mind. Her fingers dropped and sadness settled over her. She'd been told about the stages of grief but she'd been fiercely determined that it would not happen to her—she needed to remember Randy for the boys' sakes!

But what about you? whispered a little voice. Well-meaning people had hinted that she was too young to spend the rest of her life with only memories for company. In fact, some were trying to set her up with blind dates, but, she wasn't interested. She had her two sons and the café, and even in the far reaches of her imagination, she couldn't picture herself with anyone else.

Her gaze moved to the other framed picture, taken of her and Dorine at the latter's wedding. They'd been clowning around and the photographer had caught them in the act, as well as a few of the wedding guests in the background.

One of those guests was the insurance investigator, Bryce Martin, who had handled the investigation of rustlers on Dorine's ranch while she'd been away at college. He and Dorine's now-husband, Dean DeFoe, had worked together with law enforcement and other area ranchers to capture the criminals. But off the job? Bryce was a swinger!

He wasn't as tall as the DeFoe brothers, but he was well-built, with light brown wavy hair and eyes the color of warm caramel. Most people around Silverdale had become accustomed to seeing him that summer as he came and went while unobtrusively gathering information for his case.

A slight smile tilted her lips. At least *he* thought he was unobtrusive—he had no idea of how the grapevine worked in a small town. He'd been in the café a number of times and she'd caught him giving her the eye. It had amused her, but at the same time, she'd had to admit she liked the fact that she hadn't lost her attraction for the opposite sex—even after two pregnancies that left her "pleasingly plump."

She placed her hands at her sides now, having no trouble counting the ribs that used to be swaddled under that layer of "pleasing plumpness." Grief had slimmed and aged her, although

Dorine scoffed when Robin voiced her opinion of her looks. "Yeah, and pigs will fly," Dorine had retorted with her favorite saying.

Smiling faintly, Robin's gaze went back to the handsome Bryce. She'd once told Dorine that she thought he was a "hunk." He *was* a hunk, but he'd known it too, and chased after anything with skirts and a heartbeat. He'd returned to St. Louis after the rustlers were convicted, and no one heard from him again except the DeFoes, who kept in touch with Christmas cards.

She turned away, putting Bryce out of her mind, his image being replaced with the concern over her finances. Taking her Bible, she read her devotions, then slipped to her knees beside the bed to pray. She poured out her heart to the One who had been her Comforter and Friend since she was a young child. Afterwards, she fell asleep in peace, knowing her Heavenly Father was watching over her.

A small, warm body crawling into her bed awakened her. She glanced at the clock as she pulled Jeremy close to her, breathing in his sweet little boy scent. Her heart swelled with love. What would she ever do without her little ones?

"I love you, Mommie," he murmured, slipping his arms around her neck.

"I love you too, Jeremy."

She laid there a few more minutes until Jeremy's steady breathing told her that he had fallen asleep, then she rose to shower and dress in jeans and a cool white cotton blouse.

Peeking in at the boys one last time, Robin went quietly to the connecting door that opened into the café and slipped through. Laurie would arrive later through the unlocked back door, sacking out on the sofa until the boys woke up.

The sun was just peeking over the horizon behind the sleepy town, reflecting brilliant beams off the windows of the lumberyard building across the street and bouncing them back to light up the dining area of the café. Shadows still lurked in the café kitchen and she automatically flipped on the overhead lights as she prepared to make her famous German *kucken*. She chuckled. Well, famous in Jackson County, South Dakota at least!

A few hours later and a thousand miles away, Bryce Martin moved restlessly around his office, jingling his keys in his pocket and gazing at the St. Louis skyline spread out before him. Just a few more days and he would be lying on a sandy beach in the Caribbean, with a scantily-clad beauty beside him, enjoying a much-awaited vacation. The cuisine was an experience to look forward to also, but first things first: women, then food.

His reverie was interrupted by a knock at the door and Carla Williams, his assistant, came in with file folders she placed on his desk. He smiled at her absentmindedly when she gave him a coy look. "Already on that Caribbean beach?" she teased.

He nodded, not immune to the silent invitation in her green eyes. With her black hair in a stylish cut, her careful grooming and meticulous makeup, she was definite eye candy. Bryce, however, had a rule about dating co-workers, even though they often went out to business lunches together. Almost every single executive, and some of the married ones too, in the office, would give a right arm for a date with Carla, because not only was she glamorous, but there was a shrewd mind behind the glamour.

"We could go out to lunch before you go…just the two of us," she purred, sliding her well-manicured fingers along the edge of his desk. "I'm buying."

He glanced at his watch. "Sure, why not? You got time today?" He wasn't entirely comfortable with a woman buying him lunch, but this was the twenty-first century and equality reigned—if she wanted to treat, he'd take her up on it.

Lunch was pleasant but he adroitly side-stepped Carla's subtle hints for after-work drinks. At last, she took to pouting. "You and your ridiculous rules! Getting together for cocktails isn't exactly dating!"

He smiled at her, unperturbed. "Every man in this place is secretly drooling over you. You could have your pick." Carla had not been employed by the company when an inner-office scandal had rocked the business and sent one senior partner and his secretary off in disgrace. That's when Bryce's rule went into effect.

She opened her mouth again and he held up his hand. "No more talk—just let me admire your beauty from afar." She smiled smugly at his blatant flattery.

When they returned to the office, he set to work on the files but after an hour, his eyes wandered back to the window. The restlessness assailed him once again. Man, he really needed this vacation!

Swinging his chair around, he looked at the large map of the country on his back wall. The districts his company covered ranged widely across the Midwest, and his eyes were drawn almost magnetically to the Black Hills and Badlands of South Dakota.

Several years ago, he'd investigated the case of rustlers that operated in the Dakotas and Nebraska, and they'd finally been caught by the FBI, aided by his diligent surveillance. Just before they'd moved in, rancher Dorine Andrews had stumbled onto the rustlers and had been kidnapped. Bryce had helped rescue her, and shortly afterwards Dorine and her neighbor Dean DeFoe had married.

He always got a Christmas card from them. They had twin boys about a year after their marriage and his eyes shifted to a framed picture of the twins that Dorine had sent him last Christmas, along with an invitation to visit them again in the "wild west."

A sudden impulse seized him—why not? Why wait? He could always go to the Caribbean next year. Before he could rethink his impulse, he reached for the phone while wondering if he still had the western clothes and boots he had bought four years ago in Rapid City.

Chapter 2

Dorine DeFoe was chasing one of her three-year-old twins through the large kitchen when the wall telephone rang from the hallway. The little scamp was in trouble—yet again—and giggling uproariously as he dodged into the utility room.

Keeping an eye on the door, Dorine lifted the receiver and greeted the caller.

"Hey, Dorine! This is Bryce Martin—remember me?"

An image of the handsome investigator came to mind and she smiled. "How could anyone ever forget you, Bryce! How are you? Coming to visit soon?" she teased.

"You must be a mind-reader! Is your invitation still open?"

"You're kidding! I was just teasing, but *of course* you're welcome to come!"

He knew her delight wasn't feigned. "This is short notice, but I had a change of plans."

"How soon can you be here?"

"I wouldn't be putting you out?" he inquired. "How about next week?"

"We'd love to have you. It's pretty busy, but we'll put you to work!"

"Sure, I'll be glad to pitch in." He continued on in an exaggerated drawl, "Got a hankerin' for the wild west."

Dorine chuckled softly. "I'm just teasing. We wouldn't want you to work on your vacation. But," she frowned as she looked at the calendar on the wall, "we've got meetings scheduled that I'm afraid can't be postponed, and I wouldn't want to neglect a guest."

"Look, I don't need to be entertained. I'd like to fit in with your schedule, just be one of the cowboys—if I can still ride a horse. I could help on round up." His voice ended on a hopeful note.

"Sorry, Bryce, roundup was a month ago. But if you're serious about helping, we're hauling hay next week."

"That sounds…interesting."

She laughed. "It's not exactly cowboy work but has to be done to get winter feed in. When will you be arriving? Dean will be glad to see you."

"Only Dean?" he asked hopefully.

"Stop fishing! When should we expect you?"

"I'm leaving Saturday with a stop in Sioux Falls, so beginning of next week? I have three weeks but I won't have to stay all that time."

"Why not?" She paused. "Where else can we get cheap labor?"

Bryce laughed heartily before answering. "I'll work that husband of yours right into the ground!"

"Dream on," she snorted. "Have you ever even seen a hay bale?"

After finalizing details, they hung up. Dorine turned to see her tall, handsome husband come in the outer entrance, letting the screen door clap shut. He crossed the concrete floor of the sunroom to step up into the kitchen, his brilliant blue eyes glowing as he spotted her. In a few long strides, he had his arms around her, drawing her close.

Burying his nose in her hair, he murmured, "Who was that on the phone?"

"What phone?" she dreamily replied, running her hands up and down his back.

He laughed and pulled away to gaze at her flirtatiously. "I can never figure out why a good-looking woman like you would want a broken down ole cowboy like me!"

"You poor decrepit thing! All of thirty-six and we'll soon need a wheelchair for you."

He kissed her, then raised his head to listen. "It's too quiet, where are the boys?"

"*Your* son just poured bubblebath in the toilet and I was chasing him down when the phone rang, so he's hiding out," Dorine answered as she pushed out of his arms. "I saw him slip into the utility room but he may have gotten outside while I was on the phone. Speaking of which, you'll never guess who that was!" He waited expectantly as she searched his eyes, smiling mysteriously.

"You know I hate guessing games," he growled, pushing his hat back with his thumb.

"You don't like guessing games?" She pretended she didn't know about one of his pet peeves. Relenting, she answered, "That was Bryce Martin, and he wants to come visit for a few weeks. He thought he'd like to experience the 'wild west'."

"It can't get any wilder than with David and Doug," he referred to their twins as he moved to the utility room and opened the door. "Empty. Which one was it? As if I didn't know," he mumbled as he turned to go back out through the sunroom. He stopped. "And by the way, why are they *my* sons when they're bad and *yours* when they're good?"

"That's just the rule, cowboy, live with it."

He grinned and went looking for David.

Bryce loved driving with the top down on his flashy, candy red convertible, tapping his fingers on the steering wheel in time with soft rock music wafting from the radio. The air was comfortably warm as the breeze ruffled his hair. A bunch of teens roared past him in a customized pickup, giving him thumbs up as they stared enviously at his car. The sky was blue and clear, and after leaving St. Louis, the interstate was less crowded and he sailed right along.

It couldn't get much better than this.

After a time, he got out of range of the radio station and the music faded into static. Switching dials, he heard the announcer ask, "What is God's plan for your life?" He quickly flipped on past. Some long-winded preacher suckering people into his religion.

Later, he exited the freeway into Sioux Falls to hook up with a college friend/now partner who was anxious to show off the new restaurant in which the two men had invested, Bryce as the silent partner. Mark had been his roommate and had supplied them with many a gourmet meal. Bryce himself, had unexpectedly discovered a talent for cooking that he would never have been allowed to explore in his parent's elegant home. He and Mark frequently entertained their dates in their off-campus apartment, and acquired quite a reputation for the cuisine they served. Among other things.

He smiled, smoothing down his wind-blown hair—those women should not have been forgettable, but he laughed out loud as he realized he couldn't even remember their names!

Greeting Mark, he spent a pleasant evening with his friend, touring the restaurant followed by dinner. They discussed plans to expand into a chain of restaurants that already spilled over into Nebraska and was spreading west into South Dakota. Bryce was content being the "silent partner," happy that Mark looked after his interests as well as his own. They talked far into the night, but Bryce was up early the next morning, anxious to start his "wild west" adventure.

With the rising sun behind him, he hit the freeway and made very few stops during the day. Those were to gas up, eat, and snap a few scenic photos along the way.

It was a relief from the monotonous prairie when he drove off the interstate at the Silverdale exit. He noted that more freeway businesses had sprung up since he was last here, adding to travelers' comfort.

Turning left under the freeway, he found he had the two-lane state road all to himself as he drove towards his destination. All over the rural Midwest, sleepy little towns like Silverdale basked in summer heat while traffic buzzed by on the interstate, taking tourist dollars to more dramatic sights like the Black Hills and Mount Rushmore.

Approaching the "city" limits sign, he slowed, seeing children ahead on their bikes. He relished their stares at his car as he coasted past—they probably didn't see anything like his convertible out here. He was preening—so what? He'd earned it!

The township was like a green quilt block on the brows and tans of the prairie, with its tree-shaded residential area stretching off to his right, and browned pastures to his left. Ahead, the long main thoroughfare was wide and paved only in the middle, guarded by stands of towering cottonwood trees grouped here and there. A dated, white two-story high school with a proud sign announcing it was the "Home of the Silverdale Bisons," was connected with a covered walkway to a newer red brick elementary school and gym. Between the buildings, the playground and sports fields were visible at the rear.

As Bryce continued at a leisurely pace, he noted the crumbling sidewalk that paralleled the road, lined with straggly grass in front of a few small houses and newer mobile homes with postage stamp-sized lawns sandwiched between weedy lots. Along tree-lined side streets, he glimpsed heavily-shaded lawns with larger homes set back from the curbing.

The two-block business district had both old weathered buildings and a few newer ones on either side of the street, crowding up to disintegrating sidewalks. It was quiet, hot and deserted, the sound of his tires crunching on the roadside gravel echoing back from the cool shade of the cottonwoods.

He passed a tavern on his left that had a few dirt-encrusted ranch pickups clustered around it, and farther along was a new postoffice and a new fire station building, proof that the population wasn't about to sink to "ghost town" status.

The next building brought a grin to his face. A Lilliputian-sized pink stucco bank building had an eight by eight foot lobby that housed only an ATM machine, antique "wanted' posters, and fake teller windows with real iron grates in front. He chuckled as he remembered how he'd thought to do some banking there four years ago, and his surprise at learning there was nothing in the bank except that ATM machine!

Most of the older buildings had settled on their aging foundations, dried weeds along the old concrete having given up the battle for moisture. A few buildings were boarded up, others stared out through broken windows and dangling wood frames.

But there were more businesses that loudly proclaimed the town was still alive, with flower planters and hanging baskets that were a bright contrast to the dusty streets. There was a newly-built community club that flaunted a small lawn of verdant grass in front, as did the churchyard. The old community club sported a sign advertising antiques. The general store's wide cement steps, painted a soft gold, held pots of bright pink and purple flowers, sheltered by an overhead canopy of green vines twining up from more large ceramic pots. Just beyond was a junkyard, a car repair shop and the lumberyard.

The most eye-catching spot along the whole main street however, was the Sweet Schoppe where he had taken Dorine for lunch before she was married. It was tucked in between a narrow vacant lot and a two-story brick building with boarded up windows that exuded an air of abandonment. In sharp contrast to it, the flat-topped white café building had window boxes overflowing with brilliant red flowers that echoed the cherry red-and-white café curtains behind them. All along the almost non-existent curb in front, were big pots of more overflowing red flowers. He nodded approvingly as he briefly thought about the plump little woman who owned the cafe. What was her name again? Something that started with an R. Rachael? Rebecca? Oh, well, she was married anyway. He loved women but he never messed around with engaged or married women. Too much trouble down that road.

Speeding up as he exited the town, he noticed dust had settled on the car's shiny finish and he frowned. That was one thing he'd forgotten, the constant dust out here in ranch country. Even though the county roads were paved, the shoulders were gravel and dirt, and dust blew over from the fields on either side. He'd have to wash that off as soon as possible. A lively little dustdevil whirled along in the field beside him, then crossed the road, scattering dirt and leaves in his path. He braked and waited for the dustdevil to veer off into the field, then continued on.

Turning in under the impressive wrought iron entrance of DeFoe Enterprises, he slowed to let his car creep over the metal cattle guards put in the roadway to prevent animals from getting out. Picking up speed on the paved lane to the homestead, he admired red-coated Herefords grazing in pastures on either side. The family had done well for themselves and he was happy for the hard-working bunch. Dean, the oldest, and Darrell DeFoe, his younger brother, ran the ranch, as well as numerous other sidelines such as a western clothing store chain and oil rights on ranches in Texas and Oklahoma.

An oasis of towering green trees separated the homestead from the business offices and barns of DeFoe Enterprises. He took a left at the fork in the road as he approached the shelterbelt of cottonwoods, the house coming into sight around a slight curve. Cranking the wheel, he came to a stop on the gravel bib in front of the manicured lawn where the stately trees gave the impression of guarding the family home. The three-story house was surrounded by expansive lush lawns hemmed in by lilac bushes and low borders of colorful flowers along the walkway. He'd been told that Grandfather Dean had updated the stone and shake house decades ago, but it had been done in such a way as to blend the old with the new. As Bryce got out, he welcomed the cooling mist from a lawn sprinkler that caught the sun's rays and threw them out in a kaleidoscope of color.

The screen door opened as he went up the walk, and Dorine stepped out to meet him. He was struck again by her dark beauty, her fluid grace and hospitality. Four years ago, he'd hoped for a relationship with her, but her heart already belonged to her cowboy.

"Hi, we've been waiting for you!" she exclaimed, extending her hands. Her slender figure was clad in jeans, white tennis shoes and a sleeveless pink western blouse. Glancing at the car behind him she added, "Nice set of wheels!"

Grasping her hands with both of his, he smiled into her chocolate brown eyes. "Yep! My chick magnet!" he winked. "And you haven't changed a bit, darlin'! It's a wonder some Hollywood scout hasn't snapped you up!" He gave her a peck on the cheek.

"And you've been kissing the Blarney Stone!" she retorted, raising an eyebrow. "It's good to see you, Bryce," she added sincerely. "Come on in. The twins are napping, so we'll have a few quiet moments to ourselves." The cool interior of the house welcomed him as he followed her across the sunroom and into the house. "Dean is at the office and said he'd come over when he saw your car." The screen door snapped shut behind them, and she gestured for him to sit by the large, round oak table in the spacious kitchen.

Over glasses of iced tea, she brought him up to date about people he'd met previously—Dean's widowed mother Marcie, who lived with them but was gone at present to visit her daughter in Texas; Mrs. Mac, the "housekeeper" who was more family than employee, had accompanied Marcie; and Darrell, Dean's brother, who was on the rodeo circuit this year, trying for his second world championship.

Conversation turned to the ranch that Dorine had inherited, which her middle-aged cousin was supposed to be managing for her while she had been away at college. But he'd given into the greedy scheme that cattle rustlers had offered and as a consequence, had spent time in prison. Bryce remembered well, how devastated Dorine had been.

"So, have you incorporated your ranch into the DeFoe Enterprises?" he asked, sipping at his tea. He sat in a relaxed pose, his right sandaled foot resting on his left knee.

"We were going to turn it into a dude ranch, only the Lord changed our direction and the Circle A is now the base for homeless teens. They have to prove themselves before being granted the privilege of working on the ranch," she finished.

At mention of the Lord, Bryce inwardly scoffed—he didn't want anything to do with religion; it was just a crutch people used instead of common sense, but at the same time, he didn't want to alienate his hostess.

Dorine's eyes took on a faraway look. "It's strange, but I never felt the same about my place after the rustlers vandalized the house. I'd go in, even after it had been repaired and painted," she shook her head slightly, "and I always felt...violated. I'd grown up there, it was the only home I'd ever known...but suddenly it was a strange place..." she shuddered. "Something like that changes everything."

A rubber ball suddenly came bouncing down the stairs beyond the kitchen, through the short hallway and rolled past his feet. He cast a glance at Dorine, raising one eyebrow.

"The boys must be up from their naps. Boys! Come meet our guest," she called. To him she added, "We remodeled the third floor into our own quarters," she rose from her chair, "and had to put gates up when the boys were learning to walk, but they're old enough now to come down by themselves."

Even though he had pictures of the twins, he wasn't prepared for the two little charmers with dark curly hair and brilliant blue eyes that peeked around the edge of the door. They giggled and ducked back.

"Bashful?" he asked.

"Sometimes….at first," Dorine said wryly, then added, "but after that, watch out!"

On impulse, he got up and walked almost to the door, dropped on his knees and peeked around the doorjamb, growling low in his throat.

Squeals and thumps sounded as the surprised twins ran for safety. He stood up and laughed.

"Oh, *that* will win you friends and influence people!" Walking around him, she looked up the stairs. "Boys! Don't you want to meet Bryce?"

Giggles sounded from the floor above. "When you get ready to come down, there's ice cream," she called in a sing-song voice, heading back to the kitchen.

As Bryce turned to follow her, his eye was caught by photos on a bulletin board hanging on the wall by the phone. He was fairly good with a camera and always enjoyed looking at other people's photos. "Who's this cute little redhead with the two boys?"

Dorine retraced her steps to his side. "That's Robin, the one who owns the café where you took me to lunch that time, remember?"

"No way! That woman was…" his voice trailed off uncertainly.

She smiled knowingly. "Plump?"

"No, I was going to say, 'a nice armful'."

"Good save!" she chortled, heading for the refrigerator.

"I don't remember her being such a looker!" He settled back into his chair, taking a long swallow of the icy tea. When Dorine didn't answer, he glanced at her where she was filling the coffee maker. Her smile had faded and sadness filled her eyes.

"Her husband was killed two years ago in a freeway crash and she was inconsolable."

"Bummer," Bryce murmured sincerely.

"He was a long-haul truck driver and someone plowed headfirst into him. The semi burst into flames...they couldn't get him out in time..." her voice trailed off and she gazed out the kitchen window with a sorrowful expression. "They were so in love...it wasn't long before the pounds started dropping off her," she added pensively.

The nature of Bryce's job required that he rein in his emotions while dealing with unsavory characters, but the thought of Robin being widowed so young moved his heart. "That would be tough to face," he murmured, setting his glass down and turning it around and around in its own circle of moisture on the table.

Dorine heaved a long sigh, then brightened as she turned back to him. "Anyway, she's over the worst part now. The Lord is her anchor and He's uplifted her."

"So, that means she's available for dating." He ignored her reference to the Lord.

Dorine snorted inelegantly. "Not!"

"Why not? She's free to do whatever she wants."

"She doesn't have the slightest desire to date." She slanted him a questioning look. "Are you thinking of asking her out?"

"Oh," he picked up his glass and held it high enough to squint through the amber liquid, "I thought she was pretty cute when I was here before, and now...well, she's even cuter." He set his glass down and looked innocently at Dorine. "Plus, she's available."

She shook her head and moved to open a cabinet door. "No dice, Bryce. She won't go. She's been asked, but she's not in the market for a relationship. She's got the boys and the café to run, there's no room in her life for anything else."

"Well," he smiled smugly, "I'll just have to see if I can change her mind. I've got several weeks to do it."

Dorine gave him a somber look. "Bryce, even if Robin *did* date, she wouldn't be casual about it. A guy would have to mean something to her before she'd want to spend any time with him. And *definitely* no summer romances!"

"Oh," he replied cockily, "I think I can charm her around."

"Keep in mind that she's the girl next door type, not a party girl."

The screen door squeaked opened then slammed shut, followed by footsteps heading their way. Dean appeared in the kitchen doorway, and his eyes danced with welcome as he spotted their guest. "Hello there, Bryce!" He crossed the kitchen with purposeful strides, his hand outstretched. Except for more crinkles around his eyes, Dean DeFoe looked the same—scuffed boots, well-worn jeans and plaid western shirt. One would never know the way he dressed, that this man was CEO of a large business empire.

Dorine poured coffee while they chatted, and brought out a moist chocolate cake. The twins finally ventured to the kitchen and hid behind their dad's chair. Bryce leaned forward and tried cajoling the youngsters to sit next to him, while Dorine got out the ice cream.

"I suspect you have a lot of patience, but it surprises me that you can sit there so calmly and work on making friends with them! Have you been around kids much?" Dorine asked as she set small plates of cake and ice cream in front of the two men.

Bryce shook his head without taking his eyes off where the boys would peek out.

"Well, I've got the real bait, right here!" she winked as she set two bowls of ice cream on the table for the boys. That brought them out slowly before scrambling into their chairs. They eyed Bryce shyly for a few more moments, gradually warming up with Dean's encouragement, and before long, they were chattering away a mile a minute.

Bryce was thoroughly captivated. He couldn't tell the difference between the two but noticed right away that one was more outgoing than the other. "How do you tell them apart?" he asked in amazement as Dorine was pouring glasses of milk for the boys.

"We can tell the difference but you'd be surprised at how they've already learned to fool people," she answered, her gaze straying lovingly to the two little scamps. The little "scamps" in question looked at each other and grinned.

"It was hard at first," Dean admitted as he deftly caught a glass of milk bumped by a little elbow, "but after you're around them awhile, you can tell the difference."

Bryce shook his head. "I'm afraid it would take me longer than just a little while."

"Oh, surely not!" Dorine chided, using a sponge to wipe up the drops of milk that had spilled. "With your eye for detail, you'd learn fast."

Bryce leaned back and squinted at the twins, which brought giggles from their side of the table. "Which one of you is David?"

The twins looked at each other, grinned and each pointed at the other. "He is!" Their faces were endearingly smeared with ice cream.

"I don't envy you in a few years," Bryce said as Dean stood and scraped back his chair, shaking his head.

"Come on boys, let's show Bryce how cowboys work."

"Yea, yea!" The twins tumbled from their chairs and rushed towards the porch.

"Whoa, guys!" Dorine stopped them in her tracks. "Wash." She pointed towards the utility washroom.

"Awww," they complained. But they complied, then scrambled back to where the men waited. "Are we gonna make him step in some horse stuff?" asked one twin. They grabbed miniature cowboy hats from pegs that were fastened to the wall at their height.

Dean turned to Bryce. "*That* one is David."

"I'll be on the lookout for him...and for the horse stuff!" Bryce replied, laughing as they trooped out the door. The boys crammed their misshapen hats on their heads and galloped ahead like they were riding horses.

Touring the facilities, Bryce was impressed by the equipment and technology needed to run the everyday work of the ranch. No more an "Aw shucks" type of venture, DeFoe Enterprises was as modern as Bryce's own office in St. Louis. Secretaries and an office manager acknowledged his presence as they sat at state of the art computers, while a fax machine silently slid out correspondence.

The twins were obvious favorites, as they received special greetings and hugs from the women. After Bryce checked for wedding bands—and finding them—his attitude remained friendly but polite, turning his attention to the boys instead.

Watching them, Bryce had never been so entertained, nor so surprised, at the energy and curiosity of the miniature boys. Nor at the patience their big cowboy father exhibited. After they left the office and went into the barns, Dean was constantly pulling them out of harm's way as they went along.

Bryce hadn't been around children much, and he found he liked their innocent babble as the afternoon slid by. The twins exhibited a remarkable knowledge of ranch life, making him feel woefully inadequate in that department. But knowing that his ignorance kept the boys entertained, he played it up.

Helping the little ones wash up before supper left Bryce wet down the front, Dean scolding and Dorine laughing as she set a platter of fried chicken on the table. When they were seated, Bryce waited for Dorine to pick up her fork, but instead, she held out her hands to Dean on one side and David on the other.

"We ask a blessing on our food," Dean explained, "and join hands around the table."

Looking down into the expectant blue eyes of the twins, Bryce reluctantly took each of their hands and followed their example by bowing his head while Dean prayed. Inwardly, he squirmed—did they have to carry their religion even to the table?!

As soon as "Amen" sounded, the two little scamps clamored for Bryce to help them with their plates, and he had one of the most enjoyable, if messy, meals that he could ever remember.

After supper and a swim in the pool, which was enclosed in a fenced area adjacent to the house, the twins were drooping. Dorine whisked them off for baths while Bryce and Dean brought the luggage in from Bryce's car and climbed the stairs to one of the many guest rooms on the second floor.

The men had just decided to go downstairs to watch a ball game on tv, when Bryce heard the twins out in the hall, begging Dorine to let him hear their prayers. He was relieved when she replied that Mr. Martin was a guest, here to visit with their daddy.

"But Mommie, we's hafta pray for him!"

Bryce stilled, holding his breath while he waited for Dorine's reply.

"You can do that without him being there." He let his breath out.

"Mommie, we want him there! Hims gots nobody to pray for him!" They had plied him with questions earlier and seemed distraught that he had no "brovers."

The childish words crept into Bryce's heart. The twins were right—he didn't know anyone religious enough to pray, let alone pray for *him*. Their innocent concern touched a chord in his chest.

He glanced at Dean to find him grinning and stepping out into the hallway. "It looks like you're going to get prayed for whether you want it or not," he chuckled. "Go ahead, I have to check that mare one more time. I'll be back in later to watch the game."

"Mommie, pul-eeeaze?" Dorine met Bryce's gaze as he came out of the room, and raised her eyebrows. The twins, their faces scrubbed pink and smelling of soap, implored him with doleful eyes.

He crumbled.

Accompanying the scamps to their third-floor bedroom, he sat awkwardly on the bed while the little guys flopped down on their knees. They folded their hands, squeezing their eyes shut tight as Dorine leaned one shoulder against the door, her arms folded over her chest.

"Dear God, thanks for taday, for sunshine and rain, for Mommie and Daddy," prayed Doug.

"Bless Grandma D., Mrs. Mac...and, and, and Mr. Martin. Help him ta have a good vacation with us. Amen!" David almost shouted the last word before leaping to his feet and hurling himself at Bryce's chest.

"Whoa!" Bryce exclaimed as the small body propelled him onto his back. Both boys jumped on him, trying to hug him around the neck. He tickled them and before long they were all rolling around on the twin bed, laughing and shouting.

"Okay, guys, that's enough," Dorine interrupted. "Including the big guy."

Bryce looked up, his hair mussed and clothing askew. "They attacked *me*!" he complained good-naturedly as he rolled off the bed and stood, pulling his polo shirt down with one hand while running the other hand through his hair.

"A likely story." She grabbed David and flopped him down while Doug dutifully crawled into his own bed. "You guys are all red-faced and sweaty now. That means another bath."

Two pairs of blue eyes looked accusingly at Bryce. "Hims did it! It's he's fault! Make him take a baf!"

"Yes, that would be interesting," Bryce muttered slyly under his breath. "Would you wash my back?"

"In your dreams," Dorine replied, shooing him out the door while she settled the boys.

And so started his vacation.

Chapter 3

Robin rinsed out the mop and pulled it through the bucket wringer, glad the day was over. She'd propped the door open between the café and her apartment so she could keep an eye on the boys as they watched cartoons in the living room. Her mind raced with ideas of how to ease her financial dilemma. She entertained, then discarded, a number of prospects while she mopped and wiped. "Lord, how am I going to keep going?" she whispered. "You know the future but I don't. I'd really like a clue."

Trust Me.

The words weren't audible but she looked around nonetheless. She consciously relaxed her stiff shoulders and closed her eyes. "I know that You'll take care of my needs. I just have trouble remembering to bring my burdens to You."

More peaceful now, she dumped the water, rinsed the bucket and turned it upside down to dry. Hanging the mop up, she washed her hands, dried them and hurried to join the boys.

"Mommie! Mommie!" Gladness rippled through her heart and suddenly she didn't feel so weary. Playing with the boys diverted her from the pressing issues that were never far from her mind, giving her brain a much-needed rest.

They all puttered in the flowerbeds, Robin pulling weeds and the boys running back and forth with little watering cans.

But later, lying in bed, thoughts of her uncertain future kept sleep at bay. She went over her options again and again, but the months ahead were shrouded in uncertainty. She knew the Lord would provide for her and tried to focus on that. "Be not anxious, neither worry," St. Paul admonished in the New Testament. She read her devotions and fell asleep praying.

The next morning, Dorine called Robin to tell her that Bryce had arrived, and that he was the same old Bryce, a swinging bachelor with an eye for women. "So, heads up," she concluded. "He saw the picture of you on my bulletin board."

"As if!" Robin hooted, dismissing the idea of her attracting the suave man-about-town. They chatted for a few more minutes before Robin returned to baking loaves of cinnamon and raisin bread, but curiously, thoughts of Bryce continued to flit through her head while she mixed and baked.

She felt a stab of guilt for not praying consistently for Bryce when Dorine said he was still a slick-talking playboy. The two women had prayed for his salvation for months after he returned back East, but with everything else happening in her life, Bryce had slipped her memory. However, it wasn't too late to pray for him now. While her hands created bakery delights, her lips moved in silent prayer.

For the next couple of days, Bryce accompanied Dean around the ranch and was pleased that he retained most of what he'd previously learned. He was especially proud that Dean thought he had a "good seat" on his horse. They searched for stray calves and Bryce practiced his roping skills, declared "not bad" by Dean.

He helped load a semi-truck of cattle and worked out in the gym that Dean and Darrell had installed as part of their program to start a rodeo school for aspiring cowboys. He visited with the secretaries in Dean's main office and even helped them locate a computer glitch. He swam in the pool and played with the boys, amazed that he had such a rapport with kids. Who knew?

He was learning things about himself that he'd never suspected—the number one being, he was content without a woman fawning over him. Strange. Of course, there *were* no women around to impress—Dean's office personnel were all hands off. So he was stuck with himself. He wasn't one for deep soul searches, but there was no denying the peace and laid-back attitude of ranch life had affected him. He realized it the day he rode out with Dean to mend fences.

A quietness surrounded them, the stillness broken only by the sound of the horses' hooves in the soft prairie dirt path and jingling of the bridle bits. The sun beamed overhead, a breeze gently stirred the grasses, and birds flew up to soar into the blue sky, bursting with their cheerful song. The air was fresh, laden with the faint smell of sage, and Bryce could see why some people chose this life. It was a far cry from city streets choked with cars, exhaust fumes and teeming humanity. But he loved the city, the energy, the challenges, the social whirl. He gazed around him, knowing that this vacation would only point out how unsuited he would be in Dean's place. In the meantime, it was an enjoyable interlude and he was glad he could experience it.

The saddle creaked when he shifted his weight and sighing contentedly, he was lulled into drowsiness by the sway of the horse's gait. For a moment, he wondered what it would be like to live here…but only a moment. He'd never make it out here without the ladies—*that* much he knew about himself!

He was yanked out of his daydreaming and almost unseated when his horse suddenly shook its head and sidestepped, warily eyeing a buzzing insect trying to land on its nose. He adjusted his hat and shifted back into the saddle, grinning to himself. He was glad Dean was ahead of him.

They arrived at the broken spot in the fence and climbed down off their mounts. While they worked, they conversed about Bryce's job and the sometimes dangerous aspects of it, which Bryce downplayed. He watched the rancher pry sagging wire off the broken post. Bryce stood ready with the shovel when Dean pulled the broken post out so he could enlarge the hole. Their conversation eventually turned to families and Dean admitted that he couldn't imagine life without Dorine and the twins. David and Doug DeFoe were named for each of their grandfathers, carrying on the tradition of the "Double D's."

While Dean dropped the new post into the hole, he squinted at Bryce. "You ever think of settling down and having a family?"

Bryce threw a shovelful of dirt around the bottom of the post, then stood to wipe the sweat from his forehead with his arm. "Nope! I've seen too many broken marriages, the divorce rate is like what? One in three? No thanks! I like my life just the way it is."

"You don't know what you're missing," Dean grunted as he tamped the dirt around the post.

"Oh, yessss, I do!" Bryce drew out the words. Then realizing how that must have sounded, he quickly added, "Well, you and Dorine are probably in the minority of marriages that are making it, but I sure wouldn't bet on the odds. I've seen guys go off the deep end when their marriages end."

Dean stopped and took off his glove, wiping his forehead. "It used to be that farm and ranch marriages stayed for the long haul, but that isn't true anymore. Sometimes guys marry women from the city and they can't take the isolation of ranch life. Dorine and I have that going for us, we both grew up here and knew what we were getting into when we married. Plus we've known each other all our lives." He grinned at Bryce. "There isn't anything like marriage to make a man's life complete."

"I'll take your word for it!" Bryce threw the last shovelful of dirt around the post while Dean wiggled it to make sure it was solid.

"The good far outweighs the bad, I'll tell you," Dean replied as he took the tamping bar and finished packing the loose dirt. "There's nothing like having your own son come running to greet you at the end of a hard day. No matter how many troubles, they have a way of making everything right."

"Your little guys sure love you, anyone can see that. But that life's not for me!"

"You're a natural with kids, look how they swarm all over you. And believe me, dogs and kids can usually peg a person right away."

"I'm just a diversion from their usual routine, they'll forget me when I'm gone." Bryce wiped his face again and looked around. "Do we need another post, or will that do it?"

Dean moved along with the change of subject and they were soon finished, heading back to the ranch house and supper.

Bryce could smell the pot roast before they opened the door and his stomach growled. "How does she manage to cook like this with everything else she does?" he wondered aloud.

Dorine stuck her head around the washroom door. "You guys aren't the only ones with tech toys! I push buttons and food magically appears," she teased.

"Whatever. All I know is if you weren't married, I'll haul you off into the sunset."

Dorine raised one eyebrow. "And pigs will fly."

"I'd have something to say about that," Dean said at the same time. He rested a heavy hand on Bryce's shoulder, leaving no doubt what he thought about Bryce flirting with his wife. At the same time, he guided his guest toward the heavily-laden table.

Potatoes, carrots and onions were swimming in the juices from the roast that had made its own gravy for the vegetables. Completing the meal were homemade dill pickles, red beets and fresh lettuce from the garden, along with lighter-than-air biscuits hot out of the oven. He was in awe of this woman who capably ran the household and assisted in the office, even entering occasional rodeo events. All without breaking stride. He wondered if she was a vanishing breed, this focused ranch wife with so many talents—and beauty to boot. What a lucky man Dean was!

Sitting down to the table, Bryce was ready now for the prayer, shutting out the words and thinking of the bowl of steaming browned potatoes at his elbow. Apple crisp was dessert and Bryce voiced his contentment at the end of the meal.

"I enjoy cooking," Dorine commented. "But there's lots of things I *don't* do—I don't sew, I have little interest in interior decorating and I don't do scrapbooking." Bryce looked blank so she explained. "It's all the rage now, putting photographs in acid-free albums decorated with stickers and fancy background paper."

"Whatever floats your boat," he grinned. "All I know is your meals are to die for." He was almost sorry he had promised his head office to check into the Rapid City branch of the insurance company, which was on his agenda for the next day—he'd miss the noon meal here at the ranch. On the other hand, there *were* pretty women in that office.

When he passed the Sweet Schoppe on his way through town to the freeway, an idea popped into his head. Why not drop in on that little redhead on his way back? After all, there wasn't a wedding ring to deter him now. He thoughtfully rubbed his chin and smiled to himself. Yep, that was an excellent idea.

It was a sweltering day in Rapid, shimmers of heat rising from the pavement and traffic compounded by tourists intent on seeing all the sights in the Black Hills.

He completed his business at the insurance office while basking in the undisguised interest of the female staff. Some of them had been there four years ago and he vaguely remembered dating one of them. The branch manager, as he had in the past, tried to get Bryce to consider transferring to the Rapid office and once again, he refused, citing that he liked it just fine where he was in St. Louis.

When he headed back to Silverdale, thoughts of pretty office girls were replaced by the prospect of seeing the redhead at the Sweet Schoppe. Easy come, easy go. His life was one long line of women waiting for him. Ah, so many women and so little time.

Driving the speed limit through town, he made a snappy turn that brought him to the curb in front of the Sweet Schoppe. Dust curled around and settled on his car. He'd have to remember to slow and let the dust pass him by next time.

There were only a couple of other vehicles along the street at this late afternoon hour. Everything seemed deserted under the still blazing sky, except for kids in the distance trying to skateboard along the crumbling pavement near the school. Their shouts of laughter drifted on the lazy hot air, joined in by a joyously barking dog running in circles.

As he got out of the car, his gaze swept the Vayle Lumberyard and Hardware across the street on the next corner in the shade of aging cottonwoods. Always alert to his surroundings, he had to mentally force himself to relax. He wasn't on a stakeout.

Crossing the uneven sidewalk, he pulled open the screen door to the cafe, noticing the welcome sign displayed on the glass of the inner door. Good, she was still open.

Refreshingly cool air, laced with the delicious aroma of cinnamon, wafted past him as he entered, bells jangling merrily above the inner door. His peripheral vision took in the old-fashioned red and white décor, with large black and white alternating tiles underfoot that harkened back to the jukebox era. There were no customers seated at the tables, the quiet broken only by the swooshing of the ceiling fan and faint sounds of music.

He focused on the petite redhead he glimpsed through the service window beyond the back counter. The live version of Robin was even more enticing than the photograph at Dorine's house. A frisson of awareness plucked at him as he made his way towards her.

Robin turned from cutting the last of the fudge squares when the jangling bells alerted her that a customer had come in. She was not prepared for the unexpected flutter in her stomach when she saw Bryce. Soft country gospel music from her kitchen CD player floated in the stillness and she drew in a sharp breath.

He was still a hunk. And then some.

Dismayed, she shook off the inappropriate thought. Arranging a welcoming expression, she pushed through the swinging doors between kitchen and dining area.

"Hello, Bryce. I heard you were coming to spend your vacation with the Defoes. How are you?" She held out her hand, a tiny dimple appearing in one cheek beside her inviting pink lips when she smiled.

Bryce gazed into the pixie face of the woman he remembered, but now she went beyond cute, she was adorable! Her face was thinner but in spite of her smile, her intriguing hazel eyes held a hint of sadness that was hard to miss. Freckles dusted the bridge of her slightly upturned nose, her complexion devoid of anything except a bit of eye makeup. He imagined that with her light coloring, her lashes and eyebrows were almost invisible unless she darkened them. But there was no evidence she spent hours in front of a mirror.

The girl next door. Apple pie, motherhood and the flag.

Down, boy. Not your type. Remember. You're just here to say hello.

But his hormones didn't listen. She was an enticing woman and he couldn't help himself. He took her small hand in both of his and gave her his most charming smile.

"Hello," he purred. "I had the afternoon free and decided to spend it with you."

When she had put her hand in his, Robin was startled by the spark that zinged up her arm. She glanced down to see if there was really a spark! Goodness, she'd fended men off before, why had her silly emotions suddenly sat up and said "Howdy" to this man, of all people! She gently tugged her hand from his, her smile faltering.

Even though he noticed her not-so-subtle withdrawal, he was slow to release her hand, and continued to dazzle her with The Smile that brought women to his feet.

Robin only blinked.

That was it?

Un-oh. Too fast. Remember, she isn't one of your sophisticated women. He mentally backed off. Apple pie, motherhood and the flag.

"Would you like some coffee? On the house," she said, turning towards the coffeemaker, a move that smoothly took her out of his space.

Undaunted, he looked around instead. "You don't have espresso?" He was surprised at the absence of the machine. What place didn't have espresso these days?

She shook her head. "The equipment isn't in the budget. But this is *good* coffee," she stated emphatically. It helped her to keep focused on something as mundane as coffee.

He shrugged. "I'll pay for a *good* cup, then. You can't make a profit if you give it away." He slid onto one of the stools and studied her as she moved gracefully behind the counter to pick up a carafe. *Couldn't afford the equipment? What was up with that?*

He hadn't thought she would hold any appeal for him, this country woman. He'd only stopped out of curiosity since he'd seen that snapshot at the DeFoes. But from the moment he walked in the door, his awareness had gone beyond curiosity. His instincts had never steered him wrong, so he'd go with the flow. If nothing else, she could provide him with a little diversion while he was here. She'd been married and knew the score. At least that wouldn't be an obstacle.

"So how's it going?" Robin asked, unaware that she was the subject of his machinations. "Dorine said you wanted to try out the 'wild west' without having to stake out a suspect!" She poured the coffee in a thick mug and slid it across to him.

"You're going to join me, of course." His eyes were warm and suggestive as he patted the stool next to him. Even though she knew this was the way Bryce operated, disappointment flitted through her. She had so hoped he'd grown beyond the flirtatious moves that he thought made him attractive to women.

However, he was Dorine's houseguest and she didn't want to offend her best friend so would be polite. It was just that…she expected something different. *Dumb, dumb, dumb.* His practiced come-on was so obvious. But, it didn't matter, what could he possibly see in her, a single mother of two? He'd get his jollies, then leave. She relaxed. "I have to finish putting the candy into the cooler but I can talk and work at the same time."

She smiled politely and his breath hitched. *What a smile!* He'd have to think of a way to get her smiling at him all the time. He took a sip of the coffee and nodded approvingly. "This *is* good stuff." That smile was so sweet and seemed to light up the room.

The conversation switched to his vacation at the ranch and as he launched into his adventures with the twins, he morphed from playboy into a funny, articulate conversationalist, and against her will, Robin felt drawn to him.

Several customers came in, none too soon, she realized. He was enticing her into his sphere against her common sense. She needed a distraction, and was grateful for the customer who wanted a loaf of her specialty bread. Other customers wanted only ice cream. The break gave her a chance to shore up her defenses.

Bryce was intrigued by Robin's buoyant personality, how open and friendly she was with everyone. He saw her slip cookies to youngsters tagging along with their mothers, accompanied by a conspiratorial wink to shush the children from telling on her.

When a young sheriff's deputy came in, Bryce's antennae went up. He tried to detect if there was anything between the tall blond lawman and Robin. As she greeted the deputy, Bryce shamelessly eavesdropped. Adopting a neutral expression, he was silently amused as the deputy discreetly returned Bryce's scrutiny, each giving a nod to the other when Robin introduced the deputy as Jordan Langley.

After accepting the sack of donuts from Robin that he'd purchased, the deputy let his glance slide over Bryce once more before heading toward the door. As a stranger in town, Bryce knew the deputy was just checking him out. Or was he checking his competition?

"Hometown boy?" Bryce gestured at the departing figure.

"Jordan? Yes, we went to school together." She took a confection out of the refrigerated case and slid the door shut before setting the cheesecake on the counter. "He was a few grades ahead of me. He has eight brothers and his folks own a big ranch to the south," she waved with her knife.

Bryce sputtered into his coffee. "*Eight* brothers?!!"

Robin nodded as she cut slices of the mouth-watering confection. "Most of the boys have jobs away from the ranch, but they are all ranch-related, Jordan is the only one so far that has stayed this close to home." She put the cake back and slid the glass case shut.

"Any particular reason for him being around?" he asked carelessly. Robin gave him a strange look. *Cool it, man.*

"He's a pretty regular customer. With no wife to bake for him, he comes in here for his goodies."

"What is that?" He changed the subject, nodding his head at the cake.

"This is *kuchen,* a German cheesecake recipe my grandmother handed down from her grandmother. You pronounce it *'koohen,'* and it can have any kind of fruit filling, as well as other filling, like cottage cheese or even onion."

A customer came to the register as he said, "I'd like to try a piece of that." He pointed toward the case as she rang up the customer's purchase, warmly thanking the woman.

"Which kind? I only have cottage cheese, peach and prune left."

"Yes."

"Yes?"

"Yes. One of each."

She raised an eyebrow. "They're pretty rich…and filling."

"I can handle it," he boasted, grinning at her.

She chuckled as she eyed his flat stomach and got a bigger plate, carefully placing three slices of *kuchen* on it. *Never should have noticed those abs.* "Want more coffee?" She tried to keep her eyes away from his broad shoulders and muscled chest lurking under his white t-shirt. And she was never more thankful for the cooling breeze from the overhead fan, slight as it was.

He nodded while cutting into the rich confection, put a forkful in his mouth and slowly savored it. His eyes closed in ecstasy. "Oh, oh, umm, this is wonderful! I've never tasted anything like this!"

A hint of pride flickered through her. "Thank you. I try to do my grandma proud by making it exactly as she did." She filled his cup again while unsuccessfully tamping down the pleasure his words brought. *Don't forget, he knows all the tricks—be careful.*

Bryce continued to taste all three of the flavors, then pointed at his empty plate with his fork. "Have you ever thought of marketing this anywhere?"

She hesitated, looking from him to the plate. "No, I'm lucky to get some baked every day for the menu, let alone anything more."

"This is too good to be kept a secret!" he exclaimed again. "If I wasn't so full, I'd finish off the rest of those—what did you call them again?"

She carefully pronounced *"ko-o-h-e-n,"* her pink lips puckering up as she spelled, unaware that Bryce was leaning towards her, mesmerized by those kissable lips. "Now you say it."

"Umm?" he blinked, his eyes darting from her lips to her inquisitive eyes. "Oh, okay. K-*o-o-h-e-n*."

"Wonderful," she beamed at him. He stilled, experiencing a tug near his heart.

The door at the end of the booths along the wall next to the kitchen opened, and a young boy stuck his head out, glancing around the room. "Is it okay if we come in, Mommie?"

Mommie?

"Sure, Jason, come meet the DeFoe's houseguest."

Oh, yes. Robin's two boys. He'd forgotten them. He studied the youngster as he approached, guessing he was about six or seven years old. The boy had Robin's freckles and then some, but where her hair was more strawberry blonde, his was a dark auburn. He peered at Bryce with curious brown eyes.

Robin stepped around the counter, motioning her son to join her. "This is Jason, my oldest son. Honey, I want you to meet Bryce Martin."

The boy stuck out his hand and solemnly shook hands, his eyes roving over Bryce. "Do you play baseball, Mr. Martin?"

Impressed by the boy's manners but unprepared for the question, Bryce took a moment to assess the kid, whose clear gaze was fastened on him. Bryce found himself amused, and charmed, by the child's forthrightness.

"Sometimes." He returned the boy's scrutiny.

"Dorine said you were from St. Louis. Do you go to any Cardinal games?"

"I usually go with friends but my work often takes me out of the city so I don't follow the game as closely as I'd like."

Jason nodded slowly, processing the information. There was a sound by the door and Bryce looked up to see a smaller boy hanging back, staring at him.

Robin called to her other son. "Jeremy, come out and meet the twins' houseguest."

The boy barely moved, his brown eyes growing anxious, then he suddenly dashed to his mother's side and hid behind her. Bryce guessed him to be about five or so.

"Aren't you going to say hello?" Robin cajoled as she leaned sideways to pull the boy forward. Jeremy shook his head, peeking at Bryce from behind Robin's apron.

Jason announced, "He's kinda shy sometimes but he can color better'n me!"

Bryce was unexpectedly touched by the protective, brotherly words. He'd always wanted a brother. Had made up scenarios about what they would have done together. He wondered if these two were close buddies—he suspected they were, by the boy's remark.

"Robin, I'm going home now," a pretty, barely-teen girl called from the doorway. She glanced bashfully at Bryce, dropping her gaze when he winked at her.

"Laurie, this is Bryce Martin. He's visiting the DeFoes." Disgust washed through her that he would try his charm on the teen. If she'd had any charitable thoughts towards him before, they evaporated with that wink meant to overwhelm a mere child.

"Hello, Mr. Martin," the girl replied, smiling shyly at him.

Bryce tipped his head sideways, thinking what a beauty she would be in a few years, with her dark hair and striking blue eyes. "Hello Miss Laurie." The girl rewarded him with an embarrassed glance while a flush of pink stained her porcelain cheeks. He knew he shouldn't have his ego stroked by such a young female, but he was macho enough to see the admiration in those pretty eyes of hers.

"Laurie's dad owns the lumberyard and she watches the boys for me during the day," Robin explained in a voice tinged with annoyance. She hadn't missed Bryce's preening. Turning back to the teen, she said, "See you tomorrow." Inside, she was seething, not so much at Bryce as at herself, for the foolish emotions that had swirled around her ever since he had walked in the door. She struggled to tamp down the unwanted feelings, and swallowed before facing Bryce again.

"Bye, boys," Laurie called, waving her fingers. Bryce watched the attractive girl, so unaware of her charms that surely drew the boys to her.

Jeremy dashed to the teen and threw himself against her jeans-clad leg. She laughed, swinging him up in the air and moving through the door. It closed on their chatter.

"Bye, Laurie," Jason called without moving from his spot in front of Bryce. "Would you play ball with me, Mr. Martin?"

Bryce jerked his attention to the pint-sized questioner in front of him at the same time Robin frowned in dismay.

"Mr. Martin is busy, Jason, he just stopped in to say hello. He's probably expected back at the ranch." She couldn't imagine what possessed her son to be so forward.

Something about that dismissive statement irked Bryce and he raised an eyebrow. He'd been pondering the best way to ask Robin for a date, and the boy had just provided him with an opening. Setting his hands on his hips, he looked down at Jason again. "You got a ball, kid?"

Jason's face lit like a sunbeam. "Oh, boy! Oh boy, Mr. Martin, yeah, I got a ball. Wanna see it?"

Bryce raised his eyes, a challenge in the honeyed depths as he faced Robin. "Yes. If your mother says it's alright?"

She recognized a challenge when it was dumped back in her lap and raised her chin a fraction. "Of course. Jason, go get your ball. I'm sure Mr. Martin keeps his promises." He didn't miss the thinly-veiled insult and wondered where it had come from? She had no reason to doubt his word, she didn't know him. Nevertheless, her remark made him want to dig in his heels.

"But Mom—" Jason twisted to look up at his mother. "He doesn't just wanna *see* it, he wants to play too!" Jason turned beseeching eyes to Bryce. "Don't cha, Mr. Martin?"

Taken completely off-guard by the child's eagerness, he looked down into the anxious face of the little boy and melted. How could anyone refuse that pleading look? He vaguely wondered when he had become such a patsy for kids.

"Do you play Little League, Jason?"

The boy's face fell. "Naw, I'm not old enough."

Robin spoke up. "They have T-ball for his age but I'm not able to take him. And I don't want just *anyone* influencing him." Bryce got the message loud and clear. He firmed his lips and stared back at Robin.

"So I just hafta practice in the back yard and I'm no good!" The boy's discouraged tone tugged at Bryce's heart. Poor little kid.

Before he could stop his unruly tongue, the words were out. "I'll play catch with you, son." At the way Jason's face brightened, he didn't regret his statement. "Just lead the way." He glanced at Robin. "That is okay with you, isn't it, *Mother*?"

Her eyes went from a stormy gray to hazel, brightly dancing with merriment. "Oh, yes, that would be a medical miracle, considering I'm younger than you!"

For a moment he didn't catch on, then he gave her a slow grin, meant to sizzle her hair ends.

But she wasn't even looking at him, her focus was on her son. "Take Mr. Martin to the back yard to play catch, but don't go out of the yard, okay?" He nodded, beginning to fidget and edge toward the inner door. "And don't keep him too long, he wants to get back to the ranch."

"Let me be the judge of that. I'm not in a big hurry, Ms. Hudson," he said softly, his eyes roaming seductively over her face. "I can decide if I need to get back…or not."

She flushed at his gentle rebuke.

"Besides, I have something to ask you."

She gazed up at him expectantly but before he could reply, the bells over the door jangled and Robin's attention turned to her customer. "Hi, Orrie! How goes it today?"

"Faster than I want and too slow for the rest of the world!"

declared the frizzy-haired older lady. She was even shorter than Robin, her body starting to show the pull of gravity. Her hair, which might or might not have been red at one time, now showed a faint pink in the short nesting of curls. Bryce briefly wondered if the women were related. Orrie's bright blue eyes turned on Bryce, reminding him of a bird about to pounce.

"Aha! You're the DeFoe's guest. How do you like it here? A mite too dry for me right now but you'll never find a better bunch of people all clustered in one place. How about a loaf of that cinnamon raisin bread, honey?"

Bryce blinked. What a whirlwind! He was about to open his mouth when Robin spoke.

"Sure, Orrie, got one loaf left, with your name on it." She glanced at Bryce and waved her hand towards Jason. "You better hurry up. You *promised*." She left no doubt that she expected him to carry through. Orrie chattered on in disconnected sentences that Robin apparently had no trouble following.

Bryce hesitated, then shifted his attention to Jason. "Lead on, McDuff!"

Jason's face broke out in smiles. "*McDuff?!*" he squealed. "That's a crazy name!" He chortled loudly and tugged on Bryce's hand.

"Does Laurie play ball with you?"

"She doesn't wanna play ball with us 'cause she's afraid she'll break her fingernails off!" declared Jason with a hint of disgust.

Bryce couldn't help the laughter that spilled out of him and he leaned down, whispering loudly to Jason, "Girls are like that. They love pretty fingernails."

"Aren't good for anything," replied the boy, tugging Bryce's hand again. "Come on!"

Down the hall they went, with Bryce catching only a brief glimpse of the modest home—several darkened rooms that must be bedrooms and a bathroom—then they were in the living room. His first impression was one of hominess—overstuffed chairs swathed in afghans, thriving plants on every surface and videos spilling out of a bookcase onto the well-worn carpet. An upright vintage piano sat against one wall, with photographs that displayed several generations lining its top. A sure bet that Robin valued family values that was the glue that held them together.

Jason dropped Bryce's hand and raced to a wood toy box beside the back door to rummage until he came up with a softball. "Here it is! Let's go!" He darted to the screen door and pushed it open, looking back to see if Bryce was following. "Come on!" he urged Bryce out onto the flat paving stone that served as the stoop.

Laurie was standing at the edge of the yard still holding Jeremy and talking softly to him. They both glanced back as Jason and Bryce walked to the middle of the lawn, where Jason heaved the ball at Bryce, missing him by a mile. Laurie put Jeremy down and he dashed headlong to the back door, opened it and charged inside, letting it slam behind him. Laurie laughed and disappeared around the corner.

Bryce was puzzled at the young boy's distrustful attitude. Had someone scared the kid, or done something worse to make him so skittish? That thought left a bad taste in his mouth. He knew that child abuse was rampant and could only hope it hadn't happened here.

He turned his attention to Jason. The kid could hardly catch the ball, even when it was gently tossed to him. Bryce was amazed at the boy's inexperience, but brought himself up short—what did he know about kids and their skills?

Before he knew it, he was squatting on his haunches, guiding Jason's hands and working with him until he was catching the ball almost every time. The little guy's demeanor went from downhearted to confident, his eyes shining with happiness.

"Should we go show your mother what you can do?" Bryce glanced at his watch and was amazed how the time had flown by.

"Yes!" chirped Jason, dancing around and catching Bryce's hand to pull him into the house. Now would be his chance to talk to Robin.

As before, he was towed down the hallway and out into the café, but his plan deflated when he saw that Robin had a table full of customers. Jason skidded to a stop and put his forefinger over his mouth, signaling Bryce to be quiet.

Bryce chuckled and watched Robin interact with her customers. An older gentleman winked at Bryce and reached around behind Robin to playfully yank on the bow that held her red apron tied around her waist. It fluttered down before she could catch it.

The man's wife smacked his shoulder. "Leave the girl alone or she won't give you any *kucken*."

Robin grinned as she laid down her pad and pencil, cheerfully retying the apron. "Not only that, but I'll put salt in your coffee." Laughter erupted while Robin finished taking their orders. Bryce was intrigued at the interplay, his appreciation of Robin increasing.

Jason patiently waited until his mother came toward them, an expectant look on her face. "Mom! Mr. Martin showed me how to catch the ball and I'm doing it like a professor!"

She bent down and kissed his forehead. "Do you mean like a professional?"

"Un-huh!" Jason's head bobbed vigorously.

Robin straightened and smiled at Bryce, the force of it warming him. "Thank you Bryce. It was kind of you to take the time."

"I'm on vacation, I've got lots of time," he replied in a suggestive tone.

A pink flush stained her cheeks. "Thanks again." She edged by him and headed for the kitchen. "Stop in again some time."

It took him a second to realize she'd blown him off as smoothly as her city counterpart, but Jason's voice broke into his thoughts. "Mr. Martin! Will you come and play ball with me again?"

Bryce looked down into the boy's expectant eyes. Ah. Blow him off, would she? "Sure. I'm not about to miss playing ball again."

"Oh-boy-oh-boy-oh-boy!" Jason bounced around on his toes, tossing the ball into the air. He promptly missed, the ball hitting the toe of his shoe and rolling away. He ran after it and pounced on it, turning back to Bryce.

"That's okay, Tiger, you keep practicing!" Bryce chuckled.

"Thanks again, Bryce," Robin repeated as she passed him with her hands full of heaping salad plates.

Bryce gave Jason a wink before removing his wallet to place several large bills down on the counter. Moving towards the door, he passed Robin on her way to the kitchen. "We aren't finished yet, I'll be back." He had the satisfaction of seeing her falter before continuing on. *Let her chew on that awhile.*

All the way back to the ranch, he pondered his unusual attraction to Robin. She had nowhere near the sophistication of the women he usually dated and he couldn't understand this strange fascination with her. The best way to rid himself of that feeling was to wine and dine her, get her out of his system. Smiling smugly, he settled deeper into the seat and wheeled the car through the gates of the Double D Ranch.

Chapter 4

His chance to get Robin alone came sooner than he'd expected.

He had helped move cattle between corrals the next day while Dean was tied up in his office with corporate business. Dorine was working vacation for one of the secretaries, and took the boys with her to play contentedly in the conference room.

Bryce needed a shower before dinner and came downstairs to find Dorine rushing to get the noon meal ready. He helped by setting the table before casually asking, "How come Robin doesn't have espresso? She'd draw in a lot more customers if she did."

Dorine kept her eyes on the gravy she was stirring. "She just doesn't."

"She already told me she couldn't afford it, so you won't be talking behind her back."

"She did?" Dorine looked at him in surprise. "She usually doesn't talk about her finances. To other people, I mean. I mean—"

Bryce laughed, waving off her embarrassed attempt to backtrack. "Surely she can afford an espresso machine." Dorine silently shook her head. "Are her finances that bad?"

"I can't comment." Dorine poured the gravy into a bowl, leaving

Bryce to mull over what she *wasn't* saying. Dean arrived with the boys, followed by noisy washing up, then they sat down to eat.

The phone rang while they were finishing a dessert of lemon meringue pie. Bryce offered to clear the table when Dorine got up to answer the phone. Dean excused himself, taking the boys back to the office with him.

From Dorine's end of the conversation, Bryce gathered that someone needed help with transportation. Never let it be said that Bryce Martin let an opportunity go by. He motioned to Dorine that he was available if someone needed a ride. She sent him a grateful glance while telling the caller she was sending help.

"Latsy, one of the employee's wives, can't get her car started and needs to get to a doctor's appointment in Kadoka. I'd take her but I've got an important call coming into the office this afternoon. Are you sure you're okay with this?" Dorine had stepped into the utility room while she talked, returning with an armful of little jeans. Laying them on the table, she quickly began folding them.

"Sure, if anybody needs help, I'm your man!"

Dorine rolled her eyes. "Her husband will pick her up, so all you have to do is drop her off. You do realize I was kidding when I said we'd put you to work?"

"No problem." He paused. "Is Latsy good-looking?"

"Bryce!" Dorine swatted his arm as she passed him on the way upstairs. "She's very pretty but you behave yourself!" He gave her an outrageous wink as she added, "She's in the second cottage in the employee housing."

"On my way," he sang out. Boy, oh boy! Talk about things falling into your lap!

Latsy was indeed pretty with short black shiny hair, blue eyes and sweet smile, but he didn't have to say much during the ride into Kadoka. She chatted companionably to him, in that easy-going way of mid-westerners. And she was very married.

However, she was instantly forgotten after he dropped her off, as his thoughts sped ahead towards Silverdale. He'd have to very carefully plot his strategy.

At the Sweet Schoppe, the jangling bells announced his arrival and enhanced his anticipation to see Robin. He thought the place was empty at first until Robin appeared from behind the kitchen door with a broom in her hand.

"Oh!" She started, giving him a quizzical glance. "I didn't expect to see you again so soon. I'm getting an early start on cleanup. Did you want more kucken?"

"Nope. I stopped to see *you*." He was startled at how true those words were.

She grinned. "I thought you wanted to see the 'wild west,' and I'm not it."

"I'd rather spend my time with you."

Even though she was disappointed at the old line, she couldn't help a tiny jolt of pleasure. She moved past him to the first table. "Then grab a broom."

He parked his hands on his hips and looked around. "Don't you have a janitor to do this? How about that young waitress?"

She laughed, a bubbly musical sound that reminded him of a whispering waterfall. "Don't I wish! No, I'm it," she swept her hand up her body in a grand gesture. He frowned as she returned to her task. "I can't afford Marietta any more than just a few hours every day." Now why did she tell him *that*? Blabbermouth. "Besides, this is good exercise." Pulling a chair out from the table, she reached under it with the broom, using vigorous, efficient strokes. "So, why aren't you on a trusty steed, or out sightseeing?"

Undaunted by her change in subject, he replied, "Just watching you is sightseeing enough." The words flowed smoothly off his experienced tongue. "You're worth it."

"Yeah, I'm such a national monument that people are standing in line to see me." She tried to hide her disappointment at his insincere sweet talk, and pushed the chair back under the table with a little more force than was necessary.

Bryce laughed, not tuning into her irritation, and she paused as she moved to the next table. Bryce was just being Bryce, why did she let him get to her? Maybe because his laugh was so...so masculine.

He leaped to move the next chairs out of her way, replacing them when she'd swept under the table.

Touched by his show of manners, she sent him a sincere smile. "Thanks."

"I was thinking we could go out."

She stopped sweeping and straightened. "Out?"

"Yes, to a movie and drinks or whatever."

"Are we talking a *date* here?"

"Absolutely." He looked at her uncertainly. She was staring at him as though he'd asked her to dangle from the St. Louis arch. "I know it's a ways to a theater but we've got all night."

She shook her head, amusement touching her lips. "Bryce, *you're* on vacation. I'm not. I have to work tomorrow." She resumed sweeping and he kept moving chairs.

"Take the day off."

She shook her head again. "Can't." She moved to the booth area and began sweeping there.

"Can't doesn't float the boat."

"Bryce, Bryce." She sighed and leaned on the broom, her eyes twinkling. "Watch my lips...N.O. If I'm not here," she indicated the large room, "there's no one to run the café."

"Close up early or hire somebody." He perched on the edge of a table, dangling one foot like he was dangling the date in front of her.

Instead of an answer, she laughed lightly, shook her head and moved to the next booth.

"If you can't go tonight, how about tomorrow night? That'll give you time to think it over. Just the two of us, cuddled—"

"Whoa." Robin straightened and held her hand palm out to him.

"Just we two?" From her serious expression, he knew he'd hit a snag.

He plunged ahead anyway, sending her a sexy smile and a wink. "Yes! In fact, why *don't* you close up early and we can make it dinner and a mov—"

"Whoa again!" she exclaimed. "What about the boys?"

"Get a sitter," he quipped. "I'll pay her."

"No. *No way,*" she stated emphatically. "I'm away from them too much as it is. And where I go, they go. And you will *not* pay!"

"You mean you take the boys along on your dates?" he asked incredulously.

"I don't date." She gave him a pointed stare. He was beginning to get irritating.

"Well, you could make an exception while I'm here. It'll just be a couple of times. You're a good-looking woman and I'm a lonely guy. Is there anything wrong with us getting together?"

"Lonely?" she scoffed and turned to grab the dustpan. "You're about as lonely as a movie star at a press conference. I don't have time for dating. End of story." She swept the dirt into the dustpan.

"Now wait a minute! You're not even giving me a chance."

She stood up, broom in one hand and dustpan in the other, fixing a mock sorrowful expression on her face. "I'm sorry but how much plainer can I be?"

"You're not plain at all," he said softly, moving towards her.

Robin held up her hand to ward him off. Dirt spilled out of the dustpan onto the floor, unnoticed by either of them. The attraction between them sizzled in the air.

They stared at each other, neither moving until the shrill ring of the phone shattered the silence. Relief skittered across Robin's face as she hurried to answer the call. Bryce sighed and ran his hand through his hair, glancing at the spilled dirt. He took the broom and dustpan to dispose of it.

"Mom!" Jason called out as he opened the door from the apartment, peering cautiously around to check for customers.

Robin held up her finger for him to wait as she held a brief conversation with the caller, then hung up and turned to him. "Jason, remember what I told you about hollering in here?"

Crestfallen, Jason dropped his gaze. "Yes, ma'm."

"And what was it?"

"I'm not 'posed to yell or talk loud in the café."

"Right. Now, what did you want?"

"I just wanted to—" Jason suddenly spotted Bryce and his face lit with joy. "Mr. Martin! Did you come back to play ball again?!"

Jeremy appeared behind Jason, his eyes first curious, then wary.

Bryce's lips were forming a negative reply until he really looked into Jason's eyes. What he saw there rearranged his thinking.

"I had to run an errand for Dorine but I'm free now to play catch with you." He returned the boy's clear gaze. Jeremy scooted through the door and ran to Robin, ducking behind her. Jason's delight knew no bounds and Bryce chuckled at the youngster's exuberance, even while puzzling over Jeremy's retreat.

Robin studied Jason's actions and suffered a pang of guilt at how little time *she* had to spend with her children. But why did Jason have to take a shine to *Bryce*, of all people?!

Even when the café wasn't monopolizing her time, she had household chores, lawn and yard, business records. She kept the boys with her as much as possible, but at the same time, she wasn't going to let anyone else take over *any* of her responsibilities.

"Are you sure, Bryce? This is your vacation and we'll understand if you want to do something else." Robin put her hand on Jason's shoulder and squeezed affectionately. Jeremy peeked out from behind her.

"Yes, I'm sure. If I didn't want to be here, I wouldn't be." He gazed down at Jason's innocent expression, then rested his hand on the child's head, gently ruffling his hair. "Isn't that right, Tiger?"

"I'm not a tiger!" Jason grabbed hold of Bryce's wrist with both hands and grinned up at him. "I'm a St. Louis Cardinal!"

The adults both laughed, then Robin heaved an exaggerated sigh. "All right, you Cardinal! Take Mr. Martin and go play ball."

The café door opened and a gang of noisy teens pushed into the room, calling greetings to Robin. Bryce allowed Jason to drag him to the back yard again, and he enjoyed the antics of the youngster's improved confidence. Jeremy was nowhere to be seen.

When Robin pushed open the back door later and called out, "Time for supper," he looked at his watch in surprise.

"Mr. Martin! Mr. Martin! You can stay for supper...can't he, Mommie?"

Bryce smiled slyly, knowing that Jason had unwittingly aided his cause. He also knew Robin would try to wiggle out of her son's impromptu invitation.

She tilted her chin and replied, "If he wants to, he's welcome." Her gaze collided with Bryce's amused glance, then she held the door open wider. "Come in and wash your hands. We're going to eat in a booth tonight instead of at our kitchen table."

"Me too, Mommie?" Bryce said sotto voice as he ushered Jason through the door.

"Yes, even big boys have to wash their hands." Jason held his grubby hand over his mouth to smother an endearing giggle as he danced ahead of the adults. Robin swept on by them as they turned in to the bathroom. "Jeremy's already waiting for us."

Dishing up plates of meatloaf, baked potatoes, green beans and baked apples, Robin pondered her mixed feelings about Bryce eating with them. She wanted to put distance between them but she didn't want to stifle Jason's excitement either. She carried the brimming plates to the first booth as Bryce came back, Jason's hand tucked in his. Jeremy, seated in the corner of the booth, widened his eyes when he saw Bryce.

Turning to go back for the other two plates, she found her way blocked.

"I'll get the rest. You sit down and take a load off," Bryce ordered. When she opened her mouth to protest, he held up his hand. "You've been on your feet all day. It's the guys turn to serve you." Turning to Jason, he asked, "Isn't that right, Tiger?"

"Yes, sir!" Jason replied, his face shining and a grin from ear to ear. "But I'm not a tiger—I'm a *Cardinal!*" he insisted.

"That's my man!" Bryce praised and strode into the kitchen. A couple of more trips for salad, tableware, drinks and rolls, then they were all seated. Bryce hated that Jeremy seemed to shut down when he was around. The boy tried to shrink into the corner of the booth and sent fearful looks Bryce's way—when he dared to glance at the youngster.

Robin bowed her head, the boys followed suit and Bryce inwardly groaned. He should have realized she was one of "them." Why was fate against him these days?! Her simple prayer was for fellowship around the table and blessings on the food that God had provided. Bryce silently thought that farmers had provided the food, not God, but he wisely kept his mouth shut.

Then they were digging in, regaled by Jason's knock-knock jokes that only he thought were funny. Jeremy managed a few grins, sobering if he caught Bryce looking at him. Robin gradually relaxed and Bryce grew more frustrated, realizing that as long as the boys were present, there was little chance of asking Robin to go out with him.

He tried touching her foot with his under the table but she sent him a warning glance and tucked her feet under the seat. Short of pouncing on her, he was limited in what he

could say, not knowing how much a seven-year-old and a five-year-old could pick up on.

He insisted on clearing the table and rinsing the dishes for the dishwasher while Robin wiped the table. Jeremy disappeared but

Jason helped in the kitchen. "Can we go out and toss a few more balls around?" he asked eagerly when Bryce pronounced they were done.

"That's up to your mother."

Robin rinsed out her cloth and hesitated, then nodded. "It's such a nice evening. We can all go out for awhile."

Once she was settled in the lawn swing, Robin enjoyed the soft breeze, birds twittering as they settled down for the night. A few sounds of small town life drifted into the back yard, as she watched Bryce play catch with Jason. Her eyes were drawn again and again to the man's broad back and shoulders, but she jerked her thoughts away from that forbidden territory. No using window shopping when she had no intention of buying. Jeremy stayed curled up next to her. "Don't you want to go play, honey?" she leaned down, her arm around his shoulder. He shook his head and settled more closely to her.

Her gaze returned to Bryce. Strange, he almost seemed at home here in her back yard, and she would never have thought he'd have the patience to deal with a child. But he treated Jason with respect and kindness, and she was aware of adding up his good qualities. Right on the heels of that thought came the most important reason why she should not be totaling his favorable points—he did not know her Lord.

When shadows began to lengthen across the grass, she reluctantly got up and took Jeremy's hand. "Time for baths and bed, Jason."

Bryce turned and wiggled his eyebrows. "Me too?"

"Don't hold your breath," she muttered.

Jason giggled as he ran to his mother. "Mr. Martin is too big to get into our bathtub, Mommie!"

"Yes, he is, isn't he?" she agreed, trying not to sputter with laughter. "He'll have to go home for his bath, won't he?"

As they went in the door, he whispered, "I could always stand up and you could pour water over me."

She waited until the boys were ahead of them, then looked up into his handsome face. "You can be sure it would be ice water—you need cooling off!"

He threw back his head and laughed, as Jeremy ran down the hall and ducked into his bedroom, slamming the door.

"Hey, Mr. Martin, that was fun! Can you come again? Like tomorrow?" Jason gave the ball a toss in the general direction of the toybox and dropped his mitt on the floor.

"Jason, don't beg. Mr. Martin is here to visit the DeFoes, not us. And pick up your mitt, you know better than to drop it in the middle of the floor."

"You're sure a wet blanket," Bryce muttered for her ears alone. But to Jason, he said, "I don't know about tomorrow but I don't have anything planned. I can come if your mother says it's okay." He fixed an innocent gaze on her.

"You dirty dog," she muttered.

"What did you say, Mom, huh? What did you say?" Jason ran to her and grabbed her around the hips, looking up at her with a grin. "Did you invite him to come again?"

She caved. The boys needed male companionship and Jason was flowering under Bryce's praise. Not that she'd ever want him to emulate Bryce's morals, but no harm could come of a few games of catch. "I was inviting him to come again."

A choked laugh erupted from nearby.

Jason let go and whooped as he danced over to Bryce. "She said yes! She said yes!"

Bryce sent Robin a knowing look. "Didn't she though!"

Robin's heart skipped a beat at that look. Mentally shaking herself, she pointed towards the hall. "Come on now, you need to take your bath and Mr. Martin needs to go home." She walked ahead of them, aware of Bryce's eyes following her.

"Are you throwing me out, Ms. Hudson?" his whisper came from just behind her. His heavier footsteps were in contrast to the skip and jump of Jason's smaller stride.

"Fat chance." She turned and smirked as her eyes went up and down his lean, muscled body. She held the door to the cafe open and waited.

"Goodbye Mr. Martin, come again real soon!" Jason called out as he opened his bedroom door.

"Goodbye son," Bryce replied, stopping in front of Robin. Her eyes grew wide as she edged back. "How about a goodbye kiss from *you*, Ms. Hudson?"

"You, can bite the wall," she quipped.

Bryce chuckled. "I haven't laughed this much in a long time. We are going to have *so* much fun on our first date!"

"Won't happen," she replied. But at his stubborn look, she added, "You never give up, do you?" Her eyes twinkled up at him. "And you never change either." The twinkle disappeared and disappointment briefly flitted through her eyes. "No. No date."

He stood there, debating whether he should try kissing her anyway but the warning in her eyes was enough for him to draw back. He raised his hand and tapped her on the nose with one finger. "I'll just say 'good night,' not 'goodbye'." He walked through the door and turned. "But I'll be back."

"Good night, *Arnold*," she said to his retreating back and shut the door, none too gently. As she was turning on the water in the tub, a knock sounded on the door and she frowned. Had Bryce forgotten something?

When she opened the door, he leaned towards her, grinning knowlingly as she took a step back. "I'm assuming you don't want the sign on the outside door to say 'open' all night long?"

She felt the blush growing over her neck and onto her cheeks, and he smiled victoriously. Besides the sign, she'd forgotten to turn off the kitchen lights! Flustered, she managed a soft "Thanks, I'll do it later."

"What was that, I didn't hear it?" Bryce cupped his ear with his hand.

Chagrined, she looked up at him and squared her shoulders. "I said thank you." He didn't move. "If you'll get out of the way, I need to turn off the lights."

"I'll get the lights for you too," he grinned at her discomfort. Turning on his heel, he strode into the kitchen and flipped the switch. Coming out, he gave her a salute and called softly, "Goodnight, beautiful." The bells jingled above the door as he let himself out.

"Mommie, come on! I'm getting cold standing here in nothing but a towel!" complained Jason.

With one last look at the door, Robin turned to her son. "I'm coming." Her shoulders slumped. The effort to keep things light-hearted while enduring his outrageous remarks was taking a toll on her. How much longer could she bear it until she had to tell him bluntly that his suggestiveness was a real turnoff for her?

The whole time she bathed the boys, heard their prayers and put them to bed, she was on automatic rote, not really hearing their chatter.

Bryce. He had burst upon her horizon with no warning…and he'd called her beautiful.

Chapter 5

Bryce whistled as he strode to his car, hopped over the side of the convertible and dropped into the front seat. He couldn't remember enjoying an evening as much as this in a long time, and he hadn't even had anything to drink!

As he drove the country road back to the ranch, he thought about how unaffected Robin appeared to be. She had no idea of her feminine appeal and that puzzled him. He was used to women who played up their assets, using all kinds of artifice. There wasn't one devious bone in Robin's body, and that alone whetted his interest. She didn't know how sweet and appealing she was—too bad she wasn't really his type. Nonetheless, he resented her outright rejection. She was very adept at sidestepping his advances…his lips curved in a slight smile when he realized what a challenge she presented.

As he began to map out his strategy, something niggled at the back of his mind. She couldn't have much of an income with only local trade and that's why she had to be open every day. Did the woman ever take any time off? Probably Sunday, because of her religion. He snorted in derision. With her cooking skills, she could command big bucks in the city. Why was she content to stay in this little burg? Her *kucken* alone would bring gourmet prices! Had she ever thought of marketing it beyond Silverdale?

An idea began to grow as he wheeled to a stop in front of the ranch house. Opening the door, he climbed out and noted with dismay the dust again covering the shiny finish of his car. He'd have to wash it first thing in the morning, unless it rained. He glanced toward the west, where lightning flickered among clouds laying along the horizon. Dry lightning, no doubt, which meant there was no rain in those clouds. He'd heard more than one conversation among the cattlemen since he'd been here, about dried up pastures and cattle being sold because there was no feed. He hoped for their sake, that it would rain soon. Dismissing the weather, his thoughts returned to Robin again. What was he to do about the aggravating little thing?

While out on the tractor with Dean the next day, Bryce was appreciative of the air-conditioning in the cab as the hot Dakota sun beat down on them. The sky was like the inside of a blue bowl, stretching from one horizon to the other, with only a few puffy clouds visible in the far west over the Black Hills.

Birds flew up when the big machine and mower went by, clipping weeds along the fence line. Suddenly the engine missed and jerked, then ran smoothly only to miss again, the tractor jerking and sputtering, as it rolled to a dead stop. Dean turned off the key, opened the door and jumped to the ground.

"What's happening?" Bryce crawled down a little more slowly.

Dean already had his head in the bowels of the tractor, poking around in wires that resembled a jumble not unlike strings of Christmas tree lights. "I'm not sure…yet," he answered absently as he hunched down and peered up at the underside of the tractor. He began humming.

Bryce leaned back into the cab and got the straw hat Dean had given him that morning, settling it on his head while propping himself against the huge back tire.

It was still, the silence swallowing up the prairie that lay for miles in every direction. He couldn't even see the ranch buildings from here. A bird seemed to float above them, then dipped down to land on the fence wire. He cocked his head and eyed Bryce.

Dean continued humming good-naturedly as he poked and prodded. "Ouch!" he suddenly yelped, jerking back and shaking his hand, his face registering pain.

"What is it?" Bryce straightened in alarm.

"Touched a hot place—*holy cow*, that hurts!" Dean stood and stepped around him to reach for the First Aid kit on the tractor floor.

"If that was me, I'd be cussing a lot worse than saying holy cow," Bryce chuckled wryly. He watched Dean smooth ointment, then a bandage over the burn.

"That doesn't help any, and besides, it would be dishonoring to my Lord." Dean reached for a wrench, turning back to the tractor innards.

"You know," Bryce began hesitantly, "I don't get it."

"Get what?" Dean's voice floated back from where he crouched.

"This religion stuff."

"Stuff?" Dean cocked his head and gave Bryce a sideways glance.

"Yeah," Bryce gestured at the broken machine. "I've never known anyone who didn't swear when things break down, but you don't."

"People don't swear if they know the Lord. Or at least they should try to control it."

A meadowlark landed on the cab of the tractor and warbled his merry song. Bryce glanced up at the bird for something to focus on. "But you're a cowboy! Cowboys live the high life—drinking, women, living it up!"

Dean grinned, scooting farther under the tractor. "You've been watching too much television, Bryce. Not all cowboys are the way the media portrays them."

"Well, I can see why you wouldn't go after other women, not with a wife like Dorine! But I never hear you cuss and you don't have beer in your refrigerator." He shook his head as he squatted next to Dean's prone form. "I just don't get it."

"Well, Bryce, when a man gives his heart to the Lord Jesus, He makes a new man out of him. All those things you're referring to lose their appeal for a man when he accepts Christ as his Savior, no matter if he's a cowboy, a doctor or a truck driver. And whether a person has alcohol around or not is a personal choice. God doesn't condemn you for taking a drink, you know!"

Dean grimaced as he tugged on a stubborn bolt. "I choose not to drink because I feel it weakens my witness for the Lord. And then too, there's the boys. It's what comes *out* of a Christian's mouth that makes the difference," he went on. "You see, Christianity isn't a religion, it's a way of life. And you don't choose it, given man's rebellious nature, Christ chooses *you*." Dean scooted out from under the tractor and grinned cheerfully.

Bryce shook his head. "I could never do it." He stood up. "Have you always been a Christian?" He abruptly shut his mouth. *Way too personal, Martin!*

It surprised him when Dean grew serious with a faraway look in his eyes as he too, stood. It was a long moment before he answered. "Yes…"

"Do I hear a 'but' in there?" Bryce asked curiously.

"Yeah…" Dean looked down at his hands then out across the prairie. "There was a time after my dad died that I doubted God. Then when Dorine's dad died, leaving her on her own in her senior year of high school, I turned my back on God altogether." He tilted his head and looked squarely into Bryce's eyes. "I didn't understand how a loving God could allow that to happen, and I drifted away from Him, not wanting to hear anything about religion."

There was a stretch of silence. Bryce gestured with his hand. "What happened to change your mind?"

Dean took a deep breath, a look of peace coming over his face. "God allowed me to see His love when He started the healing in a very sick little baby, and, you were here when He kept Dorine from harm with the rustlers."

Bryce's eyes lit with remembrance at that frightful night four years ago. "You still think your prayers saved her?" he asked skeptically.

"No. God did." The cowboy's voice rang with certainty. "But without Dorine's unwavering faith as an example, it would have taken me a lot longer to come back to God."

"Well," Bryce wiped his hands on his jeans, "I could never do that, never give up my life-style. I'm not hurting anyone, so it suits me just fine."

Dean grinned and clapped him on the shoulder. "If God draws you to Him, you could give up anything. He has a plan for each of us, including you. You just don't know what it is yet." He grabbed a rag and wiped his hands, squinting quizzically at Bryce.

Bryce eyed him with cynicism plainly etched on his face. "I don't *think* so!" Inwardly, he was squirming. How did they get on this subject? Oh, yeah, he was the one that opened his big mouth! He mentally kicked himself.

Dean unhooked the cell phone from his belt and punched in numbers. "I better call for reinforcement—Buster? You must have been sitting right on your phone!...yeah. Can you bring the pickup out to the Toluka pasture? The tractor quit on me....yeah...okay." He snapped the phone shut and turned to grab a jug of water out of the cab and two plastic tumblers. "Want a drink? Buster is just a couple of miles away, he was checking fence lines so we're lucky we don't have to wait very long."

"Toluka?" Bryce asked with raised eyebrow.

"This piece of ground was homesteaded by a guy with the name of Toluka, but he couldn't make it ranching and it eventually became part of my dad's holdings."

They turned at the distant sound of a vehicle. "How long has Buster been your foreman?" Bryce gratefully swallowed the icy water offered to him by his host.

Dean's lips twitched. "Ever since he wrestled me for the position."

Bryce choked and spued water. *"What?!"*

"His dad worked for my dad, so we grew up together learning ranching. But it seemed like everything we did, he had to be competitive—he loved to wrestle. He'd challenge me when we were given a job to do. He said if he won, we'd do it his way and if I won, we'd do it my way. When the foreman's position opened up, Buster challenged me." Dean tipped his head back and took a long swallow.

"In spite of you being the boss's son?"

"We wrestled." Dean put the cap back on the jug.

"And?"

Dean's eyes cut towards Bryce. "He's working here, isn't he?"

"In other words, he cleaned your clock!"

Dean gave a hearty laugh just as the ranch pickup came into sight. Bryce watched Buster bouncing over the rough pasture toward them. "I thought you said he was checking fences on horseback."

"Not always, depends on where you're checking and how much time you've got," Dean replied, setting the jug back in the cab.

After the two ranchmen poked and banged around on the innards of the tractor, they removed a greasy part and announced it would have to be taken to town to be repaired, since the ranch mechanic was on vacation. "We'll ride back to the house with Buster," Dean said as he laid the part on a burlap sack in the bed of the pickup.

Bryce spoke up. "I can take the part into town. Just tell me what to do." Dean turned a questioning glance on him. Bryce grinned unrepentantly. "Gives me a chance to see Robin again." Dean's answer was raised eyebrows, then a shrug.

After hearing Dean's explanation about where to take the part, Bryce's eyes widened. "Chopsie? You want me to take that part to a guy named *Chopsie*?!!"

Buster, a tall, rangy, bowlegged cowboy, clapped Bryce on the shoulder. "When you see him, you'll know why he's Chopsie!" He slid behind the wheel of the pickup, chuckling, as the other two slid in beside him on the front seat.

Bryce found the mechanic's business on Main Street like Buster said, and knew he was in the right place when a mountain of a man came out of the garage's dim interior that housed several dismantled cars. The guy *had* to be Chopsie. He stood six-six if he was an inch, with a rotund belly that reminded Bryce of sumo wrestlers. His friendly smile, albeit with a front tooth missing, immediately put Bryce at ease and he handed over the part.

Dean had called ahead to let Chopsie know Bryce was coming and the big man assured Bryce he could return for the repairs in a few hours. "Gives you a chance to make time with our Robin," he winked.

Bryce was intrigued at how fast news traveled in this town. He hopped back in the pickup, wondering if everyone knew he was trying to date Robin. He mulled that over while driving on down the street to the Sweet Schoppe.

His heart picked up its pace at the sight of Robin in the kitchen. At this time of the day, there were only a couple of older women in deep conversation over coffee in the last booth, but they paused to watch him cross the room. He sent them a cordial smile.

Robin's heart gave that annoying little flutter when she saw Bryce come in, and couldn't help the smile that curved her lips. "Hi, how's your vacation coming along?"

"Dusty and dirty." He eyed the white dough in her hands. "What are you making? Can I have a bite?"

"Pinwheel cookies. But they're not done yet, you'll have to wait until they're baked." She picked up a rolled-out piece of cinnamon-sprinkled dough and placed it on top of another, rolling it into a long, fat tube. Conscious of Bryce's scrutiny, she experienced a wave of nerves, and took inordinate care with the dough, avoiding his gaze.

He ambled closer, watching as she picked up a knife and sliced the dough into about half inch slices. Before she knew what he intended, he reached over and snagged a piece, popping it in his mouth.

"Yuck! What are you *doing*?!!" she cried out in mock horror, the knife motionless.

"Um-m-m," he rolled his eyes and smacked his lips. "You don't need to bake those, they're good raw."

She wrinkled her nose. "Eeew! I've never understood people who want to eat dough!" She startled him by suddenly grabbing his hand. "Bryce! Is this *grease* I see?!"

He proudly held up the offending hand. "Yep. That's grease all right! I brought a part in to Chopsie to repair."

She put the knife down, her hand going to her heart. "Don't tell me you've been *working*?"

"Guilty as charged." He snagged another piece of dough.

"Stop it! You'll eat all my profits!" She grabbed up a wooden spoon, intent on lightly rapping his knuckles, but he moved at the same time and the spoon connected with a resounding *thwack!*

"Ow!" he yanked back, rubbing his hand, an injured look directed at her.

"Oh! I'm *so* sorry, Bryce, I never meant to hit you that hard!" She took his hand and began rubbing it, her face flooded with color while she struggled with emotion.

"That's a seriously mean spoon!" Her touch sent warmth up his arm and flooded his body, in spite of the stinging sensation in his hand.

"I'm *so* sorry, I can't tell you how *sorry* I am!" Her voice wobbled as she continued to rub his hand, her head down and shoulders heaving, turning her face away.

Wrapping his other arm around her, he said, "It's okay, I'm a tough guy, don't be upset." Suddenly he realized she was *laughing*, not crying!

"I am not upset, I'm embarrassed." She deftly slid out from under his arm and cast a look at the two interested women in the dining room pretending not to hear what was going on. She lost the battle not to laugh, and it bubbled out of her.

He stared down at her. "You're laughing! You're *laughing* at my poor injured paw."

"I'm not," she denied, her eyes dancing. "It's just that…that…" and she was off again, giggles erupting before she could put her hand over her mouth.

He studied her a moment. "I'm deeply offended. But…tell you what. I'll forgive you…if you let me take you out to dinner."

"Forgive *me?! You* were the one stealing my dough!" Shaking her head, the laughter died as she lowered her eyes to the worktable. "Bryce. Listen carefully. I am not going out to dinner or *anywhere* with you."

"Why not?"

Yes, why not? asked the little voice. *When are you going to tell him the real reason you won't go?*

Not yet. He'd think she was…what? "I've told you before, I don't date," was what came out of her mouth. And why should she care what he'd think of her? Unless she really *did* care what he thought?

He held out his hand where a red welt had begun to raise. "I could tell everyone that you attacked me," he remarked smugly.

"I had every right, you were thiefing my dough!"

He folded his arms over his chest and stared down at her. "If I say pretty please, will you go, Robin?" She turned sideways but not before he saw her eyes flicker and he pressed his point. "Look, we can take the boys along, if that will make you feel...safer."

She sent him a withering glance. "I am not afraid of you, Bryce!"

"—Not of me, no, but maybe of how I might make you feel," he clarified softly, leaning towards her. "You're afraid that I'll show you a good time and you'll like it."

"There's no conceit in your family—you've got it all!" *Oh, the arrogance of the man!*

"Prove you're not afraid by going out with me...and we'll take the boys."

She jerked her head up and studied his face. Uncompromising, he held her gaze. He was as determined as she.

It was time. She squared her shoulders and took a deep breath.

"Even if I felt like dating, Bryce, I can't go out with you because of...of how different we are." She let out a resigned sigh. "I'm a Christian and you're not."

He was silent, a perplexed look on his handsome face. "Your God has something against dating?" His eyes bored a hole into her.

She shifted her attention back to the dough and began working on it again. "No, Bryce, but it never works for a believer and an unbeliever to keep company."

He was silent for so long she finally had to look at him. "I don't accept that. Besides, I didn't suggest we hop into bed." He took satisfaction at the bright color sweeping up her neck and over her cheeks. "All I want is a dinner date, and if you think about it, you'll realize there's nothing wrong with that." He paused. "But don't think too long, I've got loose lips." He held up his reddened hand with a knowing look.

She gasped as he winked and walked out of the kitchen, jauntily waving at the two women who hurriedly lowered their eyes. The bells jangled, then he was gone.

All the while she finished the cookies and set them out in the glass display cases, she mulled over what he'd said. Even knowing she could never go out with him.

Dorine called Robin later that afternoon to report that she'd phoned members of the food committee to make sure everything was in readiness for the church picnic the next day. The two of them eventually got around to Bryce when Dorine explained his experience with Chopsie.

"So he got the repaired part back okay," Robin commented then unthinkingly added, "I wondered where he got so greas—"

There was a moment of silence. "How do you know he was greasy?"

Robin hated to admit that he'd been to the café, because then she'd have to tell her friend about the episode in the kitchen. Which she did.

Dorine went off into gales of laughter. "I saw that red mark but I thought he got it out in the field." Her voice dropped. "Robin, what was he doing in your kitchen?"

Robin sighed, looking down the hall out the back door to where her sons played on the lawn, turning somersaults. "He's still after a date. But Dorrie, I'd be lying if I said I'm not flattered. Nothing will come of it, but you know, it feels…."

"—Kind of nice to have a man paying attention to you?" Dorine finished.

"Yes. But why him?" Robin groaned in annoyance. "I thought once I showed disinterest, he'd turn his sights elsewhere."

"I think he sees that as a challenge," her friend replied cautiously. "The disinterest."

Robin sighed again. "And he's not easy to ignore," she admitted. "But when I'm tempted, I just remember the verse about lightness having nothing to do with darkness."

Easier said than done. In the busy hours at the café, she could keep the handsome playboy out of her mind, but just let her mind relax one little bit, and there he was, taking over her concentration while she stirred, mixed and baked.

After closing the café that evening, she took the boys with her around front to water flower boxes with the hose, "accidentally" spraying the two unsuspecting children. They squealed and ran down the sidewalk, taunting their mother to stretch the hose that far. They were so engrossed in their play that none of them noticed the red convertible until it slid in to the curb behind them. Robin jerked the hose around at the sound, spraying Bryce as he got out, shielding his face with one arm.

"Oh, I'm sorry!" Robin clapped her hand over her mouth as she released the hand-held wand to shut off the water. "You startled me!"

"Mr. Martin! Mr. Martin!" Jason jumped up and down, his bare feet leaving little prints on the dusty sidewalk. Jeremy ran to hide behind Robin.

Bryce cautiously moved toward Robin, eyeing her suspiciously. He carried a long, narrow package. "I don't know whether to believe you or not."

"It seems I'm always saying I'm sorry, but I really didn't intend to do that." Her choked-back laughter belied her apology.

"I think you're out to get me." Bryce advanced, his eyes darting to the faucet, the hose and back to her.

"Don't," she spoke softly, guessing his intention. She felt Jeremy plastered against her. "You'll frighten him." She tilted her head towards the trembling little boy.

Bryce stopped. Then, remembering the water-splattered package, he held it out to Jason. "Here, you Cardinal. I brought you something."

"What's that?" she asked curiously, edging forward at the same time Jason did.

"It's for Jason—and Jeremy too, if he wants."

"You bought my kids a gift? Are you trying to bri—" Her eyes flew to his and knew he spotted the accusation there, bringing a frown to his forehead.

Jason's eyes grew wide as he ripped off the paper. "A bat! Wow!"

"Bryce, you didn't...." Her eyes widened and her voice trailed away.

Anger edged his reply. "No! I've never had to do that to get a date!" His nostrils flared. "I *wanted* to do this—maybe it'll prove to that other one, that I'm not a monster."

"Oh, he doesn't think that!" she exclaimed, horrified.

"It's for you too, Jeremy," Bryce turned and spoke softly. But the boy shrank away, and Bryce felt an odd pain near his heart. *Why didn't the kid like him?!!*

Jason's eyes glowing, he looked up at Bryce. "Thank you, thank you so much!" Turning, he held the bat towards Jeremy. "Lookit what Mr. Martin brung us, Jer!"

Bryce sent an irritated glance towards Robin, who held her fingers over her mouth, a look of indecision flitting across her face. "Do you suppose the kids could call me 'Bryce?' 'Mr. Martin' makes me sound old."

"Aren't you?" she asked innocently.

"Why, you minx!" Bryce stopped, glancing at the boys. They were busy examining the signature on the side of the bat, and he didn't think they'd notice if he planted a kiss on their mother's sweet lips. But he'd probably get decked!

Looking contrite, Robin gently touched the slightly-reddened knuckles on his hand. "Is that still sore?" Her touch was fleeting but he missed it when she took her hand away.

"No. Yes. It will be sore until you—" he glanced again at the boys "—consider what we talked about."

Her eyes danced. "Blackmail? No dice. I've been telling everyone that I had to thump your knuckles to keep you from eating my dough." She brought the hose up, pressing the 'on' button and water splattered at his feet. "Besides, I'm still armed."

He backed up and shook his head, not even trying to stop the grin that pulled at his lips. "I'm not giving up but let's table that for now. *Is* it okay for the kids call me by my first name?" He grew serious, his hands anchored on his hips.

She glanced at the boys doubtfully. "Wel-l-l…"

"I know you want to teach them respect for adults, but it's just for a few days and won't matter once I'm gone." As he said the words, he felt a hollowness—he *was* going to leave, and, it really *wouldn't* matter. He was always in and out of people's lives in a matter of a few weeks, but for once, that idea didn't sit well with him.

"Okay, I guess," Robin said slowly "…it will be alright. I just don't want them to get in the habit of doing that, because when Jason returns to school, he'll have to call his teachers by their last names."

"And I'm starting second grade!" Jason proclaimed proudly, gazing adoringly at Bryce.

That look made him inwardly squirm. If the kid only knew…he was no one to look up to. At least he was man enough to know that. "Wow! You're getting to be an old duffer!"

Jason kept up his excited chatter about what he'd do in school, with Bryce barely listening. Uneasiness stole over him at the kid's unabashed interest.

"…and if you're still here, you could maybe come with me, with us, when Mommie takes me to school on the first day!"

Robin started and Bryce jerked his attention to the boy. Squatting, he put his hands on the small shoulders. "That makes me feel special that you'd want me to come, but I can't be here, Jason. I'm sorry. I have a job back in St. Louis."

Jason's smile faded and he glanced up at his mother with uncertainty. "But…but…you *could* come back, couldn't you?" His gaze switched imploringly to Bryce.

The kid sure could tug on his heartstrings. "I'm sorry, son, I just can't promise. My job takes me all over the country, and I don't know where I'll be when you start school."

Disappointment washed over the child's face and he turned away. "That's...okay...I guess." He stood with his back to Bryce, his shoulders looking impossibly frail while he struggled with emotion. Finally he turned with a forced smile. "Thanks again for the bat." He grabbed Jeremy's hand and the two disappeared around the side of the building.

Silence hung heavy as Bryce stood, running one hand over his hair while puffing out a long breath. "Okay, that went well."

Robin gazed after her children, worry in her eyes. "I'd better go to him." She looked up at Bryce, then away. "I'm...I'm sorry for suggesting you'd bribe the kids for a chance to be with me. That was unworthy." She took a deep breath, starting after the boys. She looked back at him. "Thanks for thinking of them."

"Wait, Robin!" She halted and half-turned toward him.

"Did...well, has anyone ever done anything to Jeremy?"

Her expression was blank.

He ran his hand through his hair again and glanced down. "I mean, because he seems afraid of men, I just wondered...if..."

She gasped as she caught his meaning. "No! I know where they are every minute of the day, and besides, I don't know of anyone around here who would do...what you're implying."

"It happens everywhere, Robin," he reminded her gently.

"I know," she admitted. "But not in this case. Besides, he's not afraid of *all* men," she stated firmly. "However, I can't explain why he has such an aversion to you." She gestured helplessly. "I just don't have a clue."

He nodded slowly. "Okay, just thought I'd ask."

After a heartbeat of silence, she managed a small smile and with an "I'll see you later," she left him standing alone on the street.

Starting his car, he thought over the past few days. He should have realized that since Dorine was so religious, Robin would be too, as they were such good friends. When Robin had told him she couldn't date him because of her faith, he'd brushed it off as an excuse on her part. And a feeble one at that. What did religion have to do with dating? He'd have to convince her that one had nothing to do with the other.

What he needed was a good stiff drink.

Chapter 6

"We're leaving for church in about an hour," Dorine announced at the breakfast table the next morning. Bryce sat between the twins, nursing his second cup of coffee. "We didn't know if you'd want to come along or not, but you're sure welcome." She eyed the scowling man across from her, staring morosely down into his coffee. "Or were you up too late last night and need more shuteye?" Her perky observation joined a sly smile.

"Naw, I'm okay," he mumbled. He wouldn't dream of sharing that he'd hit the local tavern after leaving Robin last evening. Then he peeked up at her. "Church, huh?"

"Yeah, an we's get ta see our bestest friens!" emphatically declared David as he licked at a drop of syrup on his cheek.

Bryce braced his forearms on the table and looked down at the dark-haired little guy seated next to him. "And who would that be?"

David grinned. "Jason and Jeremy, ov course!" His sweet mouth formed an "O."

Bryce's speculative gaze swung back to Dorine. "Jason and Jeremy, huh? The Jason and Jeremy as in Robin?"

She nodded while using a wet cloth on Doug's sticky hands. "Yes, and if we don't hurry, we'll be late."

Bryce leaned back, holding his cup and looked thoughtful. "Church, huh?" he repeated.

Footsteps pounded down the stairs, and Dean's younger brother Darrell loped into the kitchen. "Unca Darrell! Unca Darrell!" the twins cried as they greeted him with joy.

As far as Bryce could tell, Darrell was a cookie-cutter image of his older brother Dean, with his black curly hair, bright blue eyes and lanky build. "Hia, guys! Didja miss me?!" He scooped them up and after hugs, set them back in their chairs.

"Uh-huh," David bobbed his head. "And we rode out wif Daddy to see the cows, an Mama Cat had kittens an Bryce he's stepped in some horse stuff!" The twins almost fell out of their chairs in hilarious laughter.

Bryce stood and shook hands with Darrell across the table. "Good to see you again. When did you get in?"

"Late last night."

"Didja get bucked off?" David half-rose, leaning over his plate towards his uncle.

Darrell laughed. "Yeah, I got bucked off, *lots* of times! Sit down before you fall off." He crossed the room to the coffeepot. "Stepped in some horse stuff, you say?"

Bryce grinned, shrugging while the twins howled and cheered.

"Come on, you two laughing hyenas," Dorine ordered as she slid a plate of hot pancakes on the table. "Time to get ready for church."

"Momma, what's a hy-eee-na?" David asked as Dorine ushered them from the table.

"An animal that laughs with uncontrollable hilarity." She took their hands and headed for the stairs.

"*What?*" the boys asked as their voices grew fainter.

Darrell shook his head, leaning against the counter. "She's sure got a handful there, but she knows how to buffalo them." He took a sip of coffee and directed his gaze at Bryce. "How you been? I was hoping I'd get home to see you before your vacation was over."

"I've got lots more time, and everything's fine." Bryce sat down and leaned back in his chair again. "I don't think I've ever spent a vacation like this before. But what about you, I hear you're trying for another bull riding championship?"

Darrell moved to the table and took a seat. "I've got two more events before I'm with the top world contenders, but I was ready for the break this weekend." He rotated his shoulders. "Gives a guy a chance to rest up his bones."

Bryce leaned his forearms on the table. "I could never see the fun in climbing on a ton of mad bull."

Darrell laughed, his white teeth a contrast to his swarthy skin. "You have to be kind of nuts to do that," he agreed, stacking waffles on his plate, slathering on butter and pouring syrup over the stack. "These young guys coming up are tough competition." He cut into the stack and put the bite into his mouth. "I've only a got a few more good years."

"A guy would have to be in pretty good shape to do that all the time."

Darrell nodded and swallowed. "Rodeo riders never used to be considered athletes, just crazy guys, but we have to be in top shape for the rigors of bull riding. Guys usually quit riding bulls before they do any other event. It's dangerous if you lose your edge."

In between bites, he told Bryce about the science of riding wild bulls, then Bryce updated him with stories of how the twins tried to get him in trouble with their mother.

Wiping his mouth with a napkin, Darrell finally rose and carried his plate to the sink. "Well, if I'm going to make it to church on time, I'd better get a move on."

Bryce's smile faded. "You're going to *church?* You just got home!"

"Yep!" Darrell grinned. "Isn't a better place to be on a Sunday morning." He started toward the stairs, then stopped and turned back. "Did anyone invite you to go along?"

Bryce nodded. "But the roof would cave in if I set foot in a church."

"I've heard that before," Darrell scratched his head, "but I have to admit, I've never seen a church cave in for that reason."

"I didn't bring anything to wear to church."

"God doesn't care what you wear. He looks on the heart, not the outward appearance."

"Yeah, well, He wouldn't want to look on my heart."

"God is interested in everybody, man—" He stopped and spread his hands. "I'm not trying to pressure you, Bryce, just wanted to let you know you're welcome to go along."

"I haven't been in church except for friends' weddings. Other than that, I've never given it any thought."

"Well, today is as good as any other for giving it a thought." Darrell moved towards the stairs. "Gotta get my Bible, I'll be right back." He bounded up the steps, with Bryce thoughtfully regarding his retreating back. Church, hmm. If Robin was going to be there, this might be a good time to get her alone even if it was at a church thing.

The aged white frame church in Silverdale nestled comfortably in a grove of sheltering cottonwoods, surrounded by a lush green lawn that gradually gave way to the graveled parking lot. The sidewalk in front of the church along the street had been cracked and buckled by tree roots, but skateboarders apparently loved the natural ramp, as evidenced by the marks they left on the concrete.

Bryce got out of the ranch van after unbuckling the seat belts for the boys, who had each scrambled to get a seat next to him. Now they clamored down to reach the ground.

Dean came around the hood and opened Dorine's door, but didn't step back when she slid to the ground.

"You're in the way, cowboy," Bryce heard her whisper to her husband.

"I know, but nobody can see if I steal a kiss," Dean replied, dipping his head.

"*We* can, Daddy!" trilled David, grinning up at his parents.

Dean reached down with one hand and covered his son's eyes. "Now you can't see us smooching."

"Yeah, but I can hear you!" David made smooching noises and the boys exploded with giggles.

Bryce hid a grin as he turned away from the family moment, feeling an odd sensation near his heart. The DeFoes were so spontaneous with their affection, and he thought of his own politeness when he visited his mother and stepfather. It was always an effort to converse with them, cognizant of every word he uttered, mouthing meaningless platitudes. Not so with the DeFoes, they said what was on their minds.

"You gonna stand there all day, Martin?"

Bryce started as he glanced up to see Darrell waiting to get out of the back seat. "Sorry, man," Bryce mumbled as he stepped to the side, allowing Darrell to climb down.

"It's okay," Darrell whispered loudly, gesturing towards his brother and sister-in-law. "You have to get used to stumbling on them kissing just about anyplace. In fact, one time in the hayloft—"

"You shut your mouth, Darrell!" Dorine scolded quickly, glancing down at the twins who were intently listening to the adult conversation.

Darrell laughed uproariously as he hefted his Bible in one hand and resettled his dress Stetson more firmly on his head with the other hand. "Yee-haw," he crowed and ambled off towards the knots of people slowly making their way inside the church.

In his quick visual sweep of the crowd, Bryce saw that Robin was not among them and felt an uncharacteristic disappointment. Where was she?

Dorine gave Dean a slight shove and began brushing her top and skirt before reaching for David's hand. "See what happens when you don't behave yourself?" she hissed at her husband, indicating the retreating form of her brother-in-law.

Dean shrugged, exchanging an unrepentant look with Bryce who stifled a smile. Dean slammed the doors and took Doug's hand, moving towards the church entrance.

Inside the hushed sanctuary, muted light from stained glass windows spilled over polished wood pews, creating a reverent serenity. The old floor creaked underfoot as people quietly greeted each other before shuffling into pews. Bryce's eyes were drawn to the front, where a simple wood cross hung above an altar draped with a white cloth. Brass candlesticks stood like sentinels on either side of a large book that lay open on the altar. At the right, a podium on the platform sported a microphone and a vase of pink roses. Steps from the platform on the right led toward large double doors that opened into another room.

It wasn't until he was seated next to the window at the end of the pew with his hosts, that he became aware of soft piano music. Glancing to the left front of the church, he was startled to see Robin at the piano, her back to the congregation. He frowned. If she was *that* much into church, maybe—

David leaned over. "These ole benches useta get really hard afore they put cushions on'em." He sounded like a little old man and Bryce was hard-pressed not to chuckle out loud. He was sure that would have earned him a frown from Dorine, who sat at the end of the pew next to the aisle. He'd probably get the same look she sent the twins.

The music ended and Pastor Rick, a slightly rotund middle-aged man in thick glasses, stepped up to the podium to cheerfully greet the congregation. It startled Bryce when the people answered back in unison, "Good morning!" The few times he could remember being in church as a child, it was cold, silent and forbidding.

The pastor smiled broadly and announced the first hymn. David plucked a hymnbook out of the rack on the pew in front of them and shoved the book into Bryce's hands. Everyone stood and he felt the book burning like a hot potato as he rose to his feet. Dean rescued him by pointing to the number in his own hymnal. Surprisingly, the tune of "Amazing Grace" was familiar and he sang along as though he was in church every Sunday. David looked up at him in admiration, and an uncharacteristic warmth lodged near his heart. Who knew a look like that from the little boy could move him?

After the hymn, prayers and announcements, Dorine slid out of the pew and walked to the front to take a place next to the piano. With a slight smile and nod at Robin, she began her solo in a sweet clear voice that was enhanced by the piano accompaniment. Bryce found himself enchanted with her voice, but his feelings slowly faded to exasperation that such a talent was buried here in this little town, never to be heard outside of her family or this congregation. What was the matter with these people? Hadn't anyone ever encouraged her to develop that voice, expand her options? How about talent scouts? Had one ever heard her?

He looked around. Every face was attentive, some of the older women had their eyes closed with a rapturous expression. Dean's face mirrored pride and for once, the twins were quiet, listening to their mother sing. When the last note faded away, silence hovered over the congregation until loud applause burst out. Bryce jumped. This was supposed to be a sacrosanct place, and these people were clapping like they were at a rock concert!

As Pastor Rick stepped to the podium again, the congregation grew quiet. Robin left the piano and stepped off the platform to sit in the front pew. Bryce wondered if she knew he was in the congregation. She leaned over and he could just barely see the back of Jason's head, so Jeremy must be sitting up there too.

"Today, we're going to follow the Roman Road to Salvation. Turn in your Bibles to the book of Romans." Dean slid a book out of the rack, flipped through the pages and silently handed it to Bryce without looking at him. Bryce took the Bible, thankful for Dean's subtlety.

"While you're doing that," Pastor Rick continued, stepping out from behind the pulpit, "I want to tell you about a man who brought his wife to see the minister, complaining that they hardly talked anymore, there was very little communication. The pastor pondered for a bit then he said, 'Sir, what your wife needs is some kissing. She should have kisses every day'. The man scratched his head, then brightened. 'Can't do it every day, pastor, but I'll bring her in twice a week for those kisses!'"

The congregation burst into laughter which subsided as Pastor Rick readjusted his glasses. Bryce was struck by how genuinely happy everyone seemed. These people actually enjoyed sitting inside on a beautiful morning!

"The first signpost on the Roman Road to Salvation is in chapter three, verse ten." Bryce looked down at the page in the open Bible and noted there was larger print at the head of the columns. He easily found chapter three, and moved his finger to verse ten.

"'There is none righteous, not even one'." Bryce frowned. He didn't know that he agreed with that. He thought of the company's head secretary, a woman in her fifties. She was always bringing cookies, had pictures of her grandchildren on her desk, and in spite of difficult people to deal with, he'd never seen her angry or out of control. She was righteous if there ever was a righteous. But was she a church-goer? He didn't know.

Pastor Rick went on to explain about Adam's fall and expulsion from the Garden of Eden, and how everyone born after that, inherited sin. Bryce listened intently. "None of us could ever get back in God's graces by our own merit, we were all doomed," said the pastor. So what was the use of trying, Bryce silently questioned. He glanced around again, still wondering at the calm peace that permeated the congregation.

"Signpost two is in chapter six, verse twenty-three." There was a rustling of pages and Bryce found the reference. "'The wages of sin is death'," read the pastor. "That doesn't need a whole lot of explanation, so let's go on to signpost three. Turn to chapter five, verse nine." Bryce hurried to catch up. His thoughts were still anchored in "the wages of sin" verse but he didn't want to get behind.

Pastor Rick beamed as he read the verse, "'While we were yet sinners, Christ died for us!' Folks, we don't need to reap the wages of sin, there is a way out!" Bryce looked up from the Bible when he heard a chorus of "Amens" from around the room. Darrell glanced over the top of David's head and winked as he proclaimed, "Amen!" Bryce was struck at how natural the cowboy fit into this element, he seemed truly happy in his skin.

"We have a way out!" restated the pastor. "Sin entered the world through one man, bringing death that spread to all men, because all have sinned—" Pastor Rick paused and looked over the top of his glasses around the room. "Just because it says men, don't think you ladies are off the hook!" There was a smattering of chuckles. "Remember that when the Bible says 'men,' it is referring to 'mankind,' which includes both sexes." He grew serious again. "Adam brought sin but Christ abolished it through His death on the cross. In verse nineteen, it says 'through one man's disobedience, many were made sinners, even so through the obedience of the One, the many will be made righteous'." Bryce could follow that logic, and assumed the "One" referred to was Jesus, but in his memory, the only times he'd heard that name, it had been as a curse word. He squirmed and looked around, but no one else seemed uncomfortable with the reference to Jesus.

"In verse 21, we can see that the grace of God, through the death of Jesus Christ, His Son, grants eternal life to all who believe on His name." That was a big jump, to Bryce's way of thinking. He could concede that there was probably a God, and he knew that historically, it had been proven that Jesus lived. But as the Son of God? That would require some real faith to make *that* assumption!

"And lastly, turn to chapter ten, verse nine. 'If you confess with your mouth Jesus as Lord, and believe in your heart that God raised Him from the dead, you shall be saved'."

Pastor Rick continued on, but Bryce remained deep in thought. There was no way anybody could live once they were dead. Although there were reportedly after-death and out of body experiences, he didn't put much stock in them. They were like the people claiming to be kidnapped by aliens—

David reached over to close the Bible, bringing Bryce back from his pondering to notice that people were standing for the last hymn. He put thoughts of the sermon out of his mind. There was no way he was going to get sucked into this religion thing.

As people began spilling into the aisles, Bryce kept an eye on Robin while she continued playing, glancing up occasionally at the slowly-departing congregation. He knew the exact moment she saw him. A stillness came over her as their gazes locked but she was the first to look away. Darrell approached him just then with a petite, older woman who seemed to take Bryce's measure in one glance.

"Hello, young man!" She held out her small, age-spotted hand.

"This is Molly Schafer," Darrell grinned. "Her…daughter and I went to school together." Bryce caught the hesitation in Darrell's voice and didn't miss the quickly-hidden emotion he saw in the cowboy's eyes. He stored the information away for later.

Bryce took Molly's hand and brought it up to his lips to kiss it.

"Oh, pshaw, you young scalawag!" Molly exclaimed, "you needn't think you can charm me like that!" The rosy bloom on her wrinkled cheeks belied her words, and glancing at Darrell, he caught a glimmer of appreciation. Molly must be someone special.

Before he could ask, other parishioners came to greet him. They seemed intent on shaking his hand, welcoming him and inviting him back to church the next Sunday. No one seemed in a hurry to leave except for children as they pushed between adults in the crowded aisle. He even spotted Deputy Langley in uniform standing at the back, his arms crossed over his chest, his belt bristling with holster, radio and whatever else he had on there. *Cops in church?*

David interrupted his train of thought by grabbing his hand. "Come on, Bryce!" he demanded in a whiny voice, earning him a frown from Dorine as she chatted with others.

"You go ahead, I want to talk to Jason's mother," he answered the boy. Dorine lifted one eyebrow but turned as she led her son towards the pastor at the door.

Robin ended the song and stood to close the piano lid. She gathered her music, stepped off the platform and walked to the pew where Jason and Jeremy waited. Bryce briefly contrasted their quiet behavior with the rowdy DeFoe twins. Even knowing they were a little older, was it normal for them to act like little robots?

However, they weren't his focus.

Their red-headed mother was.

He'd spent an inordinate amount of time thinking about her last night. He'd never chased after a woman, why this one? He took a place at the end of the pew as she approached. They were alone, only a few people remained talking to Pastor Rick.

Robin's heart picked up the pace when she saw that Bryce was apparently waiting for her. What in the world was she going to do about him? There was no way she could let him think she was even remotely interested. The only positive thing in her favor was that he'd be gone soon. And temptation with him. However, he'd been under the teaching of a godly man this morning, and perhaps something of what pastor said had penetrated his heart. That lifted her spirits.

Jason caught sight of Bryce and a smile lit his little face. "Hi, Mr. Martin!" He dropped Robin's hand and moved to Bryce's side. "I mean, Bryce."

"Hi, yourself," Bryce smiled down at him, noticing Jeremy out of the corner of his eye, trying to hide behind Robin.

Robin's exuberant expression was like the sun coming up. "Well, what do you think of our little church?"

He shrugged. "I don't have anything to compare it to but everyone is certainly friendly."

"Yes, they are," she said softly, her eyes gentle. "What did you think of the sermon?"

"Your pastor is a very gifted speaker."

She continued to gaze at him, as though expecting more.

"Mommie, I'm hungry!" Jeremy whined, pulling on Robin's hand.

Giving Bryce a lingering look, she said, "We'd better hurry then before you dry up and blow away." She swept them towards the door. "You did know there was a picnic right after church today?" she asked over her shoulder. He nodded.

Robin shook hands with the minister, turning to Bryce as though to introduce him. Pastor Rick, however, surprised them both by remembering Bryce. He asked about the St. Louis Cardinals, and while the men hashed over statistics, Robin made her escape.

"Robin! Robin!" Dorine called to her from a knot of people clustered on the edge of the shaded lawn. Vehicles were leaving the parking area, dust churning up and drifting through the air. "We can run over to your place to get your food while the guys help straighten things and lock up."

Darrell waggled his eyebrows. "We don't need to have anything else if you bring *kucken*. We could fill up on that and die happy!" His gaze shifted over her shoulder. "How about you, Bryce? Have you tasted Robin's *kucken*?"

Robin already knew Bryce was close behind her, the tiny hairs on the back of her neck were all standing at attention.

"Sure have!" Bryce heartily agreed. "In fact, she should be marketing it all over the county—heck, all over the state!"

A warm flush stained Robin's cheeks and Darrell gave her a mischievous look. "See? Put old Bryce here in charge of sales, and you won't be able to keep up with the orders!"

"That is, if he wouldn't eat it all first," she quipped.

Dorine was about to comment when she saw David chasing by with a stick and a determined gleam in his eye. "Whoa, young man, where do you think you're going with that?" She grabbed him by the arm to slow him.

"I'm gonna hits that Parker kid! Hees cousins are here from Texas and they said Texas is bigger'n Souf Dakota!" Dorine firmly removed the stick from his clenched hand.

"Honey, I hate to tell you this, but Texas *is* bigger than South Dakota. That doesn't mean you can go around thumping on people."

"Huh-un! It's not eeever bigger'n Souf Dakota!"

"Hey, big guy," Darrell reached over and took the struggling boy from Dorine. "You better listen to your mother, or she'll switch you with that stick."

David grew still and looked uneasily at his mother.

"Darrell, why do you say such outrageous things?" Dorine scolded. "Maybe I should use this stick on *you*!"

"Yeah! Yeah!" David yelled gleefully, squirming to get down.

Darrell held up his finger, wagging it in front of Dorine's nose. "Ah-ah-ah! No violence in front of the kids!"

Everyone roared with laughter and Dorine threw the stick away.

Chapter 7

In no time at all, the van was traveling towards the ranch with all four boys singing "Ninety-nine bottle of coke on the wall." They'd made a quick trip to pick up the *kuchen* and a change of clothes from Robin's house.

"Coke?" Bryce wrinkled his brow. "I thought it was—"

"Coke! It's *coke* in this van!" declared Dorine with a meaningful glance.

Dean chuckled as he slowed for a gopher skittering across the road. Glancing in the rearview mirror, he said, "And if it's coke, it better be brown and wet!"

"How'd they ever learn that song anyway?" Bryce asked.

All eyes turned to Darrell, who adopted an innocent expression. "Why are you all looking at me?"

"Yeah, ole Mr. Innocence!" Dorine winked at Robin.

Bryce turned his gaze on Robin, who had remained unusually quiet. She sat with her hands demurely folded in her lap and he wondered what was going through her pretty little head. She looked up at him then quickly glanced away, staring out at the countryside. He moved to put his hand along the top of the seat behind her shoulders, and gently tugged on her seat belt, priding himself on his smooth moves.

She shifted away from him.

Well. That went good.

He had no way of knowing that her heart was pounding at his nearness and she was afraid he would hear it! Her tongue seemed to be glued to the roof of her mouth.

"Hey, Mr. Martin Bryce, yous gonna swim wif us?!!" shouted David from the back seat.

Darrell held his ears. "Ye gads! You don't have to blast my eardrums, buddy!"

Encouraged, the boys yelled all the louder until Robin turned and gave Jason a stern look. "My goodness, I haven't heard you get this loud since your dad..." her voice died away and she averted her face, but not before Bryce saw her stricken expression.

"Aww, he's not loud! Unca Darrell says loud is good!" shouted David, unaware he'd rescued the awkward moment. The boys dissolved into fits of childish laughter while Dean cleared his throat. Dorine reached back from her seat beside Dean and patted Robin's knee without looking at her.

They pulled up in front of the house and the boys tumbled from the van, followed more sedately by the adults carrying food.

Soon, cars, vans and ranch pickups filled the yard. Bryce hurried to help when the men carried picnic tables out of a nearby shed, placing them in the dappled shade on the lawn. Covered dishes appeared from nowhere and soon the tables were laden with food.

Dean called for quiet, followed by Pastor Rick asking a blessing on the food. Conversation gradually picked up again as people lined up with plates in hand, many of them urging Bryce to go ahead of them. He felt warmed by how easily people accepted him. He knew from experience that rural people weren't as jaded as their city counterparts but it still surprised him at how open they generally were towards strangers.

He followed Robin through the food line while she filled plates for the boys. He deftly slipped two of the plates away from her when he saw her juggling act.

She raised an eyebrow. "Bryce, I do that all day long, I can handle two plates."

"Not today. Today, *I* will be the jugglee," he instantly replied. Squinting, he asked, "Is that a word?" She only smiled and turned away, Jeremy tucked safely behind her. Bryce was getting used to the boy's behavior around him, but he still didn't like it.

They found a spot at a table with Paul and Melody Fisher, managers of Dorine's ranch. Bryce chuckled at Robin's deliberate ploy to put Jason next to him, then herself and Jeremy. That's okay, he'd bide his time.

He switched his attention to the couple across the table. Their daughter Kimberly, who was only a baby when Bryce was here before, was now a healthy, pretty little preschooler with dark hair and brown eyes. He recalled that she had become terribly ill while he was tracking rustlers, and Dean had flown the baby girl, her mother, and Robin to the Rapid City hospital. Bryce now commented on her glowing health and the little girl darted a look up at him, blinking her eyes flirtatiously, while her lips turned up in a pretty pout.

He laughed and shook his fork at Paul. "You're gonna have to beat the boys off with a stick in a few years!"

Paul, glancing proudly down at his daughter, nodded. "She takes after her mother."

Melody gave her husband a loving look that excluded all others and a sudden thought arrowed into Bryce's mind—would a woman ever sincerely look at *him* like that? His gaze immediately went to Robin.

No!

Not her! This was so not going to happen.

His glance flicked to family groups and knots of teens that lounged on the tree-shaded grass. The young men were trying to catch the eye of the young women, who in turn, were trying out their feminine wiles on the guys. One particularly tall blond guy with Hollywood looks was lavishing his charm on whatever female was within arm's length. Bryce watched him at first with admiration at the kid's smoothness, but then he noticed the guy was laying it on pretty thick. Couldn't he at least stick with one girl instead of calling them all his "lil' darlin's?" Did he think they were so dumb they couldn't spot his insincere flattery?

But don't you do the same thing? came the little voice. He stilled. A twinge of uneasiness touched his conscience as he remembered how he himself had lavished charm on the fairer sex at that age—and beyond. Glancing at the teen, he saw himself. Sudden clarity made him realize his tactics had not changed, only executed with more finesse—

"Bryce?"

He jerked around to meet Dorine's amused glance.

"Did you hear what I said?"

Before he could answer, Darrell got up and chortled, "No, he was too busy ogling the girls." He gestured towards the teenage bunch.

"No!" Bryce denied vehemently. "Jail bait." He heard a soft snort from Robin's direction but didn't dare look. He felt exposed, as though his sudden revelation was obvious to all. But people were still visiting, kids still running around, the sun still shone.

"Bryce?"

He looked apologetically at his host. "I'm sorry. I was thinking of something else. What did you say?"

"I said, for all the time we've known you, you've never said anything about your family. I know you don't have any brothers, but how about sisters? Cousins maybe?"

He shook his head. "Nope, I'm an only. My parents had me late in life, then my dad passed away and after a time, my mother remarried a widower with no children. So there's not even a step family lurking around."

This time there was a sound of sympathy from Robin's direction and Dorine's expression grew tender. "Well, I'm glad that you could be here with us today."

Children playing tag around the tables were a welcome diversion, the noise level increasing the more children that joined in. Robin pondered the loneliness she detected underlining Bryce's words. For all his cavalier approach to life, she sensed there was an emptiness beneath Bryce's brashness.

Jason asked permission to get away from the table, taking Jeremy with him to join the other children. Robin watched them go, her thoughts still on Bryce's family or lack thereof. Having five sisters and one bathroom in their modest house while growing up, there was no time for loneliness. What must it have been like for Bryce as a little boy, growing up with parents who seemed detached, if she read between the lines?

Dorine smiled at the antics of the youngsters dashing around the trees, racing and jumping. "The kids are sure getting wild, bet they'll sleep good tonight."

Robin jerked her thoughts back to the present and sipped at her soda. "They don't get a chance to romp and let off steam at home. That's one disadvantage of living in town." She felt a stab of guilt that thoughts of Bryce had replaced her usual vigilance over her sons, and she determined to pay closer attention.

Dean came to the table and slung one long leg over the bench to scoot close to his wife. He rested his chin on her shoulder and looked at Bryce. "Get enough to eat?" Dorine placed her hand over her husband's, giving it a squeeze.

"Man, yes! I'm full. I'll have to run twice as many laps to work all that food off." His voice lacked enthusiasm and both Dorine and Dean gave him curious looks.

Robin had stacked the boys' plates atop hers and was about to stand when Bryce put his hand on her arm. "Stay sitting. You wait on people all week long, it's time someone waited on you for a change." He slid out and carried the plates to the large garbage can set up under a tree away from the tables.

Dorine raised her eyebrows and sent Robin a questioning look. Robin felt flustered and off-center. So much for not letting him dominate her thoughts! Her arm still felt warm where he had placed his hand, touching a chord in her with his thoughtfulness.

"Is there something going on here I don't know about?" Dean murmured, reaching around to swipe Dorine's pop for a swig. He tilted his head toward Bryce.

"We all ate too much, as usual," Robin said, twisting around to search out the boys. Dean didn't miss her deliberate ploy to change the subject and glanced at his wife. She gave him a "later" look.

"Stop checking on the boys, Robin," Dorine scolded. "They're having a good time and if they get too rambunctious, Dean can go quell the riot."

"*Me?* Why me? I don't want to play the heavy."

"Two of them are yours, cowboy," Dorine blithely reminded him.

Bryce came back and sat down, leaving a respectable distance between himself and Robin. She shot him a wary glance while conversation flowed freely around them but she was extremely aware of those broad shoulders just inches away. She noticed every time he shifted on the seat, every movement of his hands. However, something had changed. She could feel it as surely as if there was a tangible link between them. As though he was still there, yet not.

Suddenly, a ruckus burst out near the edge of the lawn. Two groups of boys were lined up, yelling at each other. David stepped close to a larger boy and shoved him. Bryce more than welcomed the diversion, and noticed Jason crowding right behind David, ready to support his friend. Even though there was four years difference, it was already apparent that David would be a leader.

Bryce watched with interest as the little warriors' insults escalated. But when David picked up a twig and aimed it like a gun at the older boy, Dorine jumped to her feet. Jason also picked up a twig, and Bryce heard Robin's sharply indrawn breath. She hurried after Dorine to the now-brawling kids, while other parents also rushed to the melee.

Dorine waded into the bunch and leaning over, grabbed David by the arms. "Haven't I told you never to point anything at anyone, even pretend?"

Robin yanked the twig out of Jason's hand and looked around for Jeremy. She couldn't believe that he too, held a twig like a weapon, drawing a bead on one of the visiting boys. "Jeremy! Put that down! What is the matter with you?"

"Them guys from Texas said they's better'n South Dakota boys!"

"Yeah," David hollered, "an we ain't lettin'm git away wif it!" He struggled to escape from his mother, who held on to the back of his shirt. Dean met her, reaching for his son and trying to hide a grin.

"Yeah," Jason hollered, trying to tug his hand from Robin's grip. "We can't back down now, we have to git'm!"

Robin stretched past him to grab Jeremy's arm and pull him away from the pack of shouting youngsters. She couldn't believe her quiet, well-behaved boys were acting like a pack of wolves!

Bryce sat back enjoying the tableau, a relief from his troubled thoughts. He was surprised at the pride he felt watching Jason stand up with his buddy. The little guy would grow into a loyal friend. But when he saw Robin struggling with the boys, he surged to his feet. It was taking all her strength to gain control and he covered the space between them in a few long strides. Easily lifting Jason from Robin's grasp, he said, "Hey Jason, you're sure wasting a lot of energy! You should save it up to play baseball."

"Us Dakota boys are gonna show them Texas boys!" Jason firmly declared. He slid his arm around Bryce's neck and poked a finger towards the boys rolling around on the ground. Bryce couldn't help the grin that spread over his face. He'd never seen the kid so animated!

Robin sent him a grateful smile before turning stern. "Well, come on, you *Dakota* boys, you need to cool off!" She marched Jeremy back towards the picnic table.

Darrell entered the fray, picking up Doug. He tickled the little boy as he carried him across the lawn towards the fenced pool.

"Where do you think you're going with my son?" Dorine demanded, hands on her slim hips. "He isn't getting away without consequences."

Darrell kept walking. "Gonna dump this guy in the pool to cool off. Robin said this would work."

"*I did not!*" Robin called after him, looking horrified. "Your nose is going to grow a foot long, Darrell DeFoe, for lying!"

Dean laughed as he followed his brother with David, who was now clamoring to get into the pool.

"I'd better get their suits," Dorine shrugged and followed her menfolk.

Bryce hesitated, glancing at Robin, then at the boy in his arms.

"Don't-you-dare!" she hissed, guessing his intention.

"I'm tempted." He winked, then stopped cold. Realization shot through him that his flirty ways were so automatic, he never even thought before acting. Easing down on a bench, he settled Jason between his knees. The boy promptly leaned back against Bryce's chest. Bryce felt a tug near his heart at the boy's trust, and he put his arms around him. "Do you want to go swimming too?"

Jason wound his arms around Bryce's forearm and peeked toward the pool. "Not like that, with all my clothes on!"

Robin sat down, keeping distance between she and Bryce, Jeremy on her lap. "What in the world made you guys act like that?"

Bryce averted his eyes, having no trouble deciphering her unwillingness to get close. A feeling of inadequacy assailed him and he didn't like it one bit. He hated that he was coming up lacking, in her eyes. But since when had that ever bothered him?

Jason turned an innocent look on his mother. "Mom, we were just helpin' out Davie and Doug."

Before she could reply, Bryce spoke up. "It's good to stick up for your friends, but their mother is right. You are never to point at another person like you have a gun."

Jason squirmed and twisted his head to look up at Bryce, a question in his eyes.

"That's right," Bryce replied soberly. "Guns are a pretty serious business."

Jason studied him a long moment. "Mom said you're a 'vestigator. Does that mean you have a gun?"

"Not usually, no," Bryce answered him honestly. "But I work with police and they sometimes have to have guns."

Jeremy had been quiet, resting his head against Robin's shoulder and watching Bryce warily. Bryce smiled at him but Jeremy turned his head away.

Laughter near the pool area drew their attention to where Darrell held Doug over the water, fully clothed while the youngster giggled and hollered. Other parents had followed, and before long, jeans and shirts had been exchanged for swim trunks and the pool was filled with splashing youngsters.

Jason and Jeremy begged to go change into their suits and Robin sent them off. "No more fighting! I mean it!" She called after them. It was quiet after they'd gone.

"Thank you," she said slowly, not looking at Bryce.

"For?"

"For backing me up and making them realize that guns can be dangerous." A sharp memory surfaced of Dorine's kidnapping by the rustlers, and that Bryce had carried a gun that night when her friend was rescued.

"You thinking about the rustlers?" his voice was quiet.

She glanced at him sharply, not comfortable with his seeming ability to read her thoughts.

He wanted to reach over and take her hand, stroke her fingers, but he instinctively knew that she wouldn't welcome that. "I don't often have to carry a gun, Robin."

"I...I wish you never had to," she confessed, looking off into the distance.

His heart skipped a beat. Maybe she didn't think of him so badly anyway. "Sometimes it's part of the job."

"I don't know how women do it, married to men with careers like yours, not to mention policemen...wondering if they'll come home."

"Randy wasn't a policeman and he never came home," he gently reminded her.

She looked down at her hands, then up at him. "That's true." Her words held sadness, and it wrenched his heart.

"Do you still grieve him, Robin?"

She didn't answer at first, looking down again. Then she shook her head slightly. "There will always be a part of me that wishes him back. Sometimes a catchy tune, something someone says reminds me, but the grief has lessened. However...sometimes...I feel..." her voice trailed off.

"Feel what?" His heart sank. She was still in love with the guy.

"That I'm being...disloyal to his memory, that I should do more to keep him alive for the boys." She glanced towards the noisy crowd around the pool.

He followed her glance. "It seems to me that they're pretty well adjusted, except that Jeremy has a dislike for me, and they both seem too quiet. But I don't know anything about kids," he hastily added, "I'm just comparing them to the DeFoe kids." He paused. "But...wouldn't it be better for them to be with other kids more?"

She stiffened. "I decide what's best for them." Frost coated her words.

Un-oh, foot in mouth. "I wasn't questioning your parenting.," he backpedaled. "I told you I don't know anything about kids. In fact, I've learned more about kids this past week than I ever thought I'd want to know, thanks to David and Doug!"

She visibly relaxed and a slight smile touched her lips. "Those two! They'd give anyone a run for their money."

A shout from the impromptu ball field out near the driveway drew their attention. "Hey Bryce! Come play, we need somebody on second," shouted one of the ranch hands.

He hesitated but Robin spoke up quickly. "Go ahead, I need to check on the boys anyway." She got up and walked away from him, feeling his eyes on her. She didn't know why she had told him about Randy, she hadn't shared much about her grief with anyone except Dorine. But Bryce was just too easy to talk to, and a good listener to boot. She'd have to shore up her defenses more, he was stacking up too many good points.

Chapter 8

As shadows stretched across the lawn, people began packing their stuff, others standing in knots, still visiting. Robin rolled up the boys' wet suits in their damp towels and glanced at her sons, who were sitting tiredly beside her on lawn chairs. They had played hard all afternoon with the other youngsters under the watchful eyes of the adults who didn't want the "Dakota boys" to engage in battle again.

Bryce approached her, looking disheveled but so appealing and her heart flip-flopped. He was toweling his face as he mumbled, "I'm taking you home so Dean or Dorine don't have to leave their guests."

Glancing at the remaining people, Robin realized it would be selfish of her to refuse Bryce's offer in order to have Dorine take her home. Once again, she keenly felt the loss of her independence by not having her own transportation. Her heartbeat quickened, however, at the thought of being alone with Bryce. Good thing the boys would be an effective buffer.

On the ride back to town, she kept to general topics for conversation, asking Bryce about his childhood, learning that he'd been sent to private schools, followed by college and career. Her heart sorrowed that he hadn't had the normal life of a child in a family home, surrounded by traditions and memories, and she said as much.

Driving with his elbow resting on the window frame, he replied, "Don't feel sorry for me, Robin, I preferred school to being at home, rattling around in that big house."

"Didn't you have friends over when you were at home?" she asked curiously.

He snorted. "And risk breaking something? No way! But I was allowed to play baseball on summer teams when I was home, and the coach took a bunch of us to his house a lot. He and his wife didn't have children, and she was the best cook I'd ever seen." He had a far-away look in his eyes, rubbing his chin with his knuckle and a slight smile playing around his lips. "Those were some good times. He had an old rumpus room and didn't care when we wrestled or had pillow fights."

Robin had to smile at the boyishness in his voice. So he did have a few happy memories. The thought had her glancing in the back seat where the boys had nodded off, their little heads drooping to the side.

"Is that...why you think I'm too protective with my boys, because they aren't adventuresome and do things like wrestle around on the floor?"

He slowed to let the car glide over the cattle guard. "I hadn't thought about it, but they don't get rowdy, do they? Except for today!" he ended, laughing.

She shook her head, smiling ruefully. "I could hardly believe my eyes, but...they were having a good time, weren't they?"

"I thought it was admirable of them to join up with the twins. I can see them being good friends all of their lives." She nodded and a comfortable silence followed.

Her eyes wandered towards the western sky, where the sun was slowly slipping behind low-lying clouds. "I wish it would rain once, instead of just clouding up." Dark clouds had built up over the Black Hills, just as they had every day for the past few weeks. Lightning flickered across the charcoal mass and thunder sounded distantly.

"It's been doing that every night since I've been here, and no rain yet," Bryce agreed, giving the sky a brief glance. He was acutely aware of Robin beside him. He glanced at her hands clasped in her lap and had to squelch the urge to reach over and cover them with his fingers, to tell her…what? Give him a chance? Since when did he ever ask before he acted? He rubbed his chin again. The sense of unease that had assailed him this afternoon was back and brought friends. These unfamiliar emotions seemed to be crowding him the longer he was around Robin. He enjoyed being with her, but why did he feel like he had to prove himself to her? She seemed content to just sit and enjoy the ride, not trying to fill the silence with coy remarks and flirty innuendoes. He liked it. Liked her.

Too soon, they were at the Sweet Schoppe. Together, like a team, he helped her carry the boys into their room and laid them gently on their beds. She slipped off their shoes while he returned to the car to carry in the rest of the picnic things.

"If you want to set that stuff inside the screen door, I'll take care of it later," Robin called softly. "Thanks for bringing us home."

"I'm in no hurry to go back. I can help you with this," he remarked as he strode by the bedroom door, heading for the kitchen. She wasn't getting rid of him *that* easily!

The house was overly warm after the suffocating heat of the day, a noisy air conditioner set in the shaded living room window working overtime. He set his load on the yellow formica kitchen table and dug the *kucken* pans out of the box.

Robin hurried into the kitchen as he was filling the old porcelain sink with water. "What do you think you're doing?" she demanded, her tiny hands on her hips.

He ignored her while he opened the creaky cabinet door to hunt for dishwashing liquid. Squirting some into the stream of water from the faucet, he replied, "I'm helping out. I believe in paying my way."

She tilted her head, while warmth stole through her at his words. "You aren't going to go away, are you?" *And I'm glad...aren't I? Oh, you fickle woman, you!*

"Nope! It's been a lot of fun and noise today, now I'd like to sit down and enjoy some quiet. With you." He surprised even himself at the sincerity in his voice.

"Bryce..." She liked the idea even though it warred with her good sense.

He held up his hand. "Just sit. Talk a little." He waited.

Her shoulders relaxed. "Okay. But just for a while. I have to do the books and get my orders ready yet tonight."

"Tonight?"

She nodded as she opened the refrigerator to take out a pitcher of iced tea. "I'm too tired weeknights, so this is my special time to concentrate on my profit and loss." She wrinkled her nose. "Such as it is." She thought how incongruous it was to see him at the sink and said so while she poured two glasses of tea.

He scrubbed at the pan before answering. "It's one way to get my hands clean after that ball game."

"Not in my dishwater!" she squeaked, jerking her gaze to the sink.

He laughed. "Too late." She approached but stayed an arm's length away. "Getting back to your books...I imagine it's tough, not having a very large customer base." He concentrated on the pan while holding his breath. Had he crossed the line?

"Lately it's been more loss than profit," she easily replied." I wouldn't even need to look at the books to know that!" *Now why had she told him her dilemma?* She grabbed a towel and dried the pans he'd already washed, mulling over how easy it was to talk to him.

Bryce glanced at her. "Maybe I can help you. I've always had a head for figures. That is, if you don't mind? Then we can sit and relax." He rinsed the last pan and piled it in the dish drainer, reaching for a towel to dry his hands.

She pondered his offer. *Well, why not?* It was a lonely procedure at best, and it might be interesting to have someone else's input. "Let's have our tea first, then the books." She dried the pan and hung up her towel, shoving aside her second thoughts.

"That's called procrastination," he teased.

"With a capitol P," she quipped, taking the glasses and leading the way down the hall.

Opening the screen door, warm air washed over her. "Whew, I thought it would be cooler out here, but even though the sun's gone down, it's still pretty warm." She lowered herself into the swing. The dark storm clouds had moved closer and a whirling breeze danced across the lawn, but there wasn't a hint of moisture in the air.

To her consternation, Bryce sat beside her, resting his right arm across the back of the seat and stretching his long legs in front of him. "I had a good time today."

"Dorine and Dean always host good parties and picnics, they're so hospitable." Her heartbeat sped up at his nearness but she tried to present a façade of calm as they sipped at their tea and listened to twilight sounds. "Do your parents ever entertain? It didn't seem so when you were talking about them earlier."

He chuckled without humor. "I can't see them at a picnic like today."

"Why not? I don't know anyone who doesn't enjoy a picnic."

A variety of emotions came and went in his expression. "Oh, yeah, at the country club. But anything outdoors has to be on a bug-free patio!" He emphasized his words by swatting at a buzzing insect. "They're too sophisticated." He turned to look at her. "Tell me about your parents. I know they must have been loving and attentive, to raise such a sweet daughter." *Smooth move, to change the subject so adroitly.*

She expected a wink and was surprised when he didn't add

anything flirtatious. Warmed by his compliment, she turned sideways to face him, tucking one leg under her. He seemed genuinely interested and appeared to have dropped his phony façade. She liked that.

Launching into stories of the crazy antics she and her sisters pulled on each other, Robin commented that they were the cause of more gray hair for their parents. He laughed, a sincere, spine-tingling laugh that spurred her on.

After some time, she grew quiet. "It seems strange that you don't have siblings, you get along so well with children, like you'd had lots of practice."

He flexed his shoulders, puffing out his chest. "Must just be my natural charm."

A bit of the flirty play-boy peeked out in that remark. She didn't want *that* Bryce back to intrude on this special time. She was fascinated by this side of him that he seemed to go to great lengths to keep hidden.

"What ever made you choose to be an investigator?" Her expression was open and expectant. A gentle breeze tugged at her reddish curls, giving her a carefree look.

He knew at that moment that his interest in her had gone beyond a curvy body and tantalizing lips. He couldn't think of any other woman who was interested in his past, only what he could do for them in the present. However, Robin had substance and depth, a fact that drew him to her. But hopefully that attraction would pass in a short time.

He took a deep breath. "A police officer came to my grade school and conducted a drug prevention program for several months, and he really impressed me. I liked hanging around after his class and he took an interest in me, talked to me, let me help him pack up his material afterwards."

He leaned forward and contemplated the toes of his athletic shoes, his hands cradling the glass between his knees. Robin sensed there was something unpleasant coming.

"What happened?" she asked softly.

Bryce swallowed and looked away. "A couple of months later, he was shot during a drug raid." He swallowed again and she reached over to lay her hand on his arm. He looked at her small hand, then up to her face. "He didn't make it."

"Oh, Bryce, I'm so sorry." Her heart went out to him and her eyes misted over.

Her small hand was warm and comforting on his arm. "I decided that I would try to make things better somehow, so others wouldn't have to go through that despair. I know I can't save the world, but by going into some type of law enforcement, I could do my part. Went to college, got a degree in criminal justice and here I am."

His usual cockiness was absent and his smile crooked. Robin felt her chest tighten with emotion. "I'm sure there's a little more to it than that." He put his hand over hers.

"Yeah, there was." He chuckled as he settled back more comfortably into the corner of the swing. "While I was in college, I discovered I had a talent for details. A bunch of us played those murder weekends where you discover who the murderer is, and I really got caught up in it. Before graduation, I explored my options and decided investigative work was my niche."

Without them being aware, twilight had draped a soft mantle over the back yard, cocooning them from the rest of the world. The air was soft and created a feeling of intimacy, backed by a chorus of insects who were coming out after the heat of the day.

But the two on the swing didn't seem to notice. "That's how you ended up with the insurance group?" Robin asked.

"The cases were varied, not just drugs, which I later realized could cause burn out from all the scum a person runs into with drug cases. But with insurance, there's anything from fraud to drugs, missing children, philandering spouses," he leaned towards her, "and, missing cattle." He winked, giving her a lopsided smile. "How about you? Was college an option for you?" He'd regained his composure while wondering how she'd charmed all that information out of him, and turned the subject back to her.

"I never did want to go," she confessed. "To be honest, my grades weren't that good. Not bad," she hastily added, "but not good enough for university."

"Aha! The truth—you didn't burn the midnight oil!" He leaned closer so their shoulders touched. "Seriously, didn't you ever want to get out of this little burg?"

She shook her head. "Never. I always knew I wanted to be a cook or baker. I watched every cooking show there was on television. I realized none of my sisters wanted to stay here in Silverdale. But I did! I held my breath until the last one was gone, fearful I might not get the Sweet Schoppe!"

"It's a tight-knit, caring town, but there's a whole big world out there to explore."

"Randy saw a lot of the country and shared that with me but I never did have the wanderlust. We both decided we wanted to raise our family here. Before the boys were born, I went with him a few times, but I didn't yearn to do a lot of traveling." A far away expression entered her eyes. "I don't regret that decision, Bryce. Randy loved driving that big old truck but loved it even better when he came home to us. When he was in high school, he drove truck for Andy at the lumber yard every summer and weekends during the school year."

"Didn't that bother you that he was gone a lot?" He placed his arm on the seatback behind her, letting his fingers dangle tantalizingly close to her shoulder.

"No, I knew he'd always loved trucking and I knew what I was getting into. We made the decision together and were happy with it."

"You still love him." It was a statement not a question, but he had to know if he was competing with a dead man. Suddenly, getting closer to her didn't seem like a good idea.

"There will always be a part of me that loves him," she smiled sadly. "We were friends first, our whole lives. It was rough those first few months. I didn't know if I was going to make it. I wanted to die too," she whispered quietly. "But there were the boys. I had to keep going, for them…it's just that…I still feel married." Silence followed her words.

"Well…" he finally ventured, "I don't understand that kind of commitment because I've seldom seen it."

"Not even with your parents?" She was glad to shift the conversation away from her.

He shrugged. "I was only five when Dad died, and Mother didn't remarry for quite a few years. She never talked about Dad. I kind of got the message that it was a taboo subject. I didn't resent her remarriage but my stepdad and I don't have a lot in common."

"Even now?" He wasn't inviting pity but her heart stirred. Once again.

"I make duty calls for dinner once in awhile."

She studied him soberly. "I think I'd die if my boys ever felt that way about me."

He shrugged off the serious subject. "You'll never have to worry about that, sweet—"

A loud screech of metal brought them both to their feet.

"There goes that darn air conditioner again!" Robin took off at a run and he grinned at the cute picture her swaying hips presented. He followed her into the house to the cooling unit. She pounded on the side of it and leaned over to flip a switch, peering in at the innards of the unit. "Andy told me it was living on borrowed time, it's so old." She continued to poke around but the unit remained silent.

"Can I have a look?" Bryce asked.

"Do you know anything about air conditioners?" One pretty eyebrow rose skeptically.

"Nope!" he grinned unashamedly. "But maybe I can see something that doesn't look right." He couldn't know that the little-boy grin grabbed her heart as she moved aside. He puffed out his chest. "Give it my manly touch." He winked and turned to the machinery. Her heart gave another little hitch.

However, no matter what either of them did, the unit refused to breathe out even one little puff of cold air. The room was quickly warming up, and Robin disappeared down the hall while Bryce tinkered. She came back with a large floor fan and plugged it in.

It didn't take rocket scientist mentality for Bryce to realize that any coziness he wanted with Robin was squelched for tonight.

"All that fan is doing, is moving the hot air around." He eyed it skeptically. "You guys can't sleep in this heat."

"I'll open the door from the café and the unit in there should help cool part of the house, at least the bedrooms," she replied. "First thing in the morning, I'll get Andy over here but it probably won't help." She sighed, worry clouding her eyes.

"What about your bookwork?" He waved his hand vaguely.

She shook her head. "It's too late, I'll work it in sometime tomorrow. Thanks again for bringing us home." She walked to the door, a clear invitation for him to leave.

He considered trying for a quick kiss but decided against that when weighed against the concern in her eyes. First of all, he was sure she wouldn't have welcomed it, and secondly, he wanted to savor her lips when he did kiss her.

He settled for running the back of his knuckles down her cheek, feeling hopeful when she didn't step back. "I had a good time with you today, Robin. Let me know if I can help you in any way with that air conditioner."

She nodded, then he was gone. She stood immobile after his steps had faded, touching her cheek. She finally turned and went down the hall to open the door to the café. The welcome cool air wafting by her didn't do much to cool her cheeks. Goodness, she couldn't let him get to her like this! But at the same time, she hugged the memory of the pleasant evening she'd spent with him. Not once did she have to dodge his innuendoes. She stilled. Or had he just switched tactics? She'd sensed a difference in him on the way home…and wondered. But not for long. The worry over the broken air conditioner loomed in her thoughts. How could she squeeze out the money for a new one?

After she'd brushed her teeth and got ready for bed, she paused to look at her wedding picture. Touching her finger gently to the glass, she traced Randy's face. "Randy, dear Randy, my sweetheart. What am I going to do?" she whispered. In her heart, she had been putting Randy to rest, but had Bryce speeded up that process? Could she look to a future that might possibly contain a new relationship?

But not Bryce. Never Bryce.

Sighing heavily, she climbed into bed to read her devotions. She drifted off to sleep with the sounds of thunder in the distance but there were no telltale pitter-patters on the roof during the night.

At the ranch, Bryce laid on his back in bed, arms folded behind his head, staring at the ceiling. He'd visited with Dean and Darrell before showering and climbing into bed. But sleep wouldn't come.

His mind drifted back over the day but the only outstanding images were those of Robin. Playing the piano in church this morning, mingling with people at the picnic, their pleasant evening on the backyard swing, her worry over the air conditioner. He yearned to taste her sweet lips but she couldn't be more off-limits if she worn a sign telling him to get lost. He'd dated women who said they were church attendees but their lifestyle was nowhere near as chaste as Robin's. What was different about her faith as compared to theirs? That she was a deeply committed Christian was plain, but he was persona non grata in her book because he wasn't a believer. That made him think of the sermon this morning. It nettled him that he could remember it so clearly.

The Roman Road to Salvation. It was in neon lights in his mind. He turned over, yanked the sheet to get comfortable, but the thoughts wouldn't go away…where *would* he spend eternity? He grumped. Probably in hell, living it up with the rest of his friends.

But that wasn't as comforting a thought as it had always been.

The next morning, Robin could not believe her eyes when she went into the café. Through the front windows, she saw Bryce leaning against the fender of his car out front, arms crossed over his chest and whistling. When he saw her, he waved and moved toward the door with that self-confident stride, his shoulders back and a spring in his step.

Her heart did a funny little flip-flop. Hurrying to unlock the door, she stepped aside as he bounded in. "What are you doing here so early?" She couldn't help but smile at him.

"That air conditioner was on my mind all night." At least she seemed happy to see him! "I thought I could run over to the lumber yard so you wouldn't have to."

She studied him in the early morning light. "That's nice of you, but this is your vacation, and the air conditioner is *my* problem." Her smiled faded.

"I'm offering to help out. You have enough to do this morning." He braced his hands on his hips and hoped to distract her by asking questions. "Don't you start your baking real early? Not to mention breakfast customers?"

"Don't change the subject. I don't want you fussing about that air-conditioner." As she turned, she continued, "I do have to start baking, but I'll call Andy when he opens up at eight, and maybe he can wire that thing back together so it lasts a little longer."

"Why don't you just get a new one?" He followed her into the kitchen, where she began setting out pie pans in a row.

"Don't I wish!" she laughed, taking a red bowl and dumping flour in it.

"You have to have one, it'll be like an oven in your house today."

"One good thing, that two-story building next door casts a shadow on the café roof most of the day and that helps keep us cool. Cooler as in not roasting," she added.

He leaned against the counter and crossed his arms over his chest. "You always find the silver lining to everything, don't you?" He stopped short of calling her a Pollyanna.

"No use crying into your milk." She opened the refrigerator and slid out a tray of eggs. "Wow, that sounded like something my grandmother would have said!" Moving back to the counter, she began deftly cracking eggs and dumping them into another bowl.

"Speaking of that building next door, have you ever thought about expanding into it?"

"You mean make the café bigger?"

"Actually," he shifted his weight to the other leg, "I was thinking more about a restaurant setting, as well as bigger kitchen with more ovens and workspace."

"Where would the business come from? You know how small this community is."

"You could expand with a more diverse menu, advertise, find some kind of gimmick to draw customers. Your *kucken* alone would be a big draw." He noted the pink tinge sweeping her cheeks, knowing he'd pleased her with his compliment.

But she shook her head. "Let's not even go there. I don't have enough capital to invest in something like that. Besides, it's too risky." If he only knew—she had *no* capital!

So she was worried about finances. "People drive long distances today to find good food…I think you could do it."

"Bryce." Her voice was infused with exasperation, as though talking to a child. "This is South Dakota, not a metropolis. Folks around here cook and eat at home for the most part. Gas is too expensive to drive very far just to go out to supper."

"You're still thinking 'café.' I'm talking about a dinner restaurant, with white linens and candlelight." When she only shook her head, he went on. "I can look into it for you. If you don't have the wherewithal, have you considered taking on a business partner?"

Robin's hands stilled. *A business partner?* She angled her head and glanced at him. *He was serious.* "You would go that far just to get a date with me?" Her eyes twinkled.

"Honey, I'd do *anything* to get a chance to wine and dine you. But no, that wasn't my intent. I'm just trying to look at the big picture here."

"Bryce, Bryce." She sighed, continuing to mix ingredients. "That's not an option."

Bryce shifted his weight again and went on as though she hadn't spoken. "I've been thinking about your situation here. You know that the secret of good marketing is to go bigger. I think your *kucken* would be a tremendous angle. I told you about my friend Mark and…the restaurants. I'm certain that once he tasted one of your *kuckens*, he'd be sold on it." He'd almost let it slip about his part in the restaurant chain. Not that he wanted it to be a secret, but in light of her resistance to him, the less she knew about that part of his business proposal, the better. Let her think she would be dealing with Mark—*if* he could gain her confidence.

"And the business partner would be…." her words trailed off.

"Mark. Mostly." At her raised eyebrow, he added, "I, ah, sometimes help him in finding new cuisine. With an infusion of capital, you could expand into some of the things you've wanted to do, like adding espresso."

He couldn't know that he'd taken part of her dream and run with it. It was very tempting to consider his offer, but could she give up control to a second party in a business venture? Also, she didn't know this Mark or his background. If he was anything like Bryce, being such a good friend, mightn't his moral values be similar?

"Well, you think about it," Bryce filled in the silence, dropping his arms and straightening. "Would Andy open up any earlier if I went over there?"

All thoughts of expanding the restaurant fled as she stared at him like he had two heads. "Didn't you hear me? I don't want you going over there!"

Bryce gave her a long look, then walked to the sink and washed his hands.

"Now what are you doing?"

"I might as well help while I'm arguing with you." He leaned towards her. "Besides, you're extra cute when you argue. But just know this—I'm going to win. I always win."

She eyed him suspiciously. "You? Help?" She leaned towards him. "Read my lips. You are not going to win."

"Sure I am. But for now, just tell me what to do."

"Boy, is that a loaded comment!" Her eyes danced but she shrugged and waved a floured hand at the counter beside him. "First, grab some plastic gloves out of that box," she pointed. "I hope they're big enough to fit your hands."

"Have you ever thought of filling these with water, like balloons?" he joked, shoving his hand into a glove.

"Don't you dare suggest it where my kids will hear you!"

He laughed heartily and stood ready for her instructions. As she explained, he took mental notes, thankful again that he had a mind for details. By the time the first *kuckens* were ready for the oven, he had the recipe firmly entrenched in his mind.

An hour later, the *kuckens* were baking, the kitchen cleaned up and preparations ready for the first breakfast customers. She and Bryce had kept up a verbal tennis match of quips that had them both laughing and the time flew by. He told her more about his college roommate. "He taught me a lot and every time I visit, I work in the kitchen with him," Bryce finished. "I kinda like it."

"Better than the insurance business?" Robin asked as she washed her hands.

"At this point, no, but you never know." He walked through the door to the serving counter and poured two cups of coffee. Ducking his head to see her beyond the passthrough, he commanded, "Come on, take a load off and have coffee with me."

It had been hard enough rubbing shoulders with him in the

kitchen, she didn't need to place any more temptation in her way. But before she realized it, she found herself sliding onto a stool next to him. "Now I know why you seem so comfortable in the kitchen." She paused, setting down her cup, clearing her throat. "It was…um…fun having you help. I'm about half an hour ahead of schedule," she admitted. "Thanks."

He beamed at her. "We make a pretty good team, don't we?"

"Don't break your arm patting yourself on the back."

He squeezed her shoulder and laughed. "Your flattery is going to puff my head so big you'll have to make the doors wider."

A knock sounded at the locked café entrance and they turned to see two older men peering in through the glass. "First customers," Robin announced and slid off the stool.

The grizzled old ranchers eyed Bryce as they brushed past Robin, who held the door with one hand, and with the other, turned the "closed" sign over to "open." Shuffling to their customary booth near the front door, the men gingerly lowered their aging bodies to the vinyl seats.

"That fancy car of yourn getting' kinda dusty, ain't it, young feller?" One of the men brushed a hand down over his bristly chin, while he turned his coffee cup over, signaling he was ready for coffee.

"It wasn't too bad this morning coming into town, no one else was on the road." Bryce swiveled the stool to face them.

"I see'd you go by, when I went to let the chickens out," said the other old gent. He winked at his partner as he turned his cup over too.

Robin suddenly realized that Bryce's presence in the café so early this morning could have been compromising but he had diverted that suspicion with his remark. She thanked him with her eyes and felt heat rise in her cheeks when he winked back at her. She headed for the coffee pot. Boy, was she asking for trouble! Bryce met her halfways and took the pot from her, giving her another audacious wink. Flustered, she returned to the kitchen as he served the men and engaged in banter that had them all laughing. He even got some plates from under the counter to serve them cinnamon rolls while they chatted like they were old friends.

Men!

When she began cooking her specialty sausage, Bryce was drawn into the kitchen pretending to follow his nose to the stove. "What is that?"

"German sausage," she replied as she pricked the skin of the meat and released more savory aromas. It bubbled merrily away in its water bath, steam rising slowly above it.

"I'll bet it tastes better even than it smells."

She reached for a small plate nearby. "Hint, hint? Here, you can't drool all over my kitchen, it's unsanitary." She pretended to swat at him with one hand as she put a sample of the sausage on the plate with her other hand.

He laughed, his expression turning rapturous as he tasted the sausage. "Um-m-m." He closed his eyes, savoring the moment. Then his eyes popped open. "Who is your supplier for this?"

"I make it myself and freeze it ahead of time." The bells jingled above the door as more people came in. "It's an old family recipe. Now, I have customers to take care of, and you keep your paws out of that sausage."

"Yes, ma'm!" he quipped, while lasciviously eyeing the meat pan. Her heart took a dip at the boyishness he displayed, only half-heartedly reigning in her emotions. It *had* been a fun morning. *Please don't' spoil it with any of your innuendoes* she silently begged.

From then on, there was a steady stream of customers, and Robin suspected they were more curious than hungry when they saw that red car out front. Bryce stepped in to serve each arrival with coffee, while Robin was pleased and also touched by his actions. He had a knack for anticipating needs. With a white towel tied around his middle, he bantered with customers and took orders, then helped her serve. She was losing ground in her determination not to let Bryce get close to her, but seemed powerless to stop it.

They were the subject of speculative glances but he pointedly ignored them. He appeared to have not a care in the world as he circulated around the room. He held the chair for old Mrs. Kreil, gently sliding it closer to the table when she was seated. When Alvina Gates came in with her toddler twin girls, he hurried to bring her an extra high chair and amused the children with his silly faces. Robin didn't miss the admiring glances directed at him from almost every woman and girl in the café. She watched with sinking heart, hearing the walls of her resistance come tumbling down. Oh, he did not play fair!

At eight sharp, he whisked off his makeshift apron and headed out the door before she realized he was leaving. Puzzled, she wondered why he didn't at least say goodbye. Glancing out the window, she watched him jog to the lumberyard, where Andy was just unlocking the door. Aha! So *that* was it! They shook hands and disappeared into the store. She began a slow burn. That boy needed some straightening out!

After the breakfast crowd, Robin furiously bussed tables, replacing flatware and cups. She just finished refilling napkin holders when Bryce bounded back in the door, all smiles.

"Well?" She paused, the box of napkins in her hands, twitching to do battle. Good thing there were no customers in the café at that moment.

"Got a new air conditioner coming on the supply truck this afternoon," he replied smugly. He turned to shut the door but whipped around at her sharp response.

"*What?!!*" She dropped the box onto the counter. "Didn't you hear me earlier? I don't *want* a new unit, I want him to look at the old one!" Her hands were propped on her hips in a stance that should have warned him.

Not even looking contrite, Bryce imitated her stance. "He said there was no point looking at it, the last time he was over here it was practically worthless then."

"I know that!" Her voice dripped with disdain.

"And he said he'd order you a new one."

"I can't *afford* a new one!" She whirled towards the phone but Bryce crossed the room to stop her.

"I'm paying for it."

"*What?!* You most certainly are not!" She stared up at him, sparks flashing in those beautiful eyes.

"Robin, you have to have an air conditioner, you can't live in that house with this heat. Think of the boys," he explained reasonably.

"They can always come in here during the day." She snapped out the excuse, even knowing he was right, but she was on a roll. "Besides, I can't pay you back. I told you right from the start that I can't afford a new air conditioner!"

Her stubbornness tripped his ire, and he spread his hands placatingly. "Look—"

"No, *you* look! You think you're helping but you're just trying to get your own way without even considering my feelings!" Realizing she was close to shouting, she hesitated.

"You're being unreasonable," he snapped, "you need that AC. *Today!*"

"Give it a rest, Bryce. I cannot pay for a new air conditioner."

"Let me do this for you," Bryce cajoled. How had this escalated into such a heated argument? "I've seen how neighbors here help each other out, and that's all I'm doing, just helping out. No strings attached." He held his hands up as though surrendering.

More subdued now, she waffled for a long moment, looking him in the eye. "Alright, but I'll pay you back in installments—"

"No, you won't. This is a gift."

"Bryce," she said, warning in her voice. "I can't—"

Jingling bells announced new customers, four husky men who talked loudly as they headed for a booth. Their conversation marked them as truck drivers, probably from the state gravel pit operation. The last of them, his potbelly hanging over a well-worn leather belt, pushed himself into the booth. "Hey, sweetheart, how about some service?"

Robin's face clouded for a moment then cleared. "We're not finished with this," she muttered unhappily as she turned to get the coffee pot.

Bryce lowered himself to a counter stool while he realized he'd really enjoyed their little spat. She was so adorable and full of stubborn determination, her independence enduringly cute. His attention was diverted by a group of women trouping in the door, some carrying books, and one a baby carrier with an infant in it. They headed towards the corner table opposite the truck drivers, calling out cheerful greetings to Robin. One of them detached herself and brushed by Bryce with a quick smile, to grab a carafe of coffee and head back to the table. "Book club meeting," she flung over her shoulder. The women's chatter was filled with joking comments as they placed books and papers on the table and settled themselves around it.

Bryce's eyes swung back to where Robin poured coffee for the truck drivers, then took their orders. Pot Belly was giving her the eye, making scrambled eggs sound suggestive. Bryce took an instant dislike to the man, letting his gaze wander over the other three men. Two of them looked uncomfortable at their friend's innuendoes, and the third man met Bryce's gaze, then dropped his eyes to the menu.

Robin hurried to replace the carafe, continuing on to the kitchen. When the bells jangled again, two older couples came in. Bryce slid from the stool, grabbed a full carafe and headed to their table. From their conversation, Bryce learned they were on their way to Rapid City for a day of shopping. "You the new help around here?" one of the men said, winking at Bryce. "If I was working here, I'd take out my pay in *kucken*!" The whole group laughed. The man's wife turned to Bryce and said, "That's all we came in for, some of that *kucken*. If there's any prune left, I'll have a slice of that."

"I'll take just the plain cottage cheese."

"Me too."

"Is there any peach?"

Bryce hesitated only a second. "I'll go see. Be right back." He headed for the kitchen, bumping through the swinging doors. More customers came in, noisily filling several tables, but a glance at Robin showed that she was not flustered by having so many customers and only herself to wait on them. Of course, any of the regulars often helped themselves to coffee, realizing that Robin would get to them when she could. A far cry from his demanding city counterparts. He was doubly glad he'd come by.

In spite of herself, a chuckle escaped as Robin tried to hide her amusement at seeing Bryce juggling multiple orders. Her ire, for the moment was forgotten. "Do you even know what you're doing?" She grabbed slices of hot toast, slathering butter on them.

"You think I can't do this? Just point me in the direction of that *kucken*!" Bryce grabbed his towel and tied it around his waist. "Laugh at me, will you?!" He sent her a challenging look, but this wasn't the time to tell her just *how* proficient he was!

"In that refrigerated case out front. Labels under the pans, and you know where the plates are." Bryce nodded, heading back out to the main room. She thought again how comfortable he seemed in this element, uncaring what others thought. A man really had to be at home in his skin to face the rugged men customers with such aplomb. But if anyone could do it, Bryce could. She tried to squelch the admiration for him that grew every time he did something endearing, but it was a losing battle.

He served the couples, noting that everything was under control. Robin bustled out of the kitchen with the truck drivers' orders. When he saw it would take her two trips, he got the remaining orders and helped her serve the men. Giving him a grateful smile as she passed him with the coffee pot, she asked if the drivers wanted refills.

Bryce had walked behind the counter to see if the coffee maker needed refilling, and flicked a glance at the truck drivers. He could not believe his eyes when Pot Belly laid a beefy hand on Robin's hip, sliding down....

He slammed the pot down and stalked toward them.

Turning to Pot Belly with a pleasant smile, Robin said softly, "If you don't move your hand, you're going to be wearing this coffee in a place that may prevent your parents from having grandchildren."

Pot Belly's face turned red and angry as he dropped his hand, while his companions roared with laughter. Then he spotted Bryce standing behind Robin.

"Apologize," Bryce ground out.

Robin whipped around, almost slamming into Bryce with the carafe. "Bryce!"

Bryce's eyes never left Pot Belly's face. "You heard me."

"Aww, he didn't mean nothing by it," said the third man. "He's new on the job, and he's just getting acquainted around town." Turning to Pot Belly, he gestured. "Tell the little lady that you didn't mean any harm."

Robin felt like a spectator at a bullfight. She looked over at several old ranchers in the next booth who were eyeing Pot Belly with distaste, then her gaze darted to the table of women who thankfully hadn't noticed the interchange as they got down to their book discussion. The other customers hadn't seemed to take notice of the exchange either.

Pot Belly wore a belligerent expression, but after another look at Bryce's scowl, he apparently decided not to push the issue. He mumbled an apology, and started shoveling food in his mouth.

Bryce wasn't satisfied. He wanted to haul the guy out of that booth and throw him into the street. But his name on Robin's lips stopped him.

"Bryce!" She angrily jerked her head towards the kitchen and turned on her heel, marching ahead of him, head held high. He followed, wondering what was up now.

As the doors swung shut behind them, she turned and jabbed her finger in his chest with each word she hissed. "Bryce, I don't need you to defend me! I've been handling guys like that long before you came along and I'll be handling them long after you're gone!"

"Ow!" Bryce grabbed her little poky finger and held it away from him. "You're hurting me!" He rubbed his chest with his other hand. "What was I supposed to do, just stand there and let that jackass paw you?"

"Why can't you get it? It's none of your business!" she ground out in frustration. "I can handle jerks like him!"

He opened his mouth then slammed it shut. What was her problem? He was defending her! He looked down at her angry expression, and at the same time, they both became aware that he was still holding her hand. She jerked it away and turned her back, her shoulders trembling with emotion. He wanted to gather her up in his arms but considering her ramrod straight back, he'd better not. However, *he* was not at fault here, darn it!

"I'm not going to apologize. That...that...poor excuse of a man had no business putting his hands all over you, and I wasn't going to stand by and watch him do it."

Robin clenched her teeth and turned back. "You have no right to say who can put his hands on me and who can't. This has nothing to do with you! Does everything always have to be about *you*?!!"

Bryce stilled. The sound of silverware clinking on plates and murmur of conversation drifted on the silence stretching between them.

She slapped her fingers over her mouth, her eyes wide. "I'm sorry. I shouldn't have said that."

"Don't hold anything back, let it all out," he replied, stony-faced.

Awkwardness sat like an elephant between them. "Yeeeeach," he finally muttered, turned and left only the swinging door in his wake.

It was a good thing the meat loaf for that day's special needed lots of mixing, pounding and mashing. It was the best meat loaf she'd ever baked.

Chapter 9

Dean did a fly-over check of the herds that afternoon and Bryce went along, thankful for the diversion. But if he thought to put Robin out of his mind, it wasn't happening—she was right there in his head. Why did she have to be so stubborn? He called Andy at the lumberyard later, to learn the man had installed the air conditioner for Robin, and he hung up with a certain satisfaction. And a lot of smugness.

Darrell had business in Rapid for a couple of days, so that left only the five of them at the supper table that evening. He wondered if Dean and Dorine had ever had problems during their courtship. There was respect as well as love between his hosts, even though their conversation was often sprinkled with good-natured kidding.

"Do you guys ever argue?" he finally asked.

"Oh yes!" Dean replied emphatically.

"You bet!" Dorine said at the same time.

They looked at each other and burst out laughing.

"I hate it when he comes in and can't find a pen so he swipes mine and never brings it back. Sometimes he'll take a fork and eat cake right out of the pan inside of cutting a piece and putting it on a plate." She gave her husband a mock indignant glare.

"And I hate it when she forgets to put gas in the van," Dean countered. "I go to jump in, in a hurry, and there the needle sits on empty."

Dorine stuck her tongue out and they both laughed again. The twins laughed too but didn't have a clue as to what they were laughing about. Altogether, the little family scene tugged at his heart. He had never been a part of this kind of family, and realized the emotion he felt was one of envy.

"Yeah, but those are just little irritations," he remarked. "Surely you have serious disagreements?"

Dean folded his arms and leaned on the table. "Don't know of anyone who hasn't. But you gotta remember that we've known each other all our lives so there weren't too many surprises." He slid an affection glance at his wife. "Sometimes you have to agree to disagree. I don't have time to get a plate to put cake on. Besides, it's just one tiny little bite." Dorine opened her mouth but he held up one hand and she shut her mouth. "However," his expression grew serious as he turned to Bryce, "if you pile up enough irritations, you can have a serious problem. You can't let it get that far. We both honor Jesus as a Guest in our home, and that knowledge helps us calm down. Plus, there's a lot of compromise—if we didn't both learn to give and take, there'd be lots more trouble."

Dorine leaned over and planted a kiss on his cheek. "Just so long as you remember that I'm always right."

Dean wiped his cheek and grinned at her.

"Daddy!" shouted David. "You not 'posed to wipe off Mommy's kiss!"

"I didn't wipe it off, I was just rubbing it in," Dean explained, and there was another burst of laughter. Bryce felt the tug in his chest again, this time stronger. Dean rose to carry his plate to the sink.

As Bryce helped clear the table, he came to a decision. Casually mentioning that he was going into town to help Jason master the art of batting, he was met with a suspicious lift of Dorine's eyebrow as she told him that Robin would be at school that evening for a meeting with parents and teachers for the coming year. Bryce tried to stuff his disappointment but Dean winked at him.

"Kind of crimped your plans, there, huh?" the cowboy teased. Before Bryce could reply to his astute host, the twins pounced on him, demanding he play a board game with them, involving cards printed with candy pictures. Frustration battled with not wanting to disappoint the two little rascals, and the twins won out.

After their bedtime, Bryce watched a Mariner's baseball game with Dean—his usual mode of relaxation, but tonight only the image of Robin stayed in his mind.

The following evening after another day on horseback, Bryce was ready to apologize to Robin. He'd given it a lot of thought and she was right. She had been running her business long before he came on the scene, and knew how to handle it on her own. He didn't have a right to step in anywhere, but he didn't know of any red-blooded man who could walk away from that situation with Pot Belly. He turned his attention back to the pork chop supper that came with baked apples and baked potatoes, only half-listing to the twins.

They were finishing dessert when Dean broke into his musings by asking if he'd like to go along to prayer meeting. Bryce brightened. Robin would be at church too. Then the bugaboo of religion weaseled its way into his mind and he knew he wasn't ready to deal with that, Robin or no Robin. The idea of competing with church again soured him. Instead, he offered to babysit the twins at home rather than have them in church childcare.

Dean chuckled as he slapped Bryce on the back. "Rots of ruck!" he chortled, looking meaningfully at the boys.

Bryce realized what he meant during bathtime and afterwards, getting the boys settled down after romping all over their beds and messing up the sheets and blankets. He told them he'd nail their pajamas to their beds if they didn't settle down and go to sleep. Two pairs of bright blue eyes looked up at him in mischief as they tried tackling him again. So much for his authority.

"Stop it! I mean it!" he warned severely.

The boys quieted, looking uncertain.

"Now get in bed and I'll tuck you in." He tempered his words with a smile.

"But what 'bout prayers?"

Ohboy! What had he gotten himself into?

"Okay, get down here beside your bed like your mother taught you."

"But you hafta help us," David murmured, dropping to his knees.

Ohboy!

"You're big guys, you know what to say. Just go ahead like I'm not here."

Dutifully, two little dark heads bowed, tiny hands folded as the twins closed their eyes. "Dear God," began David. The childish trust stirred Bryce's heart.

"Thank you for taday," continued Doug.

"Forgive us sins and watch over us durin' the night."

"BlessMommyanDaddyanUncaDarrellGranmaanMrs.MacanJasonanJeremy antheirMommy…an…an…Mr. Martin!" finished Doug breathlessly.

Bryce didn't know a kid could hold his breath that long but it touched him to hear his name mentioned. The boys piled into bed and David handed Bryce a storybook.

By the time he was on the third page, the twins had drifted off so he put the book down and quietly let himself out of the room. It was still light out with twilight hovering on the tails of the last sunbeams. He turned the television on but nothing interested him.

Restless, he walked out to a lounge by the pool. Stretching out on his back, he propped his head up with his stacked hands and contemplated the stars just beginning to come out as soft darkness glided over the prairie. Gradually, his body relaxed. He heard the hooty owl's mournful call and the occasional howling of a coyote. The ever-present breezes had died down, calming the air that usually rattled the leaves of the cottonwoods above him. Animal sounds from the barn drifted to him as cattle lowed their goodnights.

Robin. What was he going to do about her? Why was she able to tie his stomach in knots with one sweet smile from those kissable lips? His desire to be with her went beyond a challenge, beyond the usual attraction. He admired her gutsy attitude, her business acumen, her infectious personality. There had never been a woman who had affected him at this level. He frowned and shifted. The little redhead had crept under his skin and he didn't like it one bit. He'd never been at this point in his life before and hated the idea of not knowing what to do. He huffed out a humorless laugh. Love'em and leave'em Martin. Being done in by a little freckle-nosed redhead in a baker's apron. The one thing he *was* sure of, his protectiveness toward her *had* crossed the line of a casual relationship—

The phone ringing brought him up out of the lounger to dash into the house to answer it before it woke the boys. He took the message, checked on the boys, and decided to do what they were doing—peacefully sleeping. He crawled into bed but laid there for some time, thinking about the petite redhead just a few miles away. She might as well have been a million miles away. He groaned and turned over, punching his pillow. He flopped on to his stomach and punched the pillow again.

He heard his hosts come home, the house creak and settle in the stillness. Gradually, sleep claimed him and he sank into oblivion. He didn't even hear Darrell come home.

The next morning, Dean and Darrell discussed how the hay harvest was coming along while Dorine cooked breakfast and Bryce sipped at his coffee. The rising sun cast a golden beam through the open door across the polished floor, almost blinding him. Outdoors, birds sang joyously. Crisp morning air wafting in the open door felt cool but he seldom paid any attention to mornings, he was a night owl. He usually wasn't up this early, and now the smell of sausage and coffee added to the pleasant atmosphere in the kitchen. He decided he rather liked it.

Dorine served waffles, Dean asked the blessing and they all dug in. After a few moments, Bryce said, "It sounds like you could use another hand with the haying."

Dean nodded as he swallowed a bite of sausage before answering. "Hauling hay is one of the itchiest jobs on the ranch. You sure you're up for that?"

Darrell looked at Bryce's almost empty plate and gestured with his fork. "Sure he is, but you better eat more, Bryce, it's going to be a long day. You want to experience the 'wild west', and hauling hay is something you city boys don't hear much about. In fact, you're going to itch in places you didn't know you had to itch!"

"I can stand it if you can, rodeo man," Bryce retorted as he followed Darrell's advice to down a hearty breakfast.

It only took a little while in the hay field to know what Darrell meant about itching. The tiniest sticks of hay had worked into Bryce's clothing and even down into his socks. Every square inch of skin was alive and demanded scratching!

He stood on top of the truckload of hay, waiting for the next bale to drop off the mobile elevator. His job was to guide and swing each bale around so the load was squared. Darrell drove the truck and had the volume on the radio turned up, singing along with the wailing western tune.

"How ya doin' up there, city boy?"

"Spoken from your cushy job out of the sun, rodeo man! I'm up here slaving!"

"That's the idea, city boy!"

Bryce didn't have time to answer as the next bale came up the elevator and they reached the end of the field.

Darrell braked, turned off the engine and hopped out, bringing a jug of water with him. "Come on down and get a drink, don't want you withering up and blowing away." He squinted up at Bryce, whose face glistened with sweat that ran down his jaw and dripped onto his bare chest.

Bryce grabbed his t-shirt and clamored over the cab of the truck, stepped down on a wooden wedge placed between the bed and cab, and dropped to the ground. He shook out his shirt, chaf and dust floating away on the breeze. Taking the water jug from Darrell, he tipped it up and let it run over his sweaty head, catching some of the cool moisture in his mouth. He spit out the first mouthful, then drank heavily from the lemon-flavored water. Using his shirt, he rubbed it over his glistening chest where furry hair arrowed down toward his waist in low-slung jeans.

"Boy, you've earned your salt today," Darrell said with a hint of admiration in his voice. "Come rest awhile." He dropped down in the shade cast by the heavily-loaded truck. Bryce followed suit.

"What do you have to rest from? All you did was sit in the cab and holler!" Bryce muttered as he wiped the shirt over his forehead and down his face. Chaff and sweat mingled to cause a dirty smudge on the light-colored fabric.

Darrell chuckled, eyeing Bryce's build. "Do you swim, work out at gym, or what, to keep yourself in shape?"

"All of the above. Makes the ladies take a second look." Bryce leaned back against the tire with a contented sigh. It felt good to have a workout without sweaty gym-mates.

Darrell picked up a stem of hay and put it in his mouth, gazing out over the almost empty hayfield. "I hear you're putting the moves on Robin."

Bryce snorted. "I didn't even get to first base."

"You won't either."

"Have *you* asked her out?" Bryce demanded sharply.

Darrell turned and grinned, his teeth white against his swarthy complexion. "Heck no! That would be like dating my sister!"

Bryce whistled. "Why? She's one good-looking woman."

Darrell was silent again, gazing into the distance where heat waves shimmered up from the baked soil. When he spoke, Bryce could barely hear the softly spoken words. "Don't hurt her, Bryce, she's had enough heartache."

"What makes you think I'll hurt her?" Bryce demanded indignantly as he sat up.

"Because you like women, and she doesn't even know what that means." Darrell replied. "She isn't naive but she's not sophisticated either, not like women you date."

"It's not my intention to hurt her," Bryce's answer was clipped.

"You like women, Bryce, but she isn't just any woman. She's a good friend, an innocent where guys like you are concerned."

"What do you mean, 'guys like me'? All I want is a date, I'm not out to seduce her!"

Darrell held his gaze. "Good. Because I wouldn't want to have to punch you out."

Bryce was about to rise to the bait when he saw Darrell's eyes dancing with mischief. The clown! It would be satisfying to turn the tables on him. "You say you won't date Robin, but come to think of it, I've never heard about *your* love life," Bryce relaxed back against the tire with a speculative gleam in his eyes.

A wariness flitted through Darrell's eyes, then was gone. "Oh, I date...but not often." His gaze wandered out over the hayfield again.

Bryce studied the other man before asking, "Does this have anything to do with Molly Schafer's daughter?"

Darrell turned in surprise, his eyebrows raised. "Yeah," he finally replied, although reluctantly. "She lives in Minneapolis."

"Your lady love?"

"I wish." The words were wistful.

"Well, come on, man, tell me about this. I've got a big shoulder to lean on."

But Darrell didn't smile. He heaved a sigh. "Her name is Sharry. We went to high school together, but she got a scholarship at a different college than I did. We continued dating and things were coming right along…then the roof fell in."

"Another guy?" Bryce murmured sympathetically.

"No, it was never that. We just didn't see eye to eye about the future." He was silent, absently brushing away a grasshopper that landed on his chest. "We had an argument a couple of years ago and shortly after that she moved to Minnesota."

"A couple of years?" Bryce was incredulous. "Why didn't you go after her?"

Darrell raised his head and looked off into the distance. "Wouldn't have done any good, wouldn't have solved the problem." He took a deep breath, and moved to get up. "I'm praying about it and if we're to get together, the Lord will have to do it." He pulled his gloves on. "Come on, city boy, back to work! I'll even let you drive!"

All the way back to the barn, Bryce pondered Darrell's words. He felt for the guy, he was obviously in love with this Sharry, who appeared to be cold and uncaring. How could such a warm-hearted guy fall for a woman like that? But he'd be hanged before he'd trust any Supreme Being to sort out *his* love life.

Love. His thoughts immediately flew to Robin. For the first time, doubt entered his mind about the wisdom of getting involved with her. He never wanted to get into the position that Darrell was in now. Love was nothing but trouble. *How about Dean and Dorine, they're in love,* asked the little voice. And why did the word "love" pop up? He snorted.

"Hey, watch where you're goin'! You wanna dump this whole load on its side?!"

Bryce replied, "Only if I can bury you in it. It's your turn to get itchy!"

Later that afternoon, white billowing thunderheads built up in the west again and by suppertime, the sky was overcast, a welcome breeze cooling the air. They finished hauling hay and Bryce experienced a certain sense of pride in a job well-done.

After the men had showered and they had their evening meal, Bryce casually announced he was going to see how Jeremy was doing with his new bat. He didn't miss the look between Dorine and Darrell, but chose to ignore it.

"You mean I didn't wear you out?!" exclaimed Darrell! "I thought your sorry behind would be dragging out your tracks!"

Bryce smiled smugly. "Fooled you, didn't I?" Heading for the door, he tossed out a "Good night, see you later."

"Hey, you've got a midnight curfew!" Darrell called as the screen door slapped shut. Bryce ignored him.

Driving into town, leaves and dust swirled across his path, coating his car. He thought about Darrell and made a note to ask Dorine about Sharry the next time they were alone. In Silverdale, the wind was picking up cottonwood fluff and whirling it around in a crazy dance that only it knew. But there wasn't a hint of moisture in the air.

He parked in front of the Sweet Schoppe, noting how the awning was swaying and one end flapping in the brisk breeze. Somebody should fix that for her.

Andy Vayle was closing up the lumberyard, holding his baseball cap on with one hand as he squinted in Bryce's direction. Andy kept the yard open later in the evenings so ranchers could get supplies that they didn't have time to get during the day.

Bryce got out and called to him. "Is this the gentle breezes of South Dakota?"

"What, *this*?" gestured the other man, looking around him. "This is just the warm up, wait till we get a real humdinger!"

Bryce chuckled and let the wind push him along the sidewalk to the door of the café. The closed sign was up, and hesitating only a second, he made his way around the side of the building and along the sidewalk toward the back of the house.

He could hear the laughter and screams before he rounded the corner, and the sight before him instantly enchanted him.

Jason and Robin were hanging on to the string of a bobbing kite that twisted and twirled in gusts of wind like a whirling dervish trying to escape its earth-bound existence. Jeremy danced around under the dragging tail of the kite as it eluded his outstretched hands. All three were shouting with excitement as they wrestled the uncooperative kite.

Bryce strode forward, and grasping the bottom of the kite, gave a mighty shove, sending it soaring.

"Mr. Martin, you did it! You did it!" Jason's face was lit with joy as he let go of the string to grab Bryce around the hips. Jeremy's smile instantly vanished and he ran to the back step. Robin struggled with the kite, now at the mercy of the mischievous wind, and Bryce moved behind her, reaching around to place his big hands over her smaller ones. "Easy, sweetheart, give it a little line, then drag back on it like this." He demonstrated, all the while marveling at the softness of her hands and how just touching her drove up his temperature. "Kind of like casting a line when you're fishing."

Robin had noticed his arrival in her peripheral vision, but was startled when his hands closed over hers. His chest at her back was warm and solid, and she got a whiff of spicy aftershave. Almost letting go of the kite string, she valiantly tried to tamp down her spiraling heartbeat. It seemed her crazy heart always went bonkers over Bryce. "I've never been fishing so I don't know how to cast a line."

With Jason cheering them on and Jeremy watching warily from the sidelines, Bryce and Robin managed to keep the kite aloft for a few minutes before a maverick gust sent it plummeting down, straight as an arrow toward the ground. Bryce yanked the string quickly to one side as Robin let go and the kite settled into the birch branches at the end of the lawn by the wall. "Well, at least it didn't crash!" he grinned down at Robin as she turned in his arms.

Their eyes met and his chest tightened. Robin was gazing at him with an unreadable expression, but he knew it was more than simple appreciation. His chest swelled a little.

She drew in a breath and glanced at the kite. "Well, that was exciting!" She ducked under his arm and took several steps away.

Jason ran to the kite, shouting at Jeremy to come join the fun. Bryce coiled the string as he walked toward the kite, his heart as buoyant as the kite had been a few minutes ago. He was a connoisseur of women and knew when one was attracted to him, and just as sure as he was a foot high, Robin Hudson was *not* immune to him! He grinned secretly while he had his back to her, untangling the string.

"Let me help!" Jason was at his side, his boyish faced tipped up to the man.

Robin had made a valiant effort to keep her mind on business the last few days but would never admit that she had been watching for that red convertible to slide to a stop in front of the café. What she *didn't* expect, was for him to appear in her back yard! She finally had to acknowledge her attraction to Bryce went beyond what it should, but sadly, she also knew there was no future for them.

Back and forth, back and forth, the internal debate went on just like when she had been bathing the boys in the evening, or serving up her famous chicken with German dumplings to customers during the day. To keep Bryce out of her mind, she focused on her financial worries that stilled loomed overhead like the threatening thunderclouds over the Black Hills. One moment she was in despair, the next moment she remembered that God would provide and care for her because wasn't she more important than the birds of the field? But always her mind veered back to the big handsome investigator.

Welcome relief from so much thinking had come when Dorine had called to tell her of Bryce's experience hauling hay with Darrell and the two women had a good laugh over the picture that presented.

Now one of those men was right here in her back yard, reaching up to untangle the kite from the tree branches. She noticed his tan had deepened from being out in the sun all day. In town, the streets had shimmered in waves of heat, and it was probably worse out in the hayfield. But he undoubtedly had reveled in it.

She watched him interact with Jason, enjoying the sight of his muscles stretching the polo shirt over his strong back. She saw muscled men every day in the café, ranchers who built up admirable bodies not from working out in a gym but from the hard work of wrestling a living from the land. Why were her eyes drawn to these particular muscles?

Glancing at her watch, she called to her son. "Okay, Jason, it's time for bed."

"Aww, already?" he whined.

"Yep! You have to get used to going to bed early because in a few weeks, you'll be getting up earlier for school."

"Aww, I don't wanna," he answered half-heartedly.

"Come on, hop to it," she firmly replied.

Bryce watched them, an amused smile on his face. "I'll put the kite away while you get the boys ready for bed."

"That sounds like you think you're staying?"

"You and I have some unfinished business," he winked.

"To quote Dorine, 'when pigs fly,'" she shot back. His laughter followed her into the house. In record time, she put the boys to bed, took out iced tea and poured two glasses. Bryce acted like he'd forgotten their disagreement of the other day and she could only hope that he'd taken it to heart when she'd told him to butt out. But then why was he here? Her heart sank, as she realized what she knew she had to tell him. This situation just could not continue. She found him sitting in the swing, gently pushing it with one foot as he relaxed, the kite beside him.

"My vacation is half-gone and we still haven't had our date," he plunged right in as he accepted the glass of tea.

"Bryce, we need to talk but first, thanks again for the air conditioner," she said as she sat beside him at the other end of the swing. "I still want to pay you for it."

He was shaking his head, and instead of commenting, he asked, "What did you want to talk about? Where we're going on our first date?" He slid her a sexy look.

"Blunt seems to be the only language you understand, Bryce. I have tried to make it perfectly clear that I don't date, and I wish you would stop asking me."

"Yeah, that's blunt enough but how about this?" He was quick with a retort. "It's time you started thinking about yourself. I can't see you spending the rest of your life buried in this little town. You've got too much zip and zest to languish here."

"Languish? Now *there's* a word that doesn't come up in everyday conversation."

He ignored her comment. "Come on, go out with me. Just once."

She looked him in the eye. "Bryce, I can *never* go out with you."

He stiffened. "Would you go out with someone else if they asked you?"

"No, because the guys around here know better than to ask."

"They're idiots," he muttered. "I still haven't heard a good reason why you won't go out with me."

"There are several reasons, the first being my son."

"What has he got to do with it?"

"Don't tell me you haven't noticed how Jason looks up to you?" He shrugged half-heartedly, as though agreeing without committing himself. "I don't want him to become attached to you and feel abandoned when you leave."

He stared at her. "He knows I'm just here for vacation, that I'll be going back."

"Does he?" she challenged. "He's a little kid, Bryce, and kids don't think like adults. They want permanence in their lives, and sometimes they think if they want something badly enough, it will happen."

Bryce remained silent, his gaze returning to his glass.

"I don't want my son hurt, Bryce."

"I have no intention of hurting him!" He finally looked at her.

"But you will, whether you want to or not. Little boys get their hopes up that the people who are important to them will become a permanent part of their lives!"

He gazed at her thoughtfully then slowly shook his head. "I would never do that to him. Maybe if I explain that I just want to be friends with his mother. Robin, I really do want to spend time with you."

She didn't answer, looking across at the roof of the abandoned building next door. Feeling his gaze, she tried again. "Bryce, we come from two different worlds—"

"Ah, Robin, men and women are the same, no matter where they come from."

"Not necessarily. You come from the big city, I'm small town. You move in a social whirl I can only read about. You date glamorous women, I'm country from head to toe." She looked down, smoothing the seam along the edge of her shorts.

"But that religion of yours is holding you back, isn't it?" he guessed. "Are you really going to hold that up as a shield between us?" he demanded as he slowly stood.

"Not as a shield—as the truth, Bryce." It hurt her to say the words but they needed saying. "Can't you understand? I can't date someone who doesn't believe in Jesus."

She gasped as he stepped forward and took her hand, pulling her up in front of him. She gazed at him, her heart thundering in her chest. He gently touched the pulse beating at the base of her throat. Finally he whispered, "You're not immune to me, Robin. Why are you fighting this attraction?"

She swallowed and took a breath, needing to be entirely honest. "You're right," she said in a low voice. "I *am* attracted to you. You'd be blind not to know it. But I'm not going to do anything about it, and...I'm asking you not to either."

"Why?" Anger simmered below the surface of the one word.

"I have already told you the most important reason of all."

He heard the determination in her voice and anger finally got the better of him. "So because of your *religion,* you won't explore this attraction?" He snorted derisively as he dropped her hand.

She hesitated, then drew herself up taller. "It's not just religion, Bryce. Christianity is a way of life, and it's the life I've chosen."

Bryce turned, pacing a few steps away. Those were almost the same words Dean had said. Placing his hands on his hips, he tipped his head back and gazed up at the heavens. "I'm surrounded by them!" he muttered. "Why? Why me?" He lifted his shoulders with a heavy sigh. Then he turned sharply, his demeanor changed.

"Okay. Okay," he rubbed his hands together, starting back towards her. "If that's the way you want to play it, I'll go along. I'll go to church with you. If that's the only way I can see you, I'll go sit in a pew."

She sadly shook her head. "Oh, Bryce." Regret coated her words. "That's not a basis for attending worship. Your focus should be on God, not a person. And I'm not playing games. This is real. This is my life."

"So what *do* you want me to do, to get a date with you?" His eyes blazed as his temper flared anew.

"Listen carefully, Bryce. I. Don't. Date. I don't want you to do *anything.*"

He turned and swept his arm in a big arc, his temper erupting.

"And all because of an obsession with a Being that nobody can even prove exists!"

Her gaze was steady and sure. "Bryce, I have never tried to hide the fact that I believe in God and He is all that matters to me. He loves me more than anyone else could."

"Lots of people believe in God and they still go on living!"

"I'm not only living the here and now, Bryce, I have eternal life because of God's love. You could know His love too, just like I do."

He made a gurgling sound, threw his hands up in disgust and stormed towards the side of the house leading to the street. "I'm going before I say something I'll really regret!"

She called after him softly. "Thanks for stopping by."

He raised one hand in acknowledgement and stalked off around the corner. She listened until the roar of his car engine faded, then took one last sip of the cold coffee. There was a heavy lump in her chest where her heart was supposed to be, but at the same time, a peace stole over her. It had hurt, but she had stood strong and resisted temptation.

She spent more time than usual that night in her conversation with God. But sleep wouldn't come and she shifted to her side, one arm bent under her head as she gazed out the window at the starry night.

Her thoughts drifted to Randy. They had shared a growing up kind of love, a comfortable warmth of rightness. But Randy had never stirred her like Bryce's nearness did. Was she being disloyal to her husband's memories? No, she couldn't think that way—her marriage vows said till death do us part. Randy was gone and she was free to seek love again. Why did it have to be an unbeliever who tempted her heart?

But, she'd done the right thing.

Chapter 10

Bryce wheeled away from the café, gravel spitting out from under the tires. He'd never met a woman so irritating and stubborn! All because of religion. He gradually slowed down, the cool air soothing his overheated face. Rubbing his chin, he silently cursed over the fact that no woman had ever gotten past his defenses like Robin did. When a woman showed disinterest, he'd usually just shrug, erase her out of his little black book, and go on to the next woman. Why was he getting so worked up over this little redhead? He didn't like to be thwarted, that's why, and Robin was a bigger obstacle than he'd ever encountered. Why didn't he just cut his losses and leave her alone? He didn't need her pious attitude. He ground his teeth together and firmed his jaw. The pastor's words chose that moment to slide into his mind:

"No one is righteous, no not one."
"All have sinned and come short of the glory of God."
"The wages of sin is death."

Well, he'd sinned plenty in his lifetime, as had most people—so what? If they were going to hell, they'd all party it up together down there.

However, for the first time, he felt an unease about his flippant attitude. Doubt settled in. What if his thinking was skewed? What if there really *was* something to that verse about the wages of sin being death? He shook it off as fanciful, but when he tried to picture the pleasure waiting for him in St. Louis, some of the glow was missing. He tried to bring up images of the women in his little black book, but they were blurred—all he could see was red hair and a cute little freckled nose. He hit the steering wheel with the palm of his hand.

It wasn't just the specter of religion hanging over him. He couldn't seem to erase the picture of Robin and her boys in their cozy family circle either, nor that of the DeFoe family, always hugging, kissing, showing affection. Even the down-to-earth men and women who peopled the area—smacking of hearth and home, a caring community that valued family life. But he'd seen the vehicles around the tavern at all hours, the community wasn't entirely a bunch of do-gooders. He smiled triumphantly. But the triumph faded as once again the homey scenes at Robin's and the DeFoes popped into his mind, letting him glimpse what he never thought he'd want. Want, as in commitment? He went cold all over. Kids? An icy trickle went down his spine. He rubbed his chin again. He couldn't picture himself in the role of husband or father, so scratch that image.

Maybe this vacation had not been such a good idea. In fact, he was sure about it now. He'd never had these unsettling thoughts until he came here. Maybe he should cut his vacation short and get back to his blissful bachelor life.

But what about Robin? His heart missed a beat at the thought of leaving her. Reluctantly, he admitted that his heart was leading him, not his head. That had never happened before. He needed to get into his own environment, the sooner the better.

Sleep didn't come easily that night.

The next morning, Dean and Darrell were hurriedly eating breakfast when Bryce came downstairs. Dorine was making lunches, packing sandwiches, fruit and cookies into a bag. From their conversation, he learned that cattle had broken down a fence to the neighboring ranch and it looked like a whole day of work ahead, just doing repairs. Bryce hesitated, torn between his desire to leave, and guilt at not offering to help when it was apparent they needed all the hands they could get.

Guilt won out. While Darrell and the hands saddled horses to round up the errant animals, Dean and Bryce tossed fence-mending equipment into the bed of the ranch pickup. Dean grinned at Bryce over the truck bed. "Well, you wanted a taste of ranch life, it doesn't get any tastier than this!" Bryce still didn't understand Dean's mellow attitude about problems, but it apparently worked—the employees Bryce had met thought highly of their boss and his ethics, and no one seemed stressed out by this latest turn of events.

As before, Bryce threw himself whole-heartedly into the task of repairing the trampled fence. They stopped working only long enough to eat lunch. Sweat beaded their faces, arms and backs, and Dean cautioned Bryce about taking off his shirt under the blaze of the overhead sun. They removed their sunglasses and dribbled water from a jug over their faces to cool off, but for once, the prairie breezes were absent—not a breath of air stirred.

"You're pretty quiet, I'm not working the city boy too hard, am I?" Dean remarked as they sat on the ground in the shade of the pickup, munching on apples.

Bryce picked a few blades of grass and pulled them between his fingers. "I've been thinking about something the preacher said in his sermon." He hesitated.

Dean remained silent, sensing that this wasn't something the other man readily shared. Bryce seemed to be wrestling with himself, then finally spoke.

"All that stuff about no one being righteous and all having sinned. I've kept up my quota of sinning, but I know lots of good people who haven't. Like a secretary in my office, grandma to three kids she dotes on. I can't imagine her being this great sinner."

"She sounds like a good woman," Dean agreed, looking across the prairie as he squinted against the brightness of the day. "But the scripture is right, everyone has sinned."

"So you're saying that, according to your religion, no one is good enough to go to heaven because of their good deeds?"

"Not if they count on that to get them there." Dean's blue-eyed gaze speared Bryce's brown eyes. "That's why Jesus came to die on the cross, and if people believe on Him, that is their ticket into heaven. No good works will ever do it."

Bryce shook his head, gazing off at the horizon. "That's too simple. There has to be more to it."

"Nope. That's it. Believe on the name of the Lord Jesus Christ and you will be saved."

Bryce absently picked up a handful of dirt, letting it trickle through his fingers. "So even if those people that work at street missions aren't saved, they're doomed? How about when people take food to the homeless on the streets? You can't tell me that your God doesn't give points for that?"

Dean nodded. "That's all good and yes, God sees that. But Jesus Himself said that He is the Way, the Truth and the Life, no one comes to the Father but by Him. If those people doing good works aren't saved, it won't matter when God opens up His books."

"No-o way," Bryce shook his head. "There's *got* to be more to it than that. You must have to *do* something!"

Dean chuckled and picked up his hat, slapping the dust out of it. "Nope, that's it. Simple as pie, like Mrs. Mac says." As they both got to their feet, he grew serious. "But if you want to read it for yourself, you can borrow my Bible. I'll mark the passages."

Bryce slowly pulled on his gloves. "I just might take you up on that. But I'll bet that I can find something to prove that good people get to heaven, with or without Jesus."

Dean grinned at him. "You know, with your drive and curiosity, you might find it worth your time to investigate the claims of Christ. After all, that's your game, investigating. Isn't it?" He slipped on his sunglasses.

Bryce clapped his hat on his head and reverted back to form with a cocky grin. "But don't hold your breath, I've got lots more living to do before I open a Bible!" He replaced his sunglasses too.

They returned to work and Bryce had no way of knowing that Dean was deep in prayer even while they dug holes and stretched barbed wire.

It was late afternoon by the time they finished and wearily loaded the equipment into the pickup. Driving back towards the ranch buildings, Dean eyed the western horizon, where both white thunderheads and dark clouds were piling up in front of the descending sun. "Don't like the looks of that sky," he remarked.

Bryce glanced that direction and shrugged, whipping off his hat. "It's been doing that every day since I've been here." He absently stripped off his t-shirt and wiped his glistening shoulders and arms.

Dean shook his head. "This seems different than the past couple of days."

Bryce took a deep breath. "The air does seem kind of heavy."

"A meteorologist would say there's something brewing in those clouds."

"Well, you've lived out here your whole life, I guess you'd know."

Dean rubbed his fingers thoughtfully over his chin and pulled the pickup into the yard.

They had just enough time for quick showers before sitting down for supper, and the twins kept them entertained while they filled up on steak, baked potatoes and buttered green beans followed by apple pie.

Bryce was unusually quiet, fiddling with his knife and fork. At last he laid them across the edge of his place and cleared his throat. "I'm thinking of heading back home."

The twins looked at him accusingly, and both Dorine and Dean's faces registered surprise. The rancher smiled but it didn't reach his eyes, as he slanted a look at Bryce. "Had enough of the wild west?"

"No…it isn't that. I've really enjoyed it here and this food is to die for," he sent Dorine an appreciative glance. She smiled sadly. The feeling was mutual—he'd really miss them. "I've got a few loose ends to tie up at home before going back to work," he hedged.

"Yous said yous was gonna stay a l-o-n-g time." David's lip poked out belligerently and Doug looked ready to cry.

Oh boy.

"Look fellas," Bryce felt like a heel. "You know I was just here for my vacation and now it's time for me to go back to work."

Doug burst into tears and slid from his chair, running from the room. David glared at Bryce. "Yous promised!"

Bryce looked helplessly at Dorine, and was humbled when he noticed a bright sheen in her eyes as she glanced away.

"I better go talk to Doug." She got up and left. David sent him one more glare and stomped after his mother.

Bryce cleared his throat and swallowed past the lump. "I never expected that kind of reaction."

"They'll get over it," Dean said kindly. "Kids bounce back pretty fast from disappointments. When were you thinking of leaving?"

Bryce ran his hand over his hair and sighed. "Tomorrow morning." Robin's words suddenly slipped into his mind. *Little kids want permanence in their lives.* "I didn't mean to hurt them."

"Don't worry about it," Dean clapped him on the shoulder as he got up. "If this is the worst disappointment they'll ever suffer, they should have smooth sailing." He carried his plate to the sink and turned. "I've got a saddle that needs repairs and a couple of bridles to oil, if you want to help me. Unless you need to pack."

Bryce had learned that there was always mending, fixing and repairs to be done in order to keep the ranch operation running smoothly. But he sensed this wasn't why Dean asked him to help. "I don't have much to pack, and yeah, I can give you a hand."

As they crossed the yard, the rancher turned and gave the sky a brief scan. Golden rays spread across the still-blue sky above them as the sun began to slip behind the clouds that seemed to grow more intense even as Bryce watched.

"I'd say we're in for a pretty good-sized storm," Dean commented. "I'll check the weather report as soon as we go back in the house." He led the way to the tackroom.

Once they were settled in, each with a bridle, Dean cleared his throat. "I hope we haven't driven you away with our talk about faith, Bryce."

"No, oh no," Bryce denied vehemently. "But I do have more questions."

Darrell ambled in later, to find Bryce and Dean deep in conversation again over Pastor Rick's sermon. As Dean answered the other man's questions, Darrell reached for the New Testament in his shirt pocket, and looked up scriptures while the other two worked linseed oil into the bridles. Even though Bryce enjoyed the feel of the leather under his fingers, his attention was more on what the brothers had to say. A thoughtful expression on his face, rather than skepticism, alerted Dean to the fact that Bryce was listening with an open heart.

Suddenly Darrell lifted his head. "Do you hear that?"

"What?" Bryce tilted his head. "I don't hear anything."

"That's just it. It's too quiet. There aren't even any birds twittering." He stepped to the door and looked out. "Hey, you guys gotta come see this." He slipped the New Testament back in his pocket.

Dean and Bryce put down the bridles and walked to the door. Bryce drew in his breath. Black ominous clouds covered the whole western sky, lightning flickering in and out like a crazed contortionist. A whitish streak, tinged with a sickly greenish color, draped like a lacy cloth in front of the dark, boiling clouds. A puff of cool air stirred the leaves on the cottonwoods before brushing across their faces, followed by the distant rumble of thunder. The writhing mass seemed to loom nearer even as they watched.

"Those are hail clouds," Dean exclaimed. He turned to Bryce. "Better get your car down to the hay barn, park in the middle alley." He reached for his cell phone and called Buster to alert the employees to get their families inside and vehicles under cover. Darrell took off running for the corral to bring the horses in. Dean snapped the phone shut while he hurried towards the office building. The wind grew stronger and cooler, gusting clouds of dust into the air and into their eyes.

Bryce felt exhilarated about the approaching storm while he drove his car into the large barn. He loved storms, the unleashed fury of them—and here was Mother Nature coming right at him. A couple of cowhands were already parking ranch vehicles in the barn but there was no panic, no mindless rushing around. Each man seemed to know what to do, like a well-orchestrated drama. When storms hit St. Louis, people holed up in stores, offices or homes, watching the weather from behind safety glass. They never experienced the untamed wind in their faces, the thrill of all that uncontrolled energy. Here, men and women stood toe to toe with nature all the time, but never losing respect for what it could do. They were prepared and acted accordingly.

He parked and jumped out of the car. His heart racing in anticipation, he charged up the slight incline out of the barn and caught the full force of the wind, lifting his face toward the gust with a smile. The air now carried the scent of rain, and the wind tore at his clothes as though to rip them off.

Noticing that Darrell was having trouble getting one of the horses to go into the barn, he veered towards the corral. An eerie twilight had replaced the setting sun, bathing the landscape in ghostly shades of gray. Quickly climbing the pole fence, he dropped down on the other side into the corral. His appearance spooked the horse towards the door into the barn.

"Thanks, man!" Darrell shouted, hanging on to his hat at a sudden gust of wind. They slammed the door and fastened it against the building storm. "That's all of them. We'd better head for the house!" The dark clouds were almost upon them, scudding along and dancing like dervishes driven before the gale forces.

Bryce leaned into the wind as it swirled around, picking up dirt and leaves in small whorls. He squinted, trying to keep dust out of his eyes, and hung onto his cap to keep it from blowing away. But he loved the roughness of the wind, the challenge it presented.

They hurried across the yard and met Dean striding from the office, his hat dipped low, one hand on it to hold it in place. Treetops began to bow low then spring back to whip in the wind, and the first raindrops spattered on the ground. As they stepped into the sunroom, they heard a faint roaring sound.

"Here it comes!" Dean grabbed the screen door and hooked it behind them. The clouds brought an unnatural darkness, far too early for nightfall, sweeping across the land like trailing witch's robes. "I hope everyone got under cover," he added worriedly.

Bryce knew the rodeo stock was sheltered but he thought of the cattle out in the open. When he voiced his concern, Dean replied, "There's a few lean-tos in the pastures and some animals crowd under the shrub trees along the coulees. There isn't anything we can do anyway." He turned a calm expression towards Bryce. "We entrust them to the care of the Heavenly Father at all times, but more so during storms like this."

Bryce stared at him and saw the steady faith in the rancher's face. For a nanosecond, he wished he had that kind of trust in a Heavenly Being. A bright flash followed by an ear-splitting crack of thunder cut off any further thoughts. The rain arrived in a sudden downpour, drumming on the roof like a thousand hammers. Lightning flashed again in a jagged streak, thunder boomed overhead, followed by more flashes and loud crashes.

"Boy, that was a close one," Dean muttered.

Dorine hurried out of the kitchen, relief apparent when she saw they were inside. The twins tumbled along behind her, and Dean scooped Doug up while Darrell hoisted David into his arms. "You guys wanna see a hailstorm? I think we're gonna get one!"

"The electricity went off a few minutes ago, so I've got the flashlights and lamps ready until you get the generator hooked up," Dorine informed them as she slipped in front of Bryce to stand next to her husband. Dean draped one arm around her shoulders.

A door slammed somewhere in the house, a gust of air blasting past them as the rain increased with the rushing noise not unlike a waterfall. Peering out through the mist-spattered screen, Bryce saw small hailstones bouncing off the sidewalk. The boys laughed in glee while their parents watched with trepidation. The hailstones became larger. Lightning flashed and the crashes of window-shaking thunder came quicker and louder. The boys gradually quieted, sensing that this was not a laughing matter. Bryce suddenly realized that he was the odd man out, no one was clinging to him. He thought of Robin, wondering how she was managing. Even she had her children.

"I'll bet some of those hailstones are as big as golf balls," Darrell muttered. Suddenly aware of the trembling child in his arms, he added, "Good thing the trees protect the windows in our house," he told David with a grin. In an aside to Bryce, he muttered, "The way the wind is blowing, they could easily break the windows at the back of the house."

Bryce started. *Those windows faced west...the same as the ones in the Sweet Schoppe!*

"What about Robin?"

Dorine turned, a quizzical expression on her face. "She's a Dakota girl, she knows what to do." She smiled confidently and laid her hand on his arm. "Don't worry about her. Remember, she's lived her whole life here."

He knew Dorine was right. No one grew up on the prairies without knowing how to ride out a storm. But the exhilaration of a few minutes before was gone, replaced by anxiety. He stared out into the rampaging weather, unable to stop thinking about Robin braving the storm by herself. The rushing sound increased to a deafening roar and when Darrell said something, Bryce couldn't hear him. Doug had curled himself in against Dean holding his hands over his ears. David was doing the same, in Darrell's arms. Lightning flashed constantly, illuminating silhouettes of the trees at the edge of the lawn. A loud clap of thunder was followed by a drawn-out crackling sound, as a large branch drifted down in slow motion to land with a thump on the hail-covered lawn. A shower of leaves, stripped from the trees by the onslaught of the hail, followed and settled over the grass and sidewalk. Rain gusted like some giant hand was flinging it over the bedraggled leaves in wave after wave, and the puffs of wind that came through the screen were cold.

It seemed like the roaring lasted for hours but in reality was only minutes.

Suddenly, it stopped, the silence loud in their ears, and even as they watched, the dark clouds scudded away to the northeast, leaving a bright moon shining down on a dripping landscape. Night had fallen, unnoticed, during the rampaging storm. Trees unbent like stooped people straightening, swaying slightly before standing tall and still again.

"I haven't seen anything like that for a long time," Dorine whispered into the quiet, broken only by the sound of water dripping off the eaves and tree branches.

"Is it gone?" David asked in a small voice as he peeped out from where he had buried his face in Darrell's shirt. Doug kept his face hidden in his father's chest, and Dean rubbed his chin over his son's head as he tightened his other arm around Dorine.

"Let's hope so." Turning to Dorine, he handed Doug to her. "We'd better go see how much damage there is." Darrell handed the other twin over to Dorine too and stepped back to grab his jacket off the peg.

Bryce had only one burning thought. "I'm going into town to see if Robin is alright!" He was halfway out the door, brushing past Dean. "You've got help here if you need it, but she's all alone!" He didn't care if they read anything in to that; he was past wondering what they'd think. All he wanted to do was get to Robin, hold her and see for himself that she was alright. Nothing could happen to her, not now, not when he'd just found her.

Dean picked up his jacket and followed him out. "You better take my pickup. Your car will never make it through the flooded low spots in the road. You'll have a better chance in a heavier vehicle." He fished the keys out of his pocket and handed them to Bryce. "There's a flashlight in the glove compartment. God go with you." Bryce gave the other man a grateful look before heading to the barn.

Chapter 11

Driving faster than what was deemed safe, Bryce was consumed with fear, wondering what he'd find in town. Dorine was confident Robin would be alright, but even the DeFoes hadn't seen a storm this bad for quite some time. What could Robin do by herself if something went wrong? The clichéd saying of having one's heart in their throat might be time-worn but that was exactly the way he felt. In all the times he'd been faced with danger in his job, none of them came close to what he was experiencing now. The fear was like acid climbing in his throat and radiating out to his very edges.

Several times he had to ease the big vehicle through low draws flooded with rain runoff, or stop and drag branches out of the way, the delays taking precious time. Curse words formed on his tongue but instead of voicing them, he sent a quick glance at the night heavens above and muttered, "If You're up there, I could sure use a little help here." It wouldn't occur to him until later that he didn't encounter any more fallen branches....

The air was cool and stars sparkled brightly overhead. If one didn't know better, the devastating storm that had just passed over could have been imagined. But the mini-lakes he saw beside the road were not there a few hours ago. He thought he may have even glimpsed a large rooftop in a pasture next to the road, but it was too dark to tell for sure. He shuddered and pushed down on the accelerator. If there were this much damage here in the country, what would it be like in town?

The road seemed to stretch out forever, but at last the headlights shone on the fading "Welcome to Silverdale" sign, hanging haphazardly on a crooked post next to an overgrown ditchbank.

Slowing, Bryce saw only darkness, then gradually made out faint bobbing lights here and there. People with flashlights were outdoors checking for damage. There were several downed trees he had to drive around, grateful the wide streets allowed him to do so.

When the silhouette of the two-story building came into sight next to the café, he let out a breath that he didn't even realize he was holding. Swinging in and parking so the headlights shown on the front of the café, he leaned over to yank open the glove compartment and grabbed the flashlight. Opening the door, he jumped out of the pickup, coming to an abrupt stop when his feet hit the ground.

A child's screams rent the air—and it was coming from inside the café!

Chills chased down his spine as he sprinted to the café door. The screen door sagged drunkenly to one side, the screen pockmarked where the hail had gone through it. Most of the glass was gone from the window in the upper part of the inside door, and to the side, one of the cheery curtains poked sadly through the blinds, dripping water on the sill.

"Robin! Robin! Can you hear me?!! He pounded on the door, dislodging shards of glass that fell with a tinkle to the floor inside. The knob wouldn't turn so he reached carefully through the remaining jagged glass and felt around for the knob on the other side. "Robin! Robin! Where are you?" he shouted, letting himself into the café. He turned on the flashlight but stopped short when he heard the crunch of glass underfoot. Shining the light around, he was amazed at the glittering mess that spread for several feet in all directions. But it wasn't all glass...he leaned down to shine the light on dark blotches on the floor.

Blood!

Large spatters that left a trail...the fear that had been in his throat now spilled into his mouth and he had to draw in a cleansing breath.

Across the room, the connecting door flew open and a small figure darted toward Bryce. The screaming continued from somewhere behind him.

"Mr. Martin! Bryce!"

Bryce's throat closed with emotion as he stepped over the glass to meet Jason mid-ways. The boy flung himself into his arms, hugging tight. "Bryce, I'm so glad you're here! I'm so scared! My mommy is bleeding and it won't stop!" He sobbed loudly, clutching Bryce tighter. Bryce's pulse pounded in his head and his ears rang. A sharp jab of fear thrust into his chest but he instinctively knew the boy needed a calming voice. He held the distraught child tightly as he made his way forward. "Where is she?" he asked gently.

With a muffled voice, Jason pointed toward the door. "In the bathroom in our house. The bleeding won't stop and Jeremy won't quit yelling!" He buried his face in Bryce's neck and plastered himself tightly to his body. The child's trust brought an unexpected surge of protectiveness, tightening his chest.

He moved through the door and down the short hall to where a faint light flickered from the bathroom. Robin leaned against the sink, her right hand wrapped in a bloody towel resting in the bowl, while she tried to console Jeremy by hugging him with her other arm. Looking up at Bryce in the wavering light from a candle sitting in the tub, she forced a smile. "I hope you don't faint at the sight of blood." The light flickered, highlighting her rioting red curls.

He'd never seen anyone so beautiful in all his life. Any doubt about his ambivalent feelings for Robin fled as he put Jason down, and with relief spiraling through him so profound it almost dropped him to his knees, he closed the distance between them. Gathering her against him, mindful of her injured hand, he tightened his hold. "I've never been so worried or scared in all my life," he whispered into her ear. Tremors racked his body and he could only hold her tighter.

He loved her.

It came to him just as simple as that. No fireworks, no loud drumbeats, just a quiet knowledge settling over him. All the excuses for not committing to anyone, his past life experiences, everything—gone. He laid his cheek on the top of her head and heaved a shuddering sigh. He could never let go of her.

When Bryce's voice had called to her from out in the café, Robin had experienced a sense of relief that weakened her knees. If she'd had any reservations about her feelings for him, they evaporated when he appeared in the bathroom doorway. Right or wrong, he had become the most important person in her life next to her boys. However, when he enveloped her in a bearhug and she could feel his big strong body trembling, she had no doubt that the self-proclaimed playboy had been sincerely worried about her. "Bryce," she whispered back. "I'm so glad you're here. I didn't know what I was going to do."

He drew back and looked down at her hand. "What happened?" he asked unsteadily. Even though the sight of blood didn't affect him, this was different—it was *her* blood. And so much of it.

"We were in here when I heard the windows break in the café, so I went out there to pull the drapes shut, thinking it would keep out the hail and some of the rain. But when I reached around to pull the cord, there was still a jagged piece of glass in the frame and it sliced across my palm." She looked down at the bloody towel. "I can't get it to stop bleeding."

Jason was gripping Bryce's leg so tight it was cutting off his circulation, but Jeremy's screaming had diminished to low moans.

Turning to the little boys, Bryce steadied his voice. "Listen very carefully, guys, we need to get Mommy to the doctor so he can fix her hand. Do you think you can help by getting her a sweater or jacket?"

"And get one for yourselves too," Robin added, slowly stepping back from Bryce and turning her attention to her injury.

Two pairs of big brown eyes overflowing with tears stared back at Bryce, but Jason took a big gulp and squared his shoulders. "Come on, Jeremy, we have to help Mommy."

Bryce handed the flashlight to him and said, "Go." Jeremy, still choking back sobs, took Jason's hand as they went out into the dark hallway, the flashlight beam bobbing ahead of them.

Bryce turned back to Robin. "Do you feel light-headed?" Bright red was spreading slowly on the towel and Robin reached for a dry towel as she shook her head.

"Not yet. I've been too busy trying to reassure the boys. But I don't think I've cut an artery, it's not gushing, it's just a steady flow." He marveled at her calmness, wondering what her city counterpart would have done in the same circumstances. He shuddered.

Helping her unwind the soaked towel, he drew in his breath at the sight. Turning on the faucet, he let cold water pour over her hand, the water turning red before gurgling down the drain. She got the clean towel ready and quickly wrapped it around her hand in a twist that put a thick layer right over her palm. Bryce tossed the used towel in the tub.

"You'd better sit down, sweetheart." He eased her down onto the edge of the tub as her hand dangled over the sink. "Jason," he called out, "do you know how to get ice?" Robin lowered her forehead to rest on her wrist, and he gripped her shoulder.

"Yes!" Jason appeared in the doorway with a jacket, Jeremy close behind him.

"Good man, there. And you know where the plastic bags are?" Jason's head bobbed up and down eagerly. "Go put some ice in a bag and bring it to me." He took the jacket, hanging it around Robin's shoulders.

"You never did say what you were doing here. Did you get caught in the storm?" Robin's voice was still calm but fainter, and she looked pale, even in the faint light.

"I was just out for a stroll and happened to pass by," he drawled. She looked up at him blankly but at that moment, car doors could be heard slamming from the direction of the street, followed by loud voices. He stepped out of the bathroom to see the beam of a flashlight come towards him through the café. Headlights played over the wall of the café and he recognized the ghostly outline of Deputy Langley.

"Everybody okay in here?"

"No! No! My Mommy's hurt!" Jeremy ran past Bryce to charge full bore into the deputy's legs and the flashlight beam bounced around as Jordan tried to juggle it and the boy.

"Hi, big guy." The deputy's voice was full of warmth and tenderness. "Mommy's hurt? Where?" His gaze came up to meet Bryce's.

Robin stuck her head around the door. "Hi, Jordan. I cut myself on some broken window glass. I was just about to call you to hitch a ride to the hospital. I'm afraid I'm going to have to have stitches."

"Phones aren't working and neither is my cell, so it's a good thing I came by. I saw Dean's pickup out front and almost didn't stop, but something just told me…" He glanced around, confused. "Aren't they here?"

"No, Bryce came to check on me. The Lord prompted you to stop," Robin said.

"It's a good thing I decided to check it out," Jordan agreed.

"I drove his pickup and I'll take Robin to the hospital." Bryce interrupted tersely. Why would she want to call on the deputy when he was right here? As to whether the Lord prompted the deputy to stop, he'd ignore that fantasy.

"Let me see." Holding Jeremy and shining the flashlight in front of him, Jordan examined the thick towel around Robin's hand, a faint stain beginning to appear. A soundless whistle escaped his lips and his eyes sought Bryce's. "Do you know where the hospital is?" He named a town some distance away.

Bryce shook his head but Robin interrupted. "I can show him, but..." her eyes anxiously searched Bryce's face. "I don't want to be a bother."

"A *bother?*" he almost shouted. "You're bleeding profusely and you don't want to be a bother?" He calmed himself. "I came to see if you were okay and you're not."

"Oh." A faint smile touched her lips, her eyes shining in understanding and unspoken appreciation. Jason arrived with the ice bag, handing it over to his mother. Between Jordan and Bryce, they bandaged Robin's hand with the ice and another clean towel, then shepherded the boys out to Dean's pickup. "Oh, I need my purse!" Robin said as she stopped on the way out the door.

"Why would you think about your purse at a time like this?" Bryce grumbled.

She gave him an impatient look. "It has my insurance card in it. You of all people must know about insurance cards!"

"I knew that," Bryce answered, chagrin coating his voice, while Jordan suffered a suspicious coughing spell. "I'll get it after you're in the pickup."

The deputy volunteered to get the purse after he had the boys buckled into their seats. His quiet voice soothed the children as Robin hesitated, eyeing the distance from the ground to the high-riding pickup.

Uttering an impatient sound, Bryce stepped forward and put his hands around her waist, lifting her to the seat. She was so slight he couldn't believe how little she weighed. She gasped and even in the shadows, he could see how flustered she'd become. He held her a moment longer, staring into her eyes, which were level with his. "I was scared for you," he whispered.

"Don't be, I'm okay. But…it was sure nice to see you coming through that door." She raised her good hand and laid it alongside his cheek. He turned his head and kissed her palm. For a moment they looked at each other in the light from the dashboard.

Suddenly aware of Jordan behind them, she dropped her hand and smoothed it over her lap as though straightening a skirt, even though she had on jeans. Bryce stepped back and closed the door.

"My purse is on the top of my dresser in the bedroom, Jordan."

"I could have gotten it." Bryce grumbled as he rounded the front of the pickup but Jordan was already heading back into the café. Bryce climbed in and settled himself behind the wheel, starting the pickup before buckling his own seatbelt. He backed up far enough so he could pull forward parallel to the sidewalk as Jordan hurried out.

Handing the purse in through the open window, Jordan smiled at Robin. "Don't worry about the café, I'll keep my eye on it while patrolling. And I'll be praying," he added softly.

Robin looked at the sorry mess of her business harshly outlined by the patrol car headlights, and a huge lump welled up in her throat. "My poor little Sweet Schoppe." Her forlorn words touched a chord in Bryce's heart, and he put a comforting hand on her shoulder. He'd never had to worry about anything monumental, but the café was her heritage and he couldn't imagine the thoughts going through her head.

"Get yourself taken care of first, then think about the café," Jordan advised. "Keep your arm up, that will slow the bleeding." He winked at her and gave her shoulder a pat.

Which Bryce didn't think was necessary and he dropped his arm, gunning the engine.

Jordan's eyes shifted to Bryce. "I just came from the freeway and a couple of trees that went down on the main road have been moved so you shouldn't have any trouble. Once you get on the freeway, it will be clear sailing to the hospital exit. The sheriff over there said the roads into town were okay, you might have to drive around a few big limbs but nothing blocking." He hesitated. "Take good care of our girl...she's the only one who knows how to make *kucken*." He winked at her again as he stepped back and Bryce tromped on the gas, shooting away from the curb.

In his peripheral vision, he could see Robin giving him a strange look.

"What?"

"You didn't need to be rude."

Bryce gripped the steering wheel tighter. "Like getting his *kucken* was more important," he muttered.

"He was trying to cover up his worry with a joke, Bryce."

He snorted and concentrated on driving, picking up speed as he left town and headed towards the interstate.

Robin's palm was still tingling from the kiss he'd pressed there and—

"How come Jordan isn't coming wif us?" Jeremy's small voice came from the darkness behind them.

Robin twisted in her seat to give her son a reassuring smile. His face was pale in the faint glow from the dashboard lights. "He has to patrol around to see if anyone else needs help, sweetie." He nodded and looked over at Jason, who was sitting ramrod straight, his little face pinched in worry. She reached through the opening between the seats and patted his knee. "It'll be alright, honey, don't worry."

Bryce glanced at the towel covering her hand and was relieved to see the stain didn't seem to be any larger. But his heart was still in overdrive during the silent trip to the hospital. What if she was injured beyond what they could tell? What if she lost the use of her hand? How could she run the café? He glanced in the rearview mirror at the boys. As upset as they were, they couldn't keep their heads from nodding, jerking upright and fighting to stay awake. He wondered if Robin had thought ahead to the same concerns he was having. He sent anxious glances her direction, thankful that she was calm enough to direct him to the hospital.

Bryce wheeled the big pickup into Emergency Room parking and cut the engine. He was relieved to see lights, courtesy of a generator no doubt.

Leaping down from the cab, he hurried around to help Robin but first, he opened the back door so the boys could scramble down. Jason had unfastened their seat belts and held out his arms to Bryce, but Jeremy was too drowsy to stand up. Realizing it was the first opportunity to touch the young boy, Bryce gathered him up and held him close as he helped Jason down. His heart was full as he held Jeremy tightly, savoring his little boy smell. He opened Robin's door and offered his hand as she slid out to the ground.

Robin had been silently praying, feeling control slipping away from her as she watched Bryce take over the care of her children. It wasn't like her to allow anything to interfere with her life, but right now, there was nothing she could do. If she had to give up control over her circumstances, she reluctantly conceded that Bryce looked as though he could handle this challenge. In spite of his questionable morals, he was a take-charge kind of guy, decisive and caring. No wonder he was so good at his job. She watched as he took Jason's hand, not missing the moment Bryce brushed a kiss over Jeremy's hair. She was fast running out of stamina, grateful that Bryce was willing to be helpful. In fact, once she thought about it, it felt rather good to give the reins to someone else for a change.

Escorting his little entourage through the electronic hospital doors, Bryce stepped up to the nurse's station. "We need some help here, right away. My friend has a deep cut, bleeding profusely and needs immediate attention." His commanding voice brought stares from the other waiting room occupants but he ignored them.

A blonde nurse seated at the desk, glanced up at him with weary impatience but after a look at the handsome face before her, the weariness evaporated. She straightened as her eyes shifted to Robin, then lowered to the towel-wrapped hand Robin held at her waist. All coyness fled as the nurse snapped into medical mode.

Rising from her chair, she grabbed a clipboard and pivoted towards curtained cubicles stretching down a hallway behind her. "Robin, what in the world did you do? Come on back, we can fill out papers there. We've already treated a broken arm, a couple of people with scrapes and scratches, one slight leg wound from a runaway chain saw. But it looks like you're priority right now."

Jeremy had come fully awake and a whimper escaped him as he realized who was holding him. Bryce carefully set him on his feet.

"Thanks, Sally," Robin breathed out. She followed the statuesque nurse, Bryce and the boys behind her. The hallway stretched miles before her; she hoped she could hold out.

Bryce shouldn't have been surprised that the nurse knew Robin, given how closely lives were intertwined in these rural communities, but he was still amazed.

Jason gripped his hand as he tried to shepherd a sleepy, stumbling Jeremy ahead of them. Sally whipped open the curtains to a cubicle and indicated that Robin should sit down. Jeremy crowded next to her knees, hiding his face against her thigh.

After introducing Sally to Bryce, Robin felt herself slowly wilting.

Bryce stood just inside the curtain with Jason by his side, feeling superfluous now that Robin was being cared for. Irritation bubbled up. He was always in control but not now and it frustrated him to no end. He kept his eyes on Robin and saw when she lost the battle to stay alert.

"Maybe you should lie down," he suggested, casting an irritable glance at the nurse.

"Good idea," Sally agreed, helping Robin stretch out. While taking Robin's blood pressure, the nurse smiled down at Jeremy.

"You must be Mommy's big helper." He peeked up at her, frowning at the equipment.

"It's okay, honey, she's listening to see if my heart is going thump-thump. Just like the doctor does when you go for a checkup." Robin smiled but Bryce could see how forced it was. It seemed unnatural for the plucky little redhead to look so done in.

Sally slipped a thermometer into Robin's mouth and picked up her clipboard and pen. Jason handed Robin her purse when she motioned towards it, and after Sally took the thermometer and read it, she briskly asked a few questions, jotting down information. She wrote on the chart and smiled at Jeremy again. "Let's let Mommy rest until the doctor comes."

Jeremy didn't look at the nurse before trying to crawl up beside Robin, but she stopped him and whispered, "You can't come up here, honey, just stand right there." Robin shivered and Sally quickly covered her with a thin white blanket, working around Jeremy who was clutching his mother's hand like his only lifeline.

"Let's go out to the waiting room, boys," Sally said, holding her hand out towards Jeremy. "We've got comic books and coloring books, tv, whatever you'd like. We're the only ones in the hospital with full power, so we're kind of special."

Robin turned her head. "Jeremy, you have to let go so Mommy can talk to the doctor when he gets here."

"No!" his lower lip protruded and tears filled his eyes.

Sally looked up at Bryce. "If you want to take the children out in the waiting room, I'll let you know when the doctor is done with Robin."

Jeremy screamed "No!" Robin immediately frowned, rolling over towards her son. "Sh-h-h, Jeremy, there are sick people here!"

"I'm n...not...ggggoing tttoo lealeave yyyou," he sobbed.

"Please, Jeremy, go with Jason, he'll take care of you—"

Bryce stepped forward to forcibly take Jeremy when the boy screamed out "No!" again. Bryce glanced uncertainly at Robin.

"It's okay," Sally said gently, leaning towards Jeremy. "You don't have to go."

Jeremy's answer was to turn his face into the clean white bedding.

Robin looked up at Bryce, pain in her eyes. "Do you mind taking Jason out?"

"You know I don't," he spoke softly. "We'll be in the waiting area. Have the nurse come get me if you need me." He looked at her lips and wanted to kiss her so badly he could taste it. She gazed back at him with what he thought was the same longing and his heart took a leap. How could he have ever thought he could leave this woman?

"Ahem," Sally cleared her throat and the look in Robin's eyes was replaced with chagrin. She glanced away, flustered.

Bryce moved out of the cubicle, and holding Jason's hand, walked the length of the hall past the nurse's station. He selected an orange plastic chair to sit, and settled Jason next to him. He'd never been this close to an emergency room before but he didn't like the feeling of being relegated to a place of waiting and not doing.

Blowing out a soft breath of air, he pondered what had happened in so short a time. Ole love'em-an-leave'em Martin, snagged by a pair of pretty hazel eyes, a dimpled smile and an independent spirit that wouldn't quit. Along with the love he now acknowledged, he had come to respect Robin. Women were usually nothing more than pleasant companions until he tired of them. He couldn't imagine ever tiring of Robin.

Glancing down at Jason, he realized he had been entrusted with one of Robin's most precious possessions. Jason's shoulders were rigid as he held himself stiffly upright by sheer determination. But what did he know about reassuring a child? Who would ever have thought that man-about-town Bryce Martin would be sitting in a hospital emergency room with an overwrought youngster? Even more important, what in the devil was he supposed to do? This situation was entirely out of his league. How did parents handle it?

How did the married guys in his office juggle jobs and parenting duties? A new respect for his co-workers nudged into his awareness and he realized that for once, he was thinking of others instead of himself.

Going purely on instinct, he gently massaged Jason's stiff shoulders, but was totally unprepared for the question that came.

"Is my Momma gonna die?"

The words sent a chill through him, and he hastily replied, "No, son, no. She isn't going to die. She's got a pretty bad cut there, but the doctor will fix her up."

Jason's shoulders remained rigid. He turned a solemn face up to Bryce. "My Daddy died."

A wave of emotion washed over Bryce and his heart melted. He could no more stop the tenderness he felt for this brave little child that he could stop the storm that had caused all this havoc. Scooping Jason into his arms, he settled him in his lap, his arms protectively around the trembling little body. Jason trustingly laid his cheek against Bryce's chest, nuzzling his shirt till he found a comfortable spot. Bryce's heart expanded even more.

"I know, buddy. I heard." Bryce rested his cheek on the top of Jason's head. The unique smell of little boy, soap and shampoo, along with the elusive scent of Robin's cinnamon, assailed his nose. He had never had anyone depend on him like this little child, and what did he have to offer him? His own needs and his wants had always come before anyone else. He'd never let anyone get close enough to need him for anything. In a glaring revelation, he saw how self-centered he had been his whole life. It was a sobering moment.

"He's not coming back. He's in heaven with Jesus." The child's voice was muffled in Bryce's shirt. "Maybe God wants my Momma in heaven with Daddy." A hiccough came, followed by another.

Talk about being out of his depth! He'd rather face a criminal on the lamb than the fears of this little boy. But he was on his own here.

He'd have to reach deep for any kind of instinct that was lurking down there to help guide him.

"Look at me, son." Jason lifted his head with sorrowing eyes. "God doesn't need your mother because He knows *you* need her." Lordy, he was on shaky ground here! He just hoped that any Almighty Being listening would take into account his ignorance of heavenly matters.

"But there's so much blood."

Bryce nodded solemnly. "The doctor will put a bandage on it, and your Momma will be fine." He hoped he wasn't giving any false assurances.

Jason turned his face back into Bryce's chest. "I don't want my Momma to die." The thin little shoulders began to shake.

Oh, Lordy. A strange, fierce emotion reared up inside Bryce, ready to take on anything that threatened Jason. But there wasn't anything tangible to fight, leaving Bryce with a helpless feeling. So he did the only thing he could.

Tightening his arms around the trembling child, Bryce cuddled Jason against his heart and let him cry. He murmured quietly, stroking Jason's back gently and slowly rocking back and forth. His throat was tight with emotion, and rubbing his cheek over Jason's soft hair, he realized he already loved this little guy as if he was his own.

A nurse walked by, captivated by the picture of the big man and small boy. Bryce barely registered her presence—his focus was to draw grief away from this little one now in his care. With a sense of wonderment, it came to him that this must be what a parent felt, this gut-wrenching emotion of wanting to shield their child from everything hateful in the world. Maybe there was hope for him yet if he could realize this.

They sat there in silence, Bryce in deep retrospect about his past life, until Jason gradually relaxed and went limp, giving in to exhaustion. Bryce gently laid him back to a more comfortable position and Jason hardly stirred. Poor little tiger. Bryce studied the boyish face, finding traces of Robin in the faint freckles scattered across Jason's nose, the shape of his lips. He was so deep in thought he missed the appreciative glances of the night nurses on their way to the cafeteria.

He adjusted Jason's sleeping form more comfortably in his arms and that was the way Robin spotted them as she stepped out of the cubicle. The sight of Bryce lovingly cuddling her son sent a warm thrill through her. There wasn't a trace of the big city playboy, only a strong male guarding a vulnerable child, cherishing him, protecting him. She had to take a deep breath and tried to still her heart. She wondered what the doctor would have said if he could take her blood pressure now!

Voices coming from the emergency area alerted Bryce that Robin was finished with the doctor. She was walking towards him, Sally by her side carrying Jeremy, slumped on the nurse's shoulder, sound asleep. Robin's hand was bandaged and her arm in a sling. She carried papers in her other hand and smiled wanly at him as they approached. "Two dead soldiers," she noted, glancing first at Jason, then at Jeremy.

Bryce stood, shifting Jason in his arms. The nurse continued walking toward the automatic doors. "I'll help you out with the children." Bryce held his precious bundle and followed the women, noticing that Robin seemed a little unsteady. He moved to her side and put one arm around her waist. She started, then glanced up at him gratefully.

Her heart went into overdrive and she hoped she could make it out to the pickup without her knees buckling. Every place Bryce's hand touched her seemed to burn through her cotton blouse. Darting a look at him however, she could see only concern and that helped to calm her. Down, girl!

They went through the doors into the night, and he took his arm from around her to open the back passenger door of the double cab. Sally deposited Jeremy on the seat and slid him over, turning to take Jason from Bryce. Robin waited patiently but found herself swaying. Reality was catching up with her and she reached out to steady herself against the door.

Bryce turned, noticed her white face and yanked open the front passenger door. He smoothly picked her up and lifted her onto the high seat. The fact she allowed him to do so without even a frown showed him that she was completely exhausted.

Sally buckled Jason in, slammed the door and stepped away, waving at Robin before she headed back inside the building.

Bryce hurried around to slide into the driver's seat, turning to buckle the seat belt around Jeremy. Settling himself in the front seat, he glanced over at Robin.

"Okay? Ready to go?" She nodded without looking at him, leaning her head wearily on the headrest and closing her eyes. The faint smell of his cologne drifted to her as she tried not to focus too much on his nearness. He was just helping out, responding to an emergency. There was nothing special attached to what he had done for her. It was the shock catching up with her, it had nothing to do with the handsome man next to her.

Yeah, right.

Lord, help me to get through this. My boys need me and I don't shouldn't be thinking about Bryce.

He slowly backed the pickup out and turned towards the exit. Robin opened her eyes, pulled the seatbelt over her and turned to check on the boys. They were both asleep, their heads lolling against the seat. Poor little things. What a night for them. She turned back around and stared out the windshield.

So many decisions to make. She tried to push them away, now was not the time to think about that. She just needed to get through the next few minutes, the next few hours. Exhaustion tightened its grip, threatening to overwhelm her. The pain pills she'd taken dulled the throb in her hand, but she could still feel it, ever so faintly. Now was not the time to weaken, she needed her wits about her. Think, girl, think!

She'd have to get the window glass replaced soon as possible. Andy would have glass in stock at the lumberyard, but a lot of people in town would be needing windows replaced. Would he have enough? She had to get hers repaired quickly. She couldn't ask people to eat with dust blowing in over their food. What about the health department? She'd have to check to see if she could open under limited circumstances. What if the power wasn't back on in the morning? How could she cook?

A sharp, jabbing pang shot across her palm and fingers. Common sense told her she could not work in the cafe using only one hand. Panic and darkness gnawed at the edges of her self-control. Hang on, hang on, she urged herself. But the unrelenting tide kept rolling over her and she felt herself giving way to it…

Bryce concentrated on maneuvering around fallen tree limbs after he was on the main street, but hearing a small sound from Robin's side of the pickup, he glanced sideways at her. After that one look, he immediately swung the pickup over to the side of the wide road, his face grim. Slamming the gearshift into park, he unbuckled his seat belt and reached for Robin, all in one smooth move. Her shoulders were slumped and her free hand covered her face.

"Come here," he murmured, reaching between them to undo her seat belt. She didn't resist, and he drew her into a loose embrace. Sobs began to shake her body and he stroked her back, much as he had Jason's earlier.

"My poor little honey. What a night you've had." He murmured softly as the storm of sobs continued. Gazing out the dark windshield, it seemed second nature to be comforting this woman, realizing how much she had come to mean to him. It had only been a couple of weeks, he mused, stroking her trembling back. Could someone learn to care for another person this much in that short a time? Heck, "care" was a wimpy word—love was the right one. A strong one. Strong enough to fill his heart with it, brimming, overflowing.

"I'm getting you all wet," her voice was muffled.

"Like that's going to matter," he replied gruffly, tightening his hold on her. He was relieved when she melted into him instead of stiffening up.

Robin told herself she should not have collapsed on Bryce, she should move, sit up and take command. Her physical strength had deserted her and on top of that, the endearment Bryce had let slip sent a flood of weakness through her. Had he realized what he said? But that didn't mean anything, those sort of phrases rolled off his tongue like newspapers off a press.

She really should move.

In a minute.

It felt so good to just lay there, her head on his chest, and close out the world. Just for a minute. She couldn't explain it, didn't want to, but she felt safe…cherished. How long had it been since she'd been held so tenderly? She turned her head a little so her cheek rested over his heart. The beat was loud. Must be from fear. He had probably never gone through an experience like tonight. He liked his women independent, not collapsing all over him. She was going to have to move from this safe haven.

In a minute.

Bryce glanced over the seat at the boys, and his heart swelled. In a flash, he realized this could be his family. His hand faltered in its stroking. Family? *Him?*

But in that instant, he knew it was true. He loved these little Dakota boys, and their mother. But the only commitment he'd ever made was to his job. He'd never allowed anything to interfere with that. He blinked and looked back at the boys. Until they entered his world. Robin slowly lifted her head and blinked up at him, her lashes wet and spiky. "I'm sorry, Bryce. I shouldn't have broken down like that." She slowly moved away as he reluctantly let her go.

"I don't know of anybody that deserved to more than you," he replied softly, brushing a curl back from her forehead. His arms felt empty without her softness. "You've had a traumatic experience tonight. You don't have to be a pillar of strength all the time, Robin, you're allowed to be human once in awhile."

"I must look a mess," she fussed, straightening her clothes.

"You're beautiful," he whispered.

She breathed in deeply at his compliment. *He probably says that to all the girls.* She leaned back and closed her eyes, a wan smile playing over her lips. "To quote our friend Dorine, 'yeah, and pigs fly'." He chuckled as she softly added, "I dread tomorrow."

"Things will look better by daylight." He buckled her seatbelt, then his, and shifted the pickup into gear. It was a test of his self control to buckle that belt, to be so near to her and yet so far.

As they approached Silverdale, Robin opened her eyes and sat forward. "It's too much to suppose the electricity will be back on. I'd like to see how much damage there is."

"I don't see any lights at all anywhere around the countryside or in town. You don't really want to go in the cafe tonight…do you? Why don't you come with me out to the ranch? I'm sure Dorine will be glad to have you, once she hears what's happened." She cast him a doubtful look and he pressed his advantage. "The night is halfways over anyway, and why stumble around in the dark? Besides, you can't do anything with your arm in a sling."

She glanced back at the road and bit down on her lip. "Well….okay. I guess you're right."

Bryce drove right on past the Sweet Schoppe and tried to ignore Robin's lingering, wistful gaze.

Chapter 12

When they pulled up in front of the ranchhouse where light streamed from the first floor windows, Bryce said with relief, "They've got the generator hooked up." Even though he liked the "wild west," he was uncomfortable without his creature comforts.

Dean peered out of the screen door and Bryce cut the lights. He hopped out of the pickup and called, "I've got Robin and the boys. She cut her hand and had to have stitches. The café is pretty much toast so I brought her along with me." Robin stirred and sat up straighter.

Dean ambled down the walk with a flashlight. "Be careful, there's still twigs all over. We got most of the big branches moved. The generator doesn't run the yard lights out here, we'll have to watch where we step." He began taking the boys out of their seat belts.

Dorine came to the door and when she saw Bryce helping Robin out of the pickup, she gave a little cry and ran to her friend. "Robin! What happened?"

Robin managed a crooked smile. "A bird kicked me."

Bryce snorted. "She cut herself on a broken window and had to have stitches. The power is off in town too, so it's better for her to be here where we can take care of her."

"You did right," Dorine declared firmly, taking Robin's other arm, guiding her towards the door. "You can tell me what happened after we get you inside."

Robin was still pondering Bryce's use of the word "we" in reference to her care. And who made him King of the World? She might have some sayso about where she went!

"The boys," she remembered suddenly. *How could she have forgotten them?*

"We'll take care of everything, you need to get inside." Dorine continued up the walk.

In no time at all, Robin was in a guest bedroom, wearing a borrowed nightgown. The boys were in the room next to her, not even waking when Bryce slid off their shoes, pants and shirts. Darrell hung their clothes over a chair while Dean pulled back the covers and helped Bryce put the boys in bed.

In her room, Robin sat on the edge of the bed and opened her purse to find the samples of pain pills Sally had given her. She took out the prescription she was to have filled the next day. Dorine brought water from the bathroom and handed the glass to her while Robin related details of the evening.

Finally laying back on the pillows, Robin sighed. "Oh, it feels good to lay down."

"You've been through a lot tonight," Dorine agreed, pulling a sheet over her friend before sinking down on the bed. "I hope you can relax enough to get some rest."

"Are the boys asleep?"

"Yes, I let the guys put them to bed, then they went downstairs to make coffee." She eyed her friend curiously. "Speaking of which, what *did* happen?"

Robin avoided looking into her friend's eyes, and shrugged. "The wind blew in—"

Dorine put her hand on Robin's shoulder. "You know I'm not

talking about that. Bryce has gone all protective about you, and can hardly keep his eyes off you."

A blush crept up Robin's neck, spreading to her cheeks. She raised her hand and scrubbed at her cheek. "Darn this complexion of mine!"

Dorine laughed softly. "You have feelings for him, don't you?"

"No!" Robin declared but still wouldn't meet her friend's eyes. "Yes...I don't know!" Dorine waited, smiling demurely, her eyes sparkling. "I don't *want* to feel this way." Robin turned to her. "It's just a case of gratitude for all he did for us tonight." She looked hopefully at her friend for verification.

"You never could hide your feelings from me—he's really tempting you, isn't he?"

Robin looked down at the sheet across her chest, her fingers picking at a loose thread. "I don't want to feel anything for him, I know it isn't right. I never thought I could get interested in anyone else after Randy, but..." she turned anguished eyes to Dorine. "What am I going to do?"

"You don't have to do anything. At least not right now," Dorine winked.

"I know." Robin put her hand up to her cheek. "I can *never* let him know that I care about him." She paused. "Maybe if I take another pain pill, this feeling will go away."

Dorine stood, soft laughter spilling out of her. "I doubt that! But right now, you need rest. No more thinking about *anything*. Mama says to go to sleep."

"Yes, mama," Robin replied sotto-voice. When Dorine was gone, Robin knew she couldn't reveal the discovery she'd made tonight, that she loved Bryce. Yes, loved.

When the object of her heart came upstairs, Robin was still awake, staring at the ceiling. He knocked gently after peeking in at her. "Can I come in?"

She turned at the sound of his voice and smiled, her heart pitter-pattering. She couldn't know that she looked like a frail angel to him. He pulled up a chair and sat beside the bed, reaching for her hand. Twining her fingers in his, he looked into her eyes.

"How you doing?" He was encouraged by her lack of resistance when he touched her.

Her heart kicked into overdrive and she swallowed, trying to quell the rush of emotion. "Thanks for all you did tonight, Bryce. I don't think I told you." She prided herself on her steady voice.

He shrugged self-consciously. "You didn't need to, I could see it in your eyes." He played with her fingers, searching her face and grinning. "You have a very expressive face, and I can usually read people like a book."

She glanced down at their entwined fingers. "Then I better not look at you."

"Is there something you don't want me to see?" His voice was low, seductive.

She looked everywhere but at him, but in the end, met his gaze. "You know that I'm attracted to you, Bryce, and tonight has shone me a new side of you. I'll be honest—"

"As though you've not been anything else," he interrupted. When he raised her hand to his mouth and kissed each knuckle, her breathing slowed to short shallow grabs of air. He looked at her hand, then raised warm, tender eyes, as though beckoning her into his world.

"—and say I didn't think you had in it you to be so...kind...and...compassionate."

"What I feel about you goes w-a-y beyond compassion, Robin, and I think you know it." There was a seriousness to him that had not been evident before.

The intimate setting, the soft light and quiet closed them in, as though they were in their own little cocoon and Robin experienced a yearning like she never had when she was married to Randy. The thought skittered through her mind that she was being disloyal, but it was only there momentarily, then was gone. Forever.

Bryce saw the indecision flicker in her eyes but dampened down his desire to take advantage of the situation. If he ever hoped to gain her confidence, he'd have to live up to her expectation of him being "kind and compassionate." He carefully kissed the back of her hand and laid it down on the bed. "Try to get some sleep, sweetheart."

She took a deep breath in relief at the change in subject. "I'm going to try, but the pain pill hasn't kicked in yet. All I can see is the wind whipping the curtains in the broken windows at the café. I'm wondering what I'll find tomorrow." This is what she needed to focus on, the problems at hand, not the handsome man gazing at her.

"You can't do anything about it right at this moment, so you might as well put it out of your mind. Tomorrow will come soon enough."

She sighed heavily, turning her eyes toward the ceiling. "Yes. Tomorrow." She held up her bandaged hand. "I can't cook with one hand, so how is that going to work?"

He shook his head and chuckled. "I doubt you'll be doing any cooking, nor will anyone else. There won't be any power for awhile, according to Dean. Nobody's going to expect you to open the café."

She turned a worried look on him. "If I don't open, I don't have any income." The shadows returned that he had seen lurking in her eyes the last few days.

"Do you really have to be concerned about that?"

She smiled mirthlessly. "No workee, no eatee. But to put it on the line, if I miss even a few days of work, I'm wading in red ink." She paused. "Ever since those new businesses opened out at the freeway, mine has been operating on a shoestring. Now, with the storm and all, I'll have to close." *Why was she telling him all this? Must be the pain pills talking.*

He steepled his fingers under his chin, his elbows on his knees as he frowned. "You've made references to that before, but are you really operating that close to the line?"

Pain flitted through her eyes. "I'm sorry, I shouldn't have said anything. But as long as I have, yes, I'm almost to the bottom line." She went on to tell him about the insurance company's bankruptcy and all it meant. The more she talked, the more he frowned.

"What sort of insurance do you have?"

She told him and his expression lightened. Oh, it felt so good to share her burden. Not that she hadn't spoken of this with Dorine, but not having a mate increasingly brought home to her how lonely she'd become. No wonder God said that it was not good for man to be alone. Or woman either. There was a certain intimacy in sharing her business concerns with Bryce but a small part of her warned not to get too comfortable with him. *Remember who he is*, warned the little voice. But the little voice was dim. She blinked.

"That's a good company and they should pay soon after your claim is filed." She heard him but he seemed to be farther away and she blinked again, trying to clear her head.

"I...don't...know when...I'll be...able to...do that." My, but her eyes felt heavy.

"Let me worry about that for you, honey." Bryce leaned forward to press a kiss on her forehead but her eyes were already closed. He watched a moment and when he saw she was breathing deeply, he whispered, "Sleep well, my love." He stood just as Dorine stuck her head in the door.

"Is she out?" She slipped in quietly and approached the bed.

"Yeah, but she's really worried about the café. I hope she stays asleep." He got up and moved aside, a frown creasing his forehead.

Dorine pulled the blanket up higher over Robin and smoothed it. "I know she's worried, but right now she needs to rest. Lots of rest."

They went out, Bryce casting lingering glances at the woman in the bed.

"Are you...are you still thinking about leaving in the morning?" she questioned softly when they'd closed the door.

He ran a hand over his head. "No, I can't leave now. This storm has changed my plans. She needs all the help she can get."

Dorine hid a Madonna-like smile, said good night and climbed the stairs to her own quarters. She and Dean had a lot of talking, *and* praying, to do tonight.

Bryce didn't think he'd sleep, knowing Robin was just down the hall but he didn't awaken until he heard birds twittering in the trees outside his window.

He dressed and checked on Robin and the boys, who were all still asleep. The house was quiet and cool in the dawn as he went silently downstairs where Dean and Darrell sat at the table, drinking coffee. He grabbed a cup while listening to them outline their plans for the day. They had both been up before dawn, assessing damage to buildings and animals. Since all the cell phones were out and phone lines down, they had no idea of how others had fared following the aftermath of the storm.

"This must be like pioneer days," Bryce ventured during a lull in the conversation. "Everybody is on their own." He took a good sip of the fragrant brew.

Dean grinned. "Kind of peaceful, isn't it? No phones ringing, no fax machine chattering, no flickers on the computer screen. Slows everything down, lets you catch your breath."

Bryce eyed him over the rim of his cup. How could the man stay so cheerful and optimistic? He himself would go bonkers without his tech toys.

As though reading his mind, Dean leaned back, flexing his shoulders. "God is still in control, and when I realized that this is His ranch, His cattle, His buildings, I quit worrying. You know what the Eleventh Commandment is, don't you?"

Bryce snorted. "I don't even know what the first one is, let alone the eleventh."

Dean chuckled. "There are only ten in the Bible but there should be eleven. God tapped me on the shoulder one day and said, '"Thou Shalt Not Sweat It.'"

Bryce's lips twitched. "That about covers it, I guess." He finished the coffee, rinsed his cup and set it in the sink. "Well, I'm going to leave you guys to it. I'm heading into town to see how much damage there is at the cafe."

Darrell snapped his fingers. "Hey, this is right up your alley, you old dog, you! Boy, did you pick a time to come visit or what?!" He got up and took his cup to the sink.

Dean cast Bryce an enigmatic look. "He's going home today."

"No, I've changed my mind," Bryce quickly corrected him. "I can't leave now...Robin needs help."

"We're here for her, like always," Darrell said defensively.

"You said it yourself, I'm in the right place at the right time. With all due respect, you don't know anything about insurance and I do."

"That's true, but people around Silverdale take care of each other," Darrell replied. "Her folks might even come back from Florida to help."

"But they're not here right now, and I am."

"You know, it's not a coincidence that you're here at this particular time," Dean drawled. "The Lord's timing is always perfect." He rose from his place at the table.

Bryce hesitated, his hand on the doorknob. "Are you saying this is Fate?"

Both brothers shook their heads. "Nope!" Dean replied. "No fate involved. If it's God's plan to have you here, here you are."

Bryce raised a skeptical eyebrow. "I don't know about that..." but his voice trailed off uncertainly.

Darrell slapped him on the back. "Go ahead, get going. Unless you want to wait for Robin? She'll want to look at the damage too."

"No!" Bryce glanced up the stairs. "She needs to rest that hand and take care of her boys. She shouldn't have to deal with that mess just yet." As he went out the door and let it clap shut behind him, Dean and Darrell exchanged knowing looks.

The bright sun shone across a branch-littered countryside, but already people were digging out and putting things to rights. When Bryce drove into town, several pickup loads of debris were headed towards the landfill, and exuberant teen boys were showing off their muscles as they used chainsaws to cut apart downed trees. Other people had rakes and wheelbarrows as they went about the cleanup.

He eased his car to a stop in front of the Sweet Schoppe and cut the engine. There was sunshine slanting across an inside wall where it shouldn't be. He frowned. The curtains drooped at the gaping windows, and even the cheery flowers out front were bedraggled and crushed. He walked to the door, pushed it open and started at the jangling of the bells. In the midst of all this chaos, those bells were still on the job.

Shaking his head, he picked his way across the glass-littered room and entered the kitchen through the swinging doors. Blue sky up above was framed by pieces of ceiling tiles, splintered wood and old tarpaper dangling from jagged wood lathes. At his feet, water covered the floor. Apparently the aged, flat roof couldn't hold up under the heavy deluge of the storm. He ran a practiced eye over the ceiling and walls, noting details.

He hoped this was the only damage as he pushed open the connecting door to Robin's living quarters, grateful the rooms seemed to be intact—until he glanced down the hall toward the back. Heading into the once cozy living room, he saw the ceiling had given way there too, sheet rock and splintered lathe dangling crazily above plaster-coated furniture that now stood in a large puddle of water.

This was going to devastate Robin. He was thankful he had come alone. Making his way back to the café, he saw Andy peering in the open front door.

"Hey! Is Robin here?" The lumberyard owner let his gaze slide over the room. "Saw your car out front. What a mess!"

Bryce realized that no one except Deputy Langley knew about Robin's injury, and quickly related the circumstances.

Andy wagged his head, frowning. "I came over at daybreak to see if she was alright an saw what happened in there. But no Robin. Couldn't figure out where she'd got herself to. Other folks stopped by too, we're worried 'cause she's nowhere 'round."

Bryce's chest tightened at the concern in Andy's voice. "I'm glad she wasn't here. That roof caved after I took her to the doctor."

Both men stared at the destruction. Bryce was the first to move. "We have to get a tarp over that roof." This was his turf, and his skills kicked in.

"I been thinkin' the same thing. I got a big stock of 'em over at the yard," Andy replied. "Got some hefty teens looking for a few bucks, we can get this done real soon."

Bryce glanced over at the lumberyard's main building and saw the roof had lost shingles too, yet here the man was, looking out for his neighbor. If this was in the city, some people would be looking to loot rather than help.

Clapping Andy on the shoulder, Bryce headed for the door. "Go for it, whatever you need to do. Be sure to save the receipts."

Andy gave him an indignant look. "We'da done that anyhow, we take care of our own around here."

"No offense, man," Bryce held out his hands, palms up. "Just making sure."

After another disgusted look, Andy trotted back across the street to the lumberyard while Bryce took out his cell phone camera. After photographing the damage, he climbed in the car and turned it toward the freeway.

Robin gradually surfaced from a deep sleep, slowly opening one eye, then the other. At first disoriented, she blinked, then the previous evening's events rushed back. She closed her eyes, not wanting to face the day. An experimental flexing of her fingers assured her she hadn't dreamed her injury. It was sore and kicking up a protest.

"Mommie? Are you awake?" Jason whispered as he peeked in the door.

"Yes, honey, I'm awake. Come on in. Did you sleep okay?"

Jason crept to the side of her bed and leaned on the mattress, looking at her with solemn eyes. "Does your hand hurt?"

She pulled it out from under the covers. "It's kinda sore, yes."

"Did you have to take pills?"

She smiled at his thoughtfulness, and reached out to ruffle his hair. "Yes, I got up once during the night. I checked on you and you were zonked, really cutting the ZZZZs!"

He looked relieved at the old joke that was a game with them. "Are you hungry? Dorine said to come down to breakfast when you're ready."

"Did you eat?" she asked as she sat up and swung her legs out of bed. The room began to tilt and she grabbed for the edge of the mattress, careful not to alarm Jason.

"Yep, and so did Jeremy. I made sure he cleaned up his plate too!" He grinned at her.

"You're a good man, Jason Hudson! Now go down and tell Dorine I'm awake and will be at the table as soon as I can." She watched him go, running a shaky hand through her tousled curls. Holding up her bandaged hand, she took a deep breath. "Well, pardner, it looks like it's you and me for the next few days!" She stood on trembling legs, and after gaining her balance, grimly headed for the bathroom.

Robin didn't have much appetite but Dorine coaxed her to eat a little breakfast. When she mentioned that Bryce had told Dean he'd be leaving for St. Louis this morning, Robin's face paled.

"Did he take his things then?" Confusion filled her mind. How could he have been so attentive last night, and still leave without saying goodbye?

Dorine hesitated. "I don't know, I haven't looked in his room."

Holding one finger up, she added, "Be right back." She took the stairs two at a time, returning in a few minutes. "His things are still there." Unexpected relief swept through Robin. Dorine continued, "Maybe he went to check the café. You know, he'd be able to estimate what the damage will be." Dorine looked thoughtful. "Come to think of it, isn't it a coincidence that he, being an insurance investigator, is here right now?" She tapped one finger by her mouth. "Hum-m, on the other hand, maybe not." She winked at Robin, who chose to remain silent.

Because Robin was anxious about the café, Dorine rounded up the four boys and they were soon on their way to Silverdale.

As they came into town, they marveled at the activity. Almost every building and house had broken windows, branch-cluttered lawns, and people were on ladders, inspecting roofs. There was almost a traffic jam around the lumberyard. Dorine had to park down a ways from the cafe. "Andy's going to do a land-slide business today, he'll probably run out of supplies."

"I don't see Bryce's car," Robin remarked, glancing at the vehicles lining the curb.

Dorine craned her neck. "Wonder where he is?"

Robin took a deep breath and opened the van door. "Well, might as well go look."

Dorine sent her a sympathetic glance. "I'll stay here with the boys."

"Thanks." Robin smiled gratefully. She approached the open doorway of the cafe, almost afraid to go in. Squaring her shoulders, she stepped in and came to a halt.

Bright sunshine poured through a hole in the roof above the kitchen.

"Oh, my goodness!" she breathed out. Skirting around the shattered glass, she crossed the dining area and stopped by the counter stools to sink down on one. Numbness slowly enveloped her.

She was finished.

The café was out of business.

Her throat filled with a huge lump and a defeated sigh whispered between her lips. She stared at the devastation with dry eyes, beyond feeling.

"Hey, Robin! There you are!" boomed Andy's voice from the doorway. She turned slowly on the stool to face him. "That Bryce guy told me what happened, and I'm glad you're here so you know what we're doing. I've got some kids putting a tarp over that hole so you don't get any more damage in case it rains again." He stepped forward and whistled as he peered at her hand. "Don't look like you'll be using that wing for awhile."

"No," she replied bleakly. At the sound of scraping noises from above, they both turned to see a teenager peering down at them through the hole in the kitchen ceiling.

"You watch out there, Kent!" ordered Andy, hurrying through the door to stand under him, looking up. "Don't need anybody tumbling in here and breaking a leg."

"Don't worry, Mr. Vayle, we got it under control," the teen grinned, giving Andy a thumbs up. His face disappeared and soon the sunlight was blocked by a blue tarp, giving an eerie glow to the room below. Laughter and pounding of hammers followed.

"Musta been the weight of the water on that old roof that brought it down. Water gets purr-ty heavy you know," Andy commented, hands on his hips as he gazed up at the tarp. "But that'll keep the weather out. And birds from coming in too," he quipped as he turned.

"Oh. Yes…well…the roof was pretty old." Her thoughts scrambled, thinking what she needed to do first, and trying not to let despair take over.

He looked kindly at her. "I know it's a shock, walking in to this. But like that feller Bryce said, it's a good thing you weren't here when it came down."

"You've seen Bryce?" It finally registered that he'd mentioned Bryce before and her spirits rose. "But where is he now?" She glanced out towards the street.

"Dunno, came in, gave a looksee, and took off."

"Took...off?" Those same spirits began spiraling down, down, down.

"Yep, headed out towards the freeway, last I saw that fancy car of his."

"You mean, he...just...left?" Bump, the spirits hit rock bottom.

"Yep, looked around in here, then headed out," repeated the lumberyard owner as he came back to where she was sitting.

"Oh. Did he...did he say where he was going?"

"Nope. Wasn't here when he left. He snapped out orders about getting this tarp on the roof and I told him we'da done that without *him* ordering us around!" Andy looked properly offended.

A small smile tilted her lips. "Thanks, Andy." Once again, she knew her choice to stay in this caring community had been the right one. Taking a deep breath, she focused on the problem at hand. "I have to get an estimate before I can file a claim but I hope the insurance gets on the ball quickly so I can pay you."

"You know I don't worry 'bout that," he patted her awkwardly on the arm and another lump joined the one already in her throat.

"I better get up there to make sure they got that on right, then we gotta go help Mizz Kingsbury with her roof. That big old cottonwood out front of her house crashed right through a corner of it."

"Is she okay?" Robin asked worriedly.

"Oh, yeah, she was in the back part of the house."

"Okay." Robin sighed. "Thanks, Andy."

She stared at the debris and thought of Bryce. Even though his belongings were still at the ranch, that didn't mean he was coming back. If he'd headed for the freeway...She stopped. Why was she concerned over his whereabouts when she should be concentrating on what *she* should be doing! *Because you love him*, said the little voice.

"Robin?" Dorine's voice came tentatively from the street entrance. "What in the world—boys! Stay back, don't go in." All four boys stood next to Dorine at the open doorway, staring in fascination.

"Wow!" exclaimed David, scrunching down to look at the broken glass. "Lookit all this mess!" His twin knelt next to him, eyes wide. Jason and Jeremy, their faces pale and worried, searched the darkened interior for their mother.

"Stay there!" Robin commanded, getting up off the stool. "I have to get the insurance policy out of the file." She paused. "Why don't you take them down to the store for...maybe an ice cream bar?" she waved her hand vaguely.

"Mommie! What happened to our place?!" Jason called fearfully, rooted to the spot, his eyes on the jagged hole in the ceiling.

Robin pasted a cheerful expression on her face. "Andy thinks there was too much rainwater up there. He's put a tarp over it to keep it dry if it rains again. But we'll get it fixed, honey, don't worry." Her ploy worked as his expression lightened. If only all the ills of the world could be fixed as simply as that.

Dorine reached for his hand. "Come on boys, who's up for ice cream?"

"Yea!" chirped David, jumping up and down. Doug looked undecided about being cheerful when he noticed his friends' downcast expressions.

"Come on, Jason, Jeremy," coaxed Dorine. "As soon as your mother is done, we'll go back to my place. You can swim in the pool and maybe have a picnic."

They reluctantly went with her, casting longing looks back at the cafe.

Robin slowly moved to the connecting door, gathering strength to plan what she had to do next. Intent on getting the policy out of the filing cabinet, she stopped when she looked down the hall towards the living room.

Oh, no!

Moving like a robot, she forced her heavy limbs along the hallway past the bedrooms until she stood under the arch leading to the living room.

The chaos here was worse than in the café—the devastation covered her personal living space. Chunks of plaster had showered down on the sofa, dusting the afghan her grandmother had crocheted for her, and water covered the crocheted rug her other grandmother had hand-made. The overstuffed chair was rain-soaked, and videos lay in the mini-lake where the bookcase had spilled them out when they were jarred by the cascading ceiling. Thankfully, the piano was far enough out of the way, still holding her prized family photographs.

Oh, Lord! She cried out silently. Sick at heart, she leaned against the doorjamb and let the tears finally come. There was no one to see her let go as her gaze flitted around the room—how was she ever going to manage now?

Bryce. His image popped into her head.

No, Bryce was gone. He wouldn't help her. She was shocked to realize how easily she thought of him before anyone else. She drew a deep breath. The St. Louis playboy had ducked under her defenses. Foolish, foolish woman, she sorrowed. She knew he'd go out of her life as quickly as he'd come in, but did her heart listen? No. Now she was alone.

Despair took over, weighing her down, and grieving for what she'd lost, Robin cried until she was spent, silently turning to God. Honesty compelled her to cry out to Him, "Why, God? I don't understand!!"

Sniffing, she finally drew herself together and walked back through the hallway to the bathroom, taking several tissues from the box there. Her gaze landed on the wet, bloody towel in the tub. Here was something positive to do. She ran water and rinsed it out as best she could with one hand. It occurred to her that there was no power to run appliances so any clothes washing would have to be done by hand. Like pioneers.

Overhead, footsteps sounded as Andy directed his crew to put another tarp over the gaping hole above the living room, followed by the sound of hammers. She stopped and listened, then squared her shoulders. Well, her great-grandparents had been pioneers on these plains, and they made it without modern conveniences. She was made of the same stuff and she would get through this, injured hand and all.

Returning to the livingroom, she gathered the videos first, letting water run off them before tossing them into a wastebasket. They were probably all ruined. She set the houseplants outside in the shelter of the arbor, shaking the leaves gently to rid them of the dusty plaster powder. Grimly, she noted she wouldn't have to water them for a few days. It was harder to shake the plaster chunks off the afghan with only one hand, but she had managed to drag it outside when Dorine came around the side of the house, the boys following, licking their cones.

"*What are you doing?*"

"Just look inside," Robin replied shortly. "Boys, don't go in the house. There's a big mess in there and I don't want you getting hurt."

"I mean, what are *you* doing? You shouldn't be moving stuff, what is the matter with you?" Dorine's voice came out sharply, as she grabbed the afghan out of Robin's hand.

"Just go look," Robin replied wearily.

"Oh...my....goodness!" Dorine breathed out as she stared through the screendoor. The boys crowded around and peered past her.

"Momma!" Jeremy whined. "Look't all that water on the floor—how're we 'posed to watch tv?"

"We won't be watching it anyway, honey, there's no electricity." She gestured towards the lawn. "Why don't you guys go play until I get through here?" David and Doug scrambled for the swing and set it in motion. Jeremy plopped down on the grass and watched them, while Jason slid his fingers into Robin's uninjured hand.

"What are we gonna do, Mommy?" He turned a worried look up at her.

Her little man. She forced a smile and put her arm around him, being careful not to bang his head with her bandaged hand. "We'll be fine, sweetheart. This is the time for trusting God to take care of us." No little boy should be made to feel that he had to be a man.

His gaze returned to the chaos in the house, a worried frown on his brow.

"Go play with the twins until I'm through here."

"I don't feel like playing, Mommie," he replied dejectedly. She squeezed his hand.

Dorine placed her slim hands on her hips and glared at Robin. "*We* most certainly will not do anything here! *You* are going to sit down!" After one look at her dark face, Robin gave in and sank down on the bench. "I'll do what I can for now and you stay put!" Dorine pulled open the screen door and Jason held it as she began carrying out sodden sofa pillows and throw rugs, spreading them out on the grass in the sun.

She made the last of many trips before glancing at Robin's slumped shoulders. "We'll leave this stuff here to dry and I'll come back later. Right now, we need to get you home."

"I *am* home," Robin pointed out wearily. But Dorine was right—no matter how staunch she wanted to be, her body was telling her it was time to lay it down.

"You know what I mean. You can't stay here, Robin. You're coming home with me."

Robin gazed around helplessly and sighed. "I suppose I'll have to."

Dorine put her arm around her friend's shoulders. "Did you get the insurance policy?"

"No, I was about to go in the bedroom when I saw this mess through the doorway. I'll go get it now." She got up and took a deep breath. That one injury to her hand was taking a toll on her whole body and she had to steady herself.

"While you do that, I'll pack a bag for the boys, then you tell me what you need."

The rest of the day passed in a blur. The return trip to the ranch was somber except for David and Doug trying to cheer up their friends. Too young to realize what the damaged café meant to Robin, the twins nevertheless knew something wasn't right and they tried their best to cheer everyone up. Several times, Robin glanced over at Dorine with a slight smile as she listened to them in the back seat. Bless their little hearts. Then Bryce popped into her mind again. Where was he? And had he abandoned her? She really couldn't blame him, she'd told him often enough to take a hike.

The trip to town and back had taken its toll however, and she willingly laid down after swallowing another pain pill. The insurance business would have to wait, her head was pounding. Sleep claimed her, and not even Dorine's soft call to come eat wakened her. She didn't hear the men come in for the noon meal, nor their conversation about Bryce.

After filling the dishwasher, Dorine left a note for Robin, then dropped the boys off at the office where the secretaries were more than happy to entertain them. Fortunately, the office building hadn't suffered any damage and generators allowed the employees to go about their work as usual, which today included one of their favorite interruptions.

She drove to Kadoka to have Robin's prescription filled, then returned to the cafe and cleaned, moving Robin's belongings into the undamaged bedrooms. Soggy items were hung on the clothesline in the backyard and in the bathroom, then she gathered up towels and other laundry to take home. Bryce's car was still nowhere in sight when she left. Her attention switched from him to the plight of neighbors who had lost a roof, and she made a couple of stops to check on several aging people living on the road out to the ranch.

Picking up the boys, she cautioned them to be quiet when they entered the house, putting in a video for them to watch while she began Robin's laundry. Once again, she was thankful for Dean's foresight in getting generators not only for the business offices, but for their private residences as well.

Late in the afternoon, Robin appeared in the door of the kitchen where Dorine was kneading bread dough. "How come you let me sleep so long?" She yawned and ran her good hand through her tousled hair.

"Because you needed it," Dorine replied, turning the dough and slapping it with her hands. "I learned that from Mrs. Mac," she said, referring to the vacationing DeFoe housekeeper and cook. "She said the bread wouldn't be any good unless you spanked it."

Robin gave her a half-hearted smile as she took a seat and watched Dorine put the lump of bread dough into a greased pan, turn it over, then cover it with a snowy white tea towel. "I got up and ate a little, read the note you left. I hate not being able to help, but I was still pretty wiped out so I laid down again and went right back to sleep!"

"You need the rest," Dorine repeated. She went on to say what she'd done at Robin's house, taking two cups from hooks and filling them with coffee. Sitting down across from Robin, she slid one of the cups towards her and fished the prescription bottle out of her pocket. "Here's more pills in case you need them."

"The coffee smells heavenly," Robin sighed. "Thanks."

Dorine smiled, cupping her hands around her coffee. "Feel better now?"

"Yes, but not quite ready to tackle the world yet." She sighed and looked at her friend. "What am I going to do?"

Dorine's heart hurt to hear the defeat in Robin's voice. "Just take one thing at a time. If you feel up to it tomorrow, we can go to Rapid City to your insurance company. Unless they get the cell tower repaired by then and you can just call." She listened as Robin outlined what she was thinking about for repairs at the café, refilling their cups once more. They mulled over the purpose God had for this circumstance, and bowed their heads in prayer before Dorine began fixing supper. Robin listlessly watched Dorine move around.

"Think about it like this—you haven't had a vacation in over two years."

"Some way to take a vacation." Robin propped her chin up with her good hand.

Dorine smiled sympathetically as she took the towel from the bread and slid the pans into the hot oven. "Chin up, we'll make the best of it." As she closed the oven, she glanced at Robin. "Have you…thought anymore about Bryce?"

"Besides the café, he's all I've thought about!" Robin candidly replied. "Do you think he really just up and left?"

Dorine emphatically shook her head. "No, he's not like that. My guess is that he went to Rapid City. He told me this morning that he could see you needed help."

Robin flushed before glancing away. "I can't get him out of my head."

"You've started to fall for him, haven't you?"

"I've never believed in love at first sight, maybe 'like,' but almost from the moment he walked in the café, my heart speeds up whenever he's around." She frowned. "But I don't see this going anywhere, we're completely wrong for each other."

Dorine reached over and put her hand over Robin's. "Maybe God has a plan for this."

Robin sighed. "He'll really have to do something big time in this case!" Dorine chuckled and got up to continue supper preparation. Robin checked on the boys in the living room, then washed her hands as best she could, and helped set the table. Soon, the aroma of baking bread wafted through the house, bringing flies to the securely-screened kitchen windows. The boys whined about being hungry and Robin herded them in to wash before supper.

Dean and Darrell came in, also washing up and sat at the table. Besides giving thanks for the food, Dean thanked God that no one had been seriously hurt in the storm, asked for healing for Robin's injury, and thanking Him for neighbors willing to help.

Passing the food around the table, Darrell glanced at Robin. "Do you have *any* idea where Bryce could have gone? Did he say anything to you last night?"

She managed to swallow past the sudden lump in her throat. "I haven't seen him since then, but Andy said he was at the café this morning, then he left."

"Left?" Darrell gestured with a slice of the warm bread in one hand and a butter knife in the other, raising one eyebrow. "He must have gone into Rapid…can't think of anywhere else he'd go." He didn't miss the bleakness in her eyes.

Darrell darted a look at his brother. "He was going to leave for home this morning but he told us last night he wasn't going now, not until after he helped out here."

"Dorine mentioned that this morning," Robin nodded, her heart skipping a beat.

"Mommy, is Bryce okay?" Jason asked worriedly.

Robin pulled herself together. "I'm sure he is, honey. He's a big man and can take care of himself," she added confidently. But where was he? It concerned her that she was worried about him, when a month ago, he hadn't even been a blip on her radar.

They finished the meal and the men took the boys outside, promising to keep them out of the mud as much as possible. "Yeah, right," Dorine muttered as the screendoor closed.

All the while Robin helped clear the table and load the dishwasher, she found herself darting anxious looks at the clock. If Bryce had gone to Rapid, he should be back by now. She finally gave up trying to keep him out of her mind, and let it run free. If he wasn't in Rapid City, he *must* have headed for St. Louis.

"Now we can relax, let's go in the livingroom," Dorine

announced. "I'm really thankful Dean got our generators going. I'm afraid my pioneer spirit is sadly lacking," she confessed sheepishly.

"You'd make a great pioneer woman," Robin assured her, as she eased onto the sofa.

They had no more than settled themselves when they heard an approaching vehicle. "I wonder if that's Bryce?" Dorine glanced out the window as Robin's heartbeat picked up. Had he come back? Dorine walked out to the kitchen while Robin held her breath.

"Hi, we were wondering what happened to you." Dorine's voice floated back into the room, and an unexpected surge of relief swept over Robin. She leaned back into the sofa cushions and expelled her breath.

"*Where* did you get so dirty?" Dorine exclaimed in mock horror.

"Crawling around in ceiling plaster," Bryce's voice answered. "Where's Robin?"

His footsteps came nearer, then he was there, looking down at her. "Hi, beautiful." She didn't want her heart to soar like it did, but she couldn't stop it anymore than she could a bird that wanted to do the same thing.

"No beautifuls here, but hi yourself. We were kind of worried that something might have happened to you." She eyed his dusty clothing. "What *did* happen to you?"

He squatted down in front of her, his eyes level with hers. "Were you worried, Robin?" he asked softly. His eyes were warm and gentle as he reached out and touched her hand, slowly stroking it. A flutter skittered up her arm.

She avoided his eyes, watching his hand. "Um-m-m, sort of...."

He laughed knowingly. "I've been in Rapid City, then came back to the café."

Her gaze shot to his. "You were at the cafe?" Her eyes roamed over the dust coating his hair, eyebrows and shoulders, hungry for the sight of him, dirt and all.

He nodded, dropping forward to his knees, which brought him

closer to her. "Since I'm a bonefide insurance inspector, I hired myself to do the assessment on your place."

"You can do that?" she asked hesitantly. "What did you find? What's the damage?"

It was his turn to hesitate. "Well, I've got bad news and I've got good news."

Chapter 13

She held her breath, her heart pounding while she searched his eyes. "Go on."

"The bad news is that the wiring in the café was so old, it's a wonder that you haven't had a fire and burned the whole place down, including your house," Bryce said gently, placing his hand on top of hers. Her eyes opened wide, filled with questions.

"The good news is that since I reported your damage right away, you'll be among the first to have your claim settled if you get your forms sent in. Like yesterday. I took photos of the café with me when I went to Rapid this morning."

She stared at him. "You didn't just…leave?"

It was his turn to stare. "No-o-o," he drew the word out, looking at her with a puzzled expression. "Oh. You heard I'd planned to leave this morning?"

"Andy said you went in the café, looked around, then left."

"You didn't think I'd just up and leave you in the lurch, did you?"

She blushed, looking away. "I don't know. Darrell said you were leaving."

"And you thought I did!" he crowed, reaching out to raise her chin with one dusty finger. "Robin, Robin," he sighed. "Don't you know by now that you are special to me? I would never leave you in a predicament like this."

She turned her face to the side, not knowing how to reply. Thoughtfulness skittered across her face, then a slow smile tilted her lips. "Praise the Lord for a broken ceiling!" she breathed out, sliding her hand out from under his and laying it on her chest.

He frowned. "I don't see any reasons for praise, Robin. Your café is as good as a total loss. Aren't you the one who said just a few days of no business might put you under?"

She laid her hand on his arm. "But don't you see? If this had not happened, we could have had a fire and I could have lost my boys," she ended on a sob. "God is watching over us, even in this."

He shook his head, pulling back. "I don't understand. You Christians mystify me—why would God allow *any* of this to happen if He has such great control?"

Her eyes shining, Robin smiled wider. "I don't have all the answers either, Bryce, but I know the One who does."

He ran his hand through his hair again and sighed in exasperation. "I guess I'll never understand." He cleared his throat, clearly uncomfortable with the conversation. "Anyway, remodeling can start as soon as your insurance company gives the word—"

"I'll have to go to Rapid to file the claims…but I can do the clean up, it will cost too much—"

He put his finger near her lips but not touching. "Your policy covers it." At her quizzical look, he admitted to getting her information—through "proper" insurance channels, of course. She raised an eyebrow and he had the grace to look uncomfortable. But she let it pass. "All you have to do is list new appliances, pick out your flooring, paint colors—and bingo!" he snapped his fingers. "I'll bet you could even have a skylight put in the kitchen area so it won't be so dark!"

Her eyes brimmed with emotion, and he thought he might die if he couldn't kiss her. He leaned forward, testing the waters. She didn't move, her eyes expectant. He leaned a little farther…

The screen door slammed, childish voices ringing through the house. "Where's Bryce? We saw him's car when we wuz at the barn!"

The twins burst into the room and flung themselves on Bryce. Jason and Jeremy hung back, watching the horseplay. Bryce rolled on the floor, pretending to fight off the boys with a sofa pillow. They each grabbed pillows and the free-for-all was on.

"Yous din't leave, yous is still here!" David crowed, smacking Bryce alongside the head with a large pillow.

"Naw, I couldn't leave, I lo-like you guys too much!" he replied, ducking.

Robin sat unmoving, her mind trying to assimilate what Bryce had revealed about the state of the café even before the fire, and a frisson of fear speared down her back, fear that a fire could have taken her boys from her. She called to them and they settled next to her, one on each side. She hugged them fiercely until Jason looked up at her. "Mommie, you're squishing me to death!"

She tried to smile but it wavered on a silent sob. "I'm just so glad you're both mine!"

Dean appeared in the doorway, his arm around Dorine's waist as they watched the wrestling match on the floor. "And you still want more kids?" he asked in a stage whisper.

"Yes!" she turned her head and tapped his chin with her forefinger. "Only they'll be nice, quiet little girls who know how to behave properly."

Darrell squeezed by them into the room, snorting. "Like *that's* gonna happen with *you* for their mother!" Dorine aimed a blow at his shoulder but he ducked and laughed, plopping down in an overstuffed chair as he tossed a pillow into the melee.

Robin's expression was tender, her eyes on the big man horsing around on the floor. He hadn't just left after viewing the café—he'd taken it upon himself to start the process that would get her business up and running again. And just like last night, when he'd cradled her in his arms, letting her cry and making her feel cherished, the warmth of his caring washed over her again.

He was a good man, deep down inside. A kind man. And he'd never pretended to be anything but what he was—a freespirited playboy. Wasn't that a kind of honesty? Oh, who was she kidding, she was so much in love with him, she'd excuse anything...

She could not love him, she berated herself. It would never work. He noticed anything with skirts on and she could never accept that. Randy had not looked at another girl after he and Robin became a couple. And she was not willing to settle for anything less. How had she left her heart unguarded? Bryce had let her know from the start that he only intended a summer fling. Then he'd be gone. That thought left a hollowness in her heart.

Her gaze remained on the wrestling match where the twins were on top, pummeling Bryce with pillows. She glanced down at her children again and squeezed them. Her little Dakota boys. It was obvious that Jason was completely taken with Bryce, completely trusted him. Her gaze slid to Jeremy. He was still frightened of Bryce...was it because he sensed his mother's attitude about men? She couldn't, wouldn't, put her boys through more heartache.

Dean's voice interrupted her thoughts. "Okay, time to break it up," he waded into the fray, picking up his sons by the backs of their jeans, one boy in each hand. David squealed, flailing his arms and legs, struggling to drop back down on Bryce. Doug merely squealed and took delight in swinging back and forth.

"Time for bed," Dorine added, moving out of the doorway.

"Where's the remote?" Darrell asked. "The dishwasher shut off so I can turn the tv on now. The Seattle Mariners are playing tonight." A faint melody cut into the noise. "Is that mine?" he checked the phone on his belt. "They must have repaired the tower."

"No, I think it's mine," Bryce said, sitting up and pulling his cell phone out of his pocket. After greeting whoever was on the other end, he quickly stood and walked into the next room.

Robin couldn't stop her eyes from hungrily following him. Jason and Jeremy turned their attention to the television when Darrell tuned into the baseball game. Robin shamelessly strained to hear Bryce's end of the conversation, but he had wandered too far into the kitchen.

"I suppose we should think about baths and bed too," she remarked vaguely.

"Aw,w, do we hafta?" Jason surprised her with his objection. He hadn't expressed very many little boy opinions lately.

"Now you're beginning to sound like David," she exclaimed. With a start, she realized that she was secretly glad. They were on the road to normal.

Bryce appeared in the doorway, a frown creasing his forehead. "I'm afraid I'm going to have to leave."

Darrell looked up. "Leave? As in you're history?"

Bryce didn't smile. "That was my supervisor. The judge has moved the hearing up in a case where I'm to testify, and I have to be in St. Louis day after tomorrow."

"Bummer," Darrell replied, while Robin's heart sank, and her knees turned weak. She leaned her head back on the sofa and stared at Bryce. Even as she knew it was for the best, her heart strained against this latest blow.

Bryce's eyes shifted to hers and softened. "I don't want to go."

Jason leaped up and dashed to Bryce, curling his arms around Bryce's waist. "I don't want you to go either, Bryce. Who's gonna help me with my baseball stuff?"

Bryce leaned down and scooped him up in his arms. "You're doing real well already, Jason, you don't need me anymore."

"Un-huh, yes I do!" the boy vigorously nodded, his arms sliding around Bryce's neck without knowing he was shackling the man's heart a little tighter.

"Next time I see you, you'll be throwing like...like one of those Mariner pitchers there on television!"

"When will I see you again?" Jason asked, his lip trembling.

"I'll be honest with you Jason, I don't know." Bryce looked into the boy's sad eyes and his heart twisted. "But we can keep in touch, maybe with emails?"

"Our computer doesn't work, no 'lectricity."

Bryce chuckled, leaning over to let the boy slip to the floor. "It will be working soon." He looked over at Robin and noticed Jeremy plastered to his mother's side, the ever-present fear in his eyes. He sighed. "I better get packed and hit the road tonight yet, if I expect to be there in time."

"Don't go, Bry—"

"Jason!" Robin's voice was stern. "Bryce told you he has to leave." The man in question appeared startled at Robin's sharp tone.

Jason hung his head, and Bryce put his hand on the boy's head, ruffling his hair. "I'm sorry, Jason. But I have to do this, it's important to my job."

Jason nodded, unconvinced as he backed towards Robin, not raising his eyes. Bryce looked at all of them, glad for the roar of the tv crowd as a Mariner hit a home run. He'd always remember them like this. He turned and bounded up the stairs.

Robin could hear him talking to Dean on the landing above, then it was quiet.

But her heart wasn't. She tried to quiet its pounding, telling it that this was for the better, it was good for him to leave now, before she became any more enamored of him. The battle raged within while on the television, the battle went on between the ball teams.

When Bryce came down the stairs carrying two duffle bags, her heart lurched. He stepped to the door of the living room and caught her eye.

"Walk me out," he mouthed.

She wanted to refuse, to let him go without him knowing how foolish she'd been. But her treacherous heart took over the rest of her body and she found herself getting up. After Bryce hugged a tearful Jason, and winked at Jeremy, he nodded towards the door with an expectant look. She told the boys to stay and watch the game with Darrell, moving towards Bryce. He stilled, his eyes drinking her in, his mouth unsmiling. She felt tension rolling off him and hesitated, then one side of his mouth tilted up in a sexy smile and the tension eased. She brushed past him and led the way through the kitchen to the screen door. She sensed how close he was behind her and turned, looking up at him.

He dropped the bags and cupped his hands on either side of her face. "I don't want to leave you," he whispered. "You have become so dear to me."

Her heart did a little jig and her naughty mouth joined her traitorous heart by saying, "I'll...I'll miss you." *Was that her voice, so soft and...loving?*

His eyes gentled and he leaned forward. "Will you really?" His heart cheered for joy! "Am I getting to first base, Robin?"

She had to get things back under control. "You've been watching too much baseball." But even that came out sounding breathy. Was her whole body ganging up on her, not willing to go along with what her head was telling her?! She tipped her chin up, watching as his head came nearer and nearer...

"No!"

The childish shriek had them jerking apart, their attention directed to where Jeremy stood in the doorway of the living room, his face white and eyes full of fear.

"Jeremy! What in the world—"

Jeremy screamed "No!" again and darted not to Robin, but...to Bryce.

Bryce's expression was bewildered as he bent to catch the child. Lifting him up, he held him tightly against his chest. His heart expanded, letting in one more little boy. Jeremy was crying as if his heart would break as he wound his thin arms around Bryce's neck. Bryce sent a questioning look at Robin, who appeared just as bewildered.

Darrell and Jason appeared in the doorway, but Darrell ducked back when Bryce waved him off, shaking his head to let the other man know he had the situation in hand. Jason hurried to his mother's side, gazing up at his brother in consternation.

Robin had frozen at her son's actions, now she raised her hand and stroked Jeremy's back. "What is it, honey, what's wrong?"

Through the sobs, they heard him choke out, "He's g-going to go a-away, just like my d-daddy and he's n-never going to c-come back! My Daddy said g-goodbye t-too and h-he never c-came b-back! Don't go!"

The two adults looked into each other's eyes in confusion, then dawning awareness. Robin gasped, sliding her arm around her son.

"Oh, honey." She'd thought Jeremy was too young to understand when the accident had happened to his father. He'd never given any indication that he'd harbored the fear his loved ones wouldn't come back if they said goodbye. All this time…she drew her hand over his sweaty hair. Some mother she was! She was so busy guarding her own heart that she didn't see her son was doing the same. His fear of Bryce became all too clear. Perhaps he'd sensed at the very start, that Bryce would come to mean something to them, and felt that if he kept him at a distance, his little heart wouldn't be broken again.

"What happened?" Dorine charged down the stairs, skidding to a stop when she saw the group by the door.

"I've got it covered." Hugging the boy tighter, Bryce looked at Robin and said fiercely, "Yes! I'll come back, Jeremy." But his promise was more to Robin than to Jeremy. "Nothing is going to happen to me. I *will* come back!" His eyes blazed as he made the firm declaration.

Robin's resolve wavered. Were Bryce's words just meant to calm the child, words that would be forgotten? Or did he really mean them?

Without any of them noticing, Dorine silently made her way back up the stairs with a perplexed expression furrowing her brow.

Bryce dropped one arm to curve around Robin and bring her close. He looked down at Jason who snuggled between them. "I've still got some vacation coming, and I promise I'll come back as soon as I can."

Jason's face cleared and he beamed up at Bryce. "Then you can help me with my baseball again!"

Robin choked and closed her eyes but the tears oozed out anyway. "I never had any idea, Bryce, that Jeremy felt this way. He never said a thing..." She looked up at him, the wetness curling her eyelashes into spikes. He thought she had never looked more beautiful. Her gaze was warm and appealing...if he leaned over just a little, he could touch her lips with his...Jeremy shifted and Jason caught hold of his brother's hand. "Come on, Jeremy, Bryce says he has to go but he promised he'd come back! If we let him go, the faster he can come back!" Jeremy glanced shyly at Bryce, ducking his head when Bryce planted a kiss on his forehead.

"I did promise, son." He wouldn't remember calling him that until later but Robin heard it, and reality hit with a bang.

He could never call him his son...because she and Bryce would never have a relationship. She eased out of his arms, helping Jeremy to slide to the floor. "Come on boys, Bryce has to leave and we're keeping him." She stepped back, taking the boys by their hands. "Bye...drive careful."

Bryce sensed her withdrawal and he looked into her eyes with a question in his. She gazed back at him steadily. It was a moment out of time but he knew something had shifted. Frustration welled up in him and he ran a hand over his hair. His job was beckoning and if he didn't get moving, he wouldn't make much time tonight. He was torn in two. Robin or his job. But without a job, there could be no Robin either.

He picked up his bags and stared solemnly down at the boys. "Take good care of your mother. I'll be back, as soon as I can." He raised his eyes and gazed at this woman who had become so important to him. "Bye…sweetheart," he whispered. "I'll call."

"God go with you," she managed to whisper but he would never know the storm she battled in her heart. It cried out, "Don't go!" but her soul knew he had to. He was not for her.

The following evening, Dean answered the phone in the hallway just as the family finished supper. His face broke into a smile. "Hi, Bryce! Glad to hear you got there okay!" He listened for a few more minutes, then turned towards Robin, holding out the phone. "He wants to talk to you." He winked and smiled.

"Me?" she squeaked, as she rose from the table on trembling legs.

He waved the phone at her and she reluctantly moved forward to take it. "Hello?"

"Hi, beautiful, missing me yet?"

His voice washed weakness through her and she backed around the corner from the interested group still seated at the kitchen table. She cleared her throat. "Did you have a good trip?"

He chuckled knowingly. "It would have been better if you'd been with me." A beat of silence went by. "Hello? Are you still there, or is this a one-sided conversation?"

"I'm here." Dean and Darrell walked past her into the living room to watch television with Darrell wiggling his eyebrows at her as he passed. She childishly stuck out her tongue and he laughed.

"Cat got your tongue?" Bryce's voice came over the line.

"I never expected to hear from you," she blurted out honestly.

"That hurts me right down to the bottom of my black little heart."

In spite of her own fluttering heart, she managed to chuckle. "You are a nut."

His voice came back serious. "It's good to hear you laugh, Robin. Why didn't you expect my call? You think I won't keep my promise?"

"To be honest, I don't know what to think, Bryce." She glanced up as Dorine brushed by her, pointing up, indicating she was taking the boys upstairs to give Robin privacy. Shifting backwards, Robin lowered herself to the bottom step, stretching out the long coiled phone cord.

"Oh, I meant it, Robin, have no doubt about that." He waited and when she didn't reply, he sighed and switched the subject. "How are the Dakota boys?"

"They're f-fine."

"Are you nervous, Robin?"

She cleared her throat. My goodness, she was reacting like a high school sophomore! "No, I-I'm not n-nervous."

"Is it because everyone is listening? Maybe I should get you a cell phone—"

"No!" she blurted out. "No," she repeated more quietly. "I can't accept that."

"Well, since you asked, my trip was uneventful." He shared details, and she listened, soaking up the sound of his voice. She asked about the trial and he filled her in, adding. "I don't know how long this is going to take, Robin. I want to call you every day but don't know if I'll be able to."

Un-oh. His first excuse. "You don't need to do that, it isn't necessary."

"It is to me," he replied seriously. "It's necessary for me to hear your voice. It keeps me going."

Shivers went down her spine. Oh, he was *good*. "I hope that everything goes well for you, Bryce."

"That sounds like a kiss-off, sweetheart, but it won't work."

"What does work for you?" she whispered.

"You waiting by the phone for me."

Suddenly aware they were flirting over the phone, Robin sent a guilty look towards the living room where strains of music from a well-known sitcom drifted out to her.

"I-I'd better go now."

There was a heavy sigh. "I'm not giving up on you, honey. I *will* be calling again."

She wanted to tell him not to waste his dime but decided that sounded immature.

"Still there?" he asked.

"Ummm."

He chuckled. "Goodbye, beautiful."

"No beautifuls here, just me."

"You'll do, sweetheart, you'll do." The phone clicked in her ear as she absorbed that last "sweetheart."

Bryce relaxed in his recliner, smug over the fact he'd unsettled Robin. He leaned his head back and sighed. On the return trip to St. Louis, his mind had been filled with her image, still hearing her laughter the day she'd sprayed him with the hose, remembering how her eyes lit up when she was happy. But the remembrance of the shadows that chased through those beautiful eyes brought out a protectiveness in him that he'd never guessed he had. If only he *could* solve her problems. The stubborn woman didn't want his help but she'd get it anyway—he'd seen to that on his trip to Rapid City the day after the storm. Glancing at the clock, he dreaded the long hours in court the next day. After showering and crawling into bed, he hugged his pillow and imagined he could smell the scent of cinnamon.

Within a few days, Robin's hand had healed to the point she could wear a smaller bandage and no sling. Bryce called every night and she hated that she anticipated those calls. What would she do when he stopped calling, stopped thinking of her as "beautiful" and calling her "sweetheart?" Why couldn't she remember that he was a live-in-the-moment kind of guy? After a few weeks, he'd never give her another thought.

She had to regain her focus and start thinking of how life had been before Bryce breezed into her world. She knew this with her mind but her heart longed after what could never be. They were just too different, but it didn't stop her from hugging her pillow at night and dreaming of spicy cologne.

When she and Randy had married, they were still in their teens and approached life with an invincible attitude, loving and living through rose-colored glasses as though there would be no end to those helicon days. And while she would treasure those times, the feelings she had for Bryce were much deeper, more mature, an eyes-wide-open kind of emotion, knowing that life was full of uncertainties but loving anyway. The teen love she'd shared with Randy was sweet, first love, and she would never have it any different.

But it was time to put away those memories. Of course, in time, the boys' memories of their father would fade, but her duty was to remember him for them. However, the past few weeks had brought her farther along the road of grief recovery than she'd ever thought possible. That was one thing Bryce had done—pulled her out of her comfort zone, made her aware of her womanliness, and that there could be a bright future with the right man. "But Lord, it can't be Bryce," she whispered in prayer one night. "Not unless You do a great work in his life."

The repair crew sent to the Sweet Schoppe by her insurance company worked tirelessly, and within a few weeks, her living quarters were done. As it turned out, her parents had gone on a cruise and hadn't been able to come help, much to their regret.

When it came time, Robin was able to move the boys home with her, even though it would be a while longer before she could open the café for business again. She had a sneaking suspicion that Bryce had pulled a lot of strings to make those repairs happen so quickly, but when she asked him over the phone, he sidestepped her questions.

She was glad to be on site when inspections were done so she could sign papers, and could hardly believe the top-of-the-line equipment that was installed in the café kitchen. There was even a new skylight overhead and she marveled at the brightness of her workspace. Her heart gave a little skip at the joyous reminder of Bryce. She knew she shouldn't be this happy, that she should be prepared for when his nightly calls would stop. However, when she stepped into her remodeled living room, smelled the newly painted walls where up-to-date windows had been installed, a new outside door and new light fixtures, her heart overflowed with happiness for Bryce's thoughtfulness.

And there were other blessings. Most of her suppliers had given her 90 days credit when they learned of her plight, and for the ones that didn't, she'd reluctantly accepted financial help from Dorine with the promise to repay her as soon as possible.

Her sons never lost faith in Bryce, however. Their talk was peppered with when he would be coming back, and they tussled over which one would get to talk with him first every night. They always handed the phone over with a glow on their faces and her own face, she was sure, reflected her happiness when they ended their calls.

Then came the night when the phone remained silent. The boys, watching a cartoon video in front of the new tv set, grew restless, glancing at the phone. "Isn't Bryce going to call, Mommie?" Jason finally blurted out. He turned from where he and Jeremy were sprawled on the new carpet, to face Robin who sat on the new sofa with business papers spread out around her.

"He said there might be times when he couldn't call," she

reminded them, but her heart grew heavy at the disappointment in their eyes. This was just what she had feared all along, the hurt that followed in Bryce's wake. She began to grow angry. How dare he tromp all over their little hearts and hurt them like this?! Outwardly, she appeared calm and eventually got the boys into bed. She tried to find comfort in the Scriptures but finally closed the Bible and took her concerns to the Lord.

The day came to open the café again for business, and Dorine came in to help, as they expected a rush of business. About mid-morning, a Rapid City florist van drew to a stop at the curb and the driver hopped out to unload a huge bouquet of red roses. Customers crained their necks to catch a glimpse of the flowers as they were brought inside.

"Robin!" Marietta squealed. "Look at the flowers!" Dorine stopped in the middle of pouring coffee for a customer, her eyes on the bouquet. A number of other bouquets had been delivered earlier, some from local businesses, some from individuals, but nothing surpassed the beauty or size of this rose bouquet.

Robin hurried out of the kitchen, her eyes wide in surprise. "Oh, my goodness!"

"Who's it from? Who's it from? Read the card, hurry!" Marietta clapped her hands. Dorine had a knowing look on her face as she finished refills and returned the carafe.

"Don't get excited, we'll see here in a minute," Robin flustered. The scent of the roses wafted over her as she slit open the tiny envelope with trembling fingers and pulled out a card. "Am busy at court. Welcome back on your first day. Affectionately, Bryce."

"Ooo, how romantic!" Marietta clasped her hands, a dreamy look on her young face.

"I'll bet it's from that young insurance feller," Molly Schafer exclaimed.

"He was sure abuzzin' around our little honey here for awhile," cackled Mrs. Kreil.

"Well, you gonna keep us in suspense?" questioned Mr. Olson.

Robin smiled, feeling color rising in her cheeks as she buried her nose in the blossoms. "Yes, it's from Bryce. He's just wishing me well on my reopening."

Molly snorted and returned to her coffee, as Mrs. Kreil leaned over to whisper to her.

Robin placed the bouquet on top of the glass cases of candy and cookies, where they could be seen from all over the room. Her gaze met Dorine's and knew that her friend had read the relief in her own eyes. The entire day, her gaze returned again and again to the beautiful roses. She wished she had time to appreciate them more, but people had flocked from miles around, even from Kadoka, to get her first *kucken* hot out of the oven. She carried a perpetual lump in her throat, grateful for the support of her neighbors and the townspeople. However, they took second place in her heart where Bryce was firmly entrenched, but she had to keep a firm hold on that fickle heart. Just because he sent flowers didn't mean anything. Perhaps this was just his method of kissing her off.

However, when he called the following night, her heart sped up when she heard his voice but at the same time, she detected a note of distraction. This, then, was it. His calls would gradually taper off until he felt he had let her down easily.

She had no way of knowing how frustrated Bryce felt as the trial dragged out. Recesses and delays had him pacing the floor both in courthouse halls and in his office, running his hands fruitlessly through his hair. He couldn't talk to anyone about the trial and in his frustration, he shortened his nightly calls to Robin, even skipping them occasionally. He'd given his deposition but the defense would not excuse him yet. When he wasn't needed in court, he spent most days in his office. He couldn't accept new investigations, making him a desk jockey, not something he dealt with very well. Restlessness settled over him again, and he took to staring out his window at the St. Louis skyline. In his mind's eye, he saw wide-open prairie, breezes gently stirring the grass, birds warbling and a faint scent of…cinnamon. He was startled to realize he was comparing all that to his present environment, which had gradually lost its appeal. What was wrong with him? He'd always been content here up to now. But it didn't take a genius to know that he was content where his heart was, and that was back in South Dakota.

One day, walking back with Carla from a staff meeting, she approached the subject of his distracted attitude.

"You've changed since you came back from the beach. Did you meet someone special?" she asked casually.

He opened the door to his office and answered absently, "I didn't go to the beach."

"Where did you go then?" She moved close enough for his arm to brush hers. He retreated behind his desk and sat down, picking up a file.

"To South Dakota."

Carla's eyebrows rose. "South Dakota?" He nodded, scanning the contents of the folder. "What in the world is in South Dakota?"

My future. I hope. Luckily, his phone rang and he didn't have to answer Carla. But he smiled to soften his disinterest in the beautiful woman. She pouted prettily but moved gracefully out of his office, shutting the door behind her.

On weekends, the lure of parties no longer held any appeal, even though they had been an integral part of his lifestyle. He knew now that they were a feeble attempt to fill a void in his life that he didn't even know he had.

But mostly, he wanted a certain little redhead by his side. Every time he thought about her not being a part of his future, his heart sank. He couldn't imagine life without her.

And the Dakota boys. One evening he laid on his back in his kingsize bed and folded his hands behind his head, grinning up at the ceiling as he recalled how they had not wanted him to leave

South Dakota. Had anyone else ever wanted him that much? Jeremy's hug that last evening remained in his heart, and Jason's clear-eyed trusting gaze made him feel ten feet tall. Who would ever have thought that two little pintsized boys could transform him into wanting to give instead of take?

However, in order for him to have a real chance at the future he was beginning to envision, he had to persuade the little guys' mother that he was worthy of her. He shifted to his side drowsily and hugged his pillow to his chest. As he drifted off to sleep, he knew what the first step had to be.

During lunch hour the next day, Bryce ducked into a bookstore not far from his office and browsed until he spotted the religion section. Glancing furtively around, he ran his fingertips over the many versions of the Holy Bible, amazed at the variety. Perplexed, he stood staring at the assortment.

"Havin' a hard time pickin' one out?" came an amused drawl from nearby. Turning, he met the dark brown gaze of a young African-American man dressed in the universal uniform of t-shirt and jeans.

"Yeah, I never realized there would be so many." After further conversation, during which the young man introduced himself as Jeremiah, the two men narrowed the choices down until Bryce was comfortable with the Bible he'd chosen. When he hesitantly admitted he was looking for a church, Jeremiah invited Bryce to attend services with him. If Bryce could learn what Robin's fascination with religion was, he'd have a better chance with her. Plus learning some of the lingo so he would sound confident. He didn't have to believe any of it, just enough to let Robin know that he respected her faith.

Bryce began attending Sunday morning services and a weeknight Bible study with Jeremiah. He was truly living outside the box, but he faced up to this new challenge, especially at the Bible studies.

He found his companions were intelligent, sincere seekers, some questioning the same things he did. Others were like Robin, grounded in their faith and able to answer questions. Discussions were energetic and sometimes loud, leaving him chuckling at their intensity.

However, when he was home alone, he plunged into the Scriptures with the goal of disproving the claims of Christ. He started out with confidence but as time went on, he found himself seriously pondering what he read. During the days in court, he'd catch himself thinking of a certain verse while listening to testimony dragging on. He had to shake himself out of it and pay attention to court proceedings, to give the persons involved his direct attention.

One evening, after reading far beyond his usual bedtime, he was startled to realize that the image of Robin's pleased reaction when she found he was reading the Word, had been replaced with his personal quest for truth. He leaned back into the recliner and closed his eyes, mulling over that thought. The trial was drawing to a close but his request for the rest of his vacation time had been denied. An investigator scheduled for a case in another state, had had an emergency appendectomy, and Bryce was needed to replace him.

He didn't want to go. For the first time ever, he wasn't ready to sink his teeth into a new challenge, his adrenaline flowing as he went methodically about his work.

He wanted to go back to South Dakota, back to Robin. She filled his mind, her beautiful eyes sparkling, her pink lips tilted in that special smile. Now that his knowledge of scripture had grown, he could hardly wait to tell her. He raised his head and contemplated the Bible open on his lap, then eyed the phone laying near his elbow on the end table. What would she say when he told her...

Told her what? That he was reading the Bible?

Everything came to a screeching halt.

She'd never believe him.

Remembering her reaction when he'd offered to go to church

just to be near her, made him wince. No wonder she had resisted him. Even in their nightly phone calls, while she seemed more relaxed, he sensed her reserve.

No, he couldn't tell her. Not just yet, anyway.

He'd been in this investigative business too long not to have seen conmen in action, greedily luring trusting women with smooth talk. He squirmed as he realized that in his social life, he also, had put the moves on women with his own insincerity. Smooth, oily, self-serving talk.

He looked at the phone again. No, he couldn't tell her.

A sorrow filled his heart at his past indiscretions. Flipping through the Bible, he stopped when a verse seemed to leap off the page at him. "Therefore, there is no condemnation for those who are in Christ Jesus." He lifted his eyes and stared off in space. Could it really be true that his previous life could be pardoned? His eyes dropped back to the page to see the phrase "...Christ Jesus has set you free from the law of sin and of death." He glanced at the top of the page and realized he was in the book of Romans.

Romans. It was that book of Romans that had started all this. It was the book Pastor Rick had preached from, when Bryce had first arrived in Silverdale. He quickly got up and went to his desk, rummaging through papers until he came up with the bulletin from the church. At the time he'd tossed it in here, he'd wondered why he'd saved it...now he knew. He felt a prickling along the back of his neck. Could God be trying to tell him something...no, He wasn't that interested in a sinful bachelor playboy from St. Louis. On the other hand, had Dean been right when he said that God loved everybody, regardless, and had a plan for his life? He had no interest in his previous life, no desire to return to it. But that didn't make him a Christian either...did it? Was it possible there was a plan for *him*?

Taking the bulletin back to his chair, he sat down and looked up the references for the Roman Road to Salvation. When he'd finished, he felt the pull on his heart, knew that, without a doubt,

God had just spoken to him through His Word. He leaned back and stared up at the ceiling, clearing his throat nervously.

"Un...God, I've never prayed before so I don't know what to say or if You can hear me. But I want to understand what Your Word means. I'm a pretty intelligent guy..." he stopped. *Did God need to know that?*

He cleared his throat and tried again. "I mean, if I understand this rightly, Your word says that if I believe that Jesus is Your Son, I will be saved, and that I'll have eternal life." He stopped and cleared his throat again. He was about to utter the words that he somehow knew was going to change his life—permanently. He felt on the brink of a vast discovery, a cliff edge and he was about to step out in thin air.

He took a deep breath and said out loud, "I am confessing with my mouth that I believe that You raised Jesus from the dead, and that I want Him for my Savior...like Robin. Like Jeremiah. Like Dean and Dorine. I ask you to forgive all my sins." He stopped, not knowing what else to add. "I guess that's all, God, You'll have to take it from here." Was that all there was to say? He waited. No booming voice from above. Then he remembered.

"Amen."

A quiet peace settled over him, a peace such as he'd never known before. He let his head rest on the back of the lounger and closed his eyes. The quietness wrapped him in a blanket of contentment, slowly ebbing away in a peaceful tide that carried him to sleep.

When the rising sun sent its first bright beams across his face, Bryce opened his eyes and shook his head. Where was he? It took a moment to gain his bearings, grimacing as his muscles protested sleeping in the recliner all night.

Then it came flooding back to him, the commitment he'd made a few hours ago. In the bright light of day, could he still feel the same way? He tensed before he realized the sense of peace was still with him, and a slow smile spread over his unshaven cheeks.

"Thank you, God," he murmured as he climbed out of the chair. Another day in court awaited him. "Oh, and God?" he stopped and looked up at the ceiling. "If You could do just one thing for me? Help this—" he stopped as he realized how close he came to swearing. "I mean," he gestured helplessly with his hands, "You know, I'd really like You to fix it so I can go back to South Dakota!" He waited, then shook his head and grinned as he headed for the bathroom. What did he expect, a loud baritone out of the air conditioning vent?

When he got to work, he headed to his supervisor's office before making his appearance at the courthouse. There were things that needed to be put into motion.

Robin leaned against the front door of the café and folded her arms over her chest. Taking a deep breath, she savored the perfume of the petunias in the flowerboxes, and lifted her face for the breeze to dance over her skin. The autumn sky was a soft baby blue from horizon to horizon.

Jason had started school, as had Laurie, her job ending as a companion for the boys. Jeremy attended kindergarten at the church twice a week since his birthday fell at the wrong time for him to start public school. The town had slipped into its usual fall routine, school buses coming and going mornings and afternoons, their duel tires stirring up dust as the first fall leaves swirled down from the trees. Groups of chattering kids passed the café door on their way to school, and again on the way home. It brought memories of when she had joined the throng with her sisters every morning and afternoon. Melancholy gripped her briefly but she shook it off.

A few things had changed, though—Mr. Jordan had passed away and she'd played the piano at his funeral. The Ruffs had a new baby. And there was a new business down the street in the old hardware store. A tanner had opened a leather shop, making chaps and other accessories for the ranchers in the area, and by all reports, it was going well, the talk being that he was considering hiring extra help to start a mail order business. It was an economic addition that hopefully would draw other businesses.

And she'd fallen in love. She sighed. Bryce was always there, lingering at the edge of her mind. But he wasn't *here*, he was hundreds of miles away. He still called, not every night of course, his job demands curtailed that, but even when he did call, Robin felt he was holding something back from her.

Across the street, the lumberyard door slammed and a tall lanky rancher made his way towards his dirt-encrusted pickup. Lifting a hand in greeting, he yelled, "Hia, Robin! How goes the battle?"

"It's going, Fred, it's going!" They both grinned and she waved as he drove off, the dust from his tires settling down like a lacy shawl dropped on the ground. Joyous sounds of kids at play during recess over at the school drifted to her, their boisterous voices carrying on the morning air. A few cars were parked in front of the former insurance office that had been turned into a senior center.

But no matter how familiar everything was, she felt an emptiness, a void. She took another deep breath, closed her eyes and tipped her face towards heaven. *Father God, I don't know why Bryce came into our lives and because he's not one of yours, I can't guess what his purpose is. Is it just my willful heart wanting to be loved? I can't forget him. Show me what to do now.* She paused, listening to the stillness and feeling a quietness steal over her. The Lord would work it out in His own time.

She turned and went back into the café.

That evening, Robin laid back on the hammock, idly watching the boys romp on the lawn in the late afternoon fall sunshine. It wouldn't be too many more evenings they could be outside without sweaters. She had thought more about Bryce today than ever, and was reminded of the schoolgirl's version of a love barometer, the wild sunflower. As each yellow petal was pulled off, the chant was, "He loves me, he loves me not, he loves me…"

Gazing up through the tree branches that were dressing themselves in yellow finery for Indian summer, she wondered what the future held. Could there be a future for she and Bryce? Maybe she should try picking off sunflower petals…

The next morning, she readied herself and the boys for church, checking one last time that she had everything as she hurried them out the back door.

A loud, off-key rendition of "Take me out to the ball game" froze her in place.

Bryce!

Jason moved first. He squealed, "Mr. Martin! Bryce!" and took off at a dead run, followed by Jeremy. Robin's breath caught in her throat as she stood stock still, her heart beating a rapid tattoo and her knees growing weak.

Bryce came into sight around the corner and the boys threw themselves on him with shrieks of joy. Robin clutched her sheaf of music tighter to her chest, as though to shield her heart from exposure. The sun gleamed off his hair, his eyes danced with amusement, and she devoured the sight of his dear face like a thirsty sponge after a drought and rain.

He gathered the boys up in both arms and hugged them tightly. If ever he had lingering doubts about his feelings, they were washed away in the flood of emotion and love that swept through him for these two little ones.

"You came back," Jeremy said, wonder in his voice as he stroked Bryce's cheek.

"I sure did!" he boomed out, moving towards Robin. Jason kept his face hidden in Bryce's neck and hung on for dear life. Robin twisted her fingers in uncertainty as he came to a stop in front of her, letting the boys slide to the ground.

"Aren't you going to welcome me home too?" he murmured softly, his warm, brown gaze never leaving hers.

She hesitated for only a moment, then stepped into his extended arms, dropping her face into his chest. Oh, it felt so good to have his arms around her! She inhaled his fragrance and almost wiggled like a puppy! No matter how wrong it was, for that one moment, she'd cherish this haven. She raised her eyes and he kissed her on the forehead. "Do you realize you said 'home'?"

"So I did," he replied mysteriously. The boys were dancing around them like high school students at a pep rally. "I'd like to kiss you more thoroughly but too many eyes," he whispered softly.

"Bryce, I didn't forget anything you teached me about baseball!" Jason declared.

"Taught," Robin automatically corrected him, still bemused.

Bryce reluctantly released Robin and knelt down to ruffle the boy's hair. "We'll have to check that out, won't we?"

Jeremy beamed at him, his grin ear to ear. "You did come back, just like you said." He rubbed his hands over Bryce's shoulders as though to make sure he was really there.

"I always keep my promises," Bryce assured him, as he rose to his feet again. "How about Mommy? Does she believe I keep my promises?"

She could only nod mutely, her eyes devouring his dear face. *Oh, Lord, help me here!*

"Bryce, we're just going to church. You can go with us!" Jason said, reaching up to touch his own head. "Hey, you messed up my hair!"

"I sure did!" Bryce exclaimed, ruffling the boy's hair again. Both boys giggled in delight while Robin tried to look indignant.

"But hey, if I'm just in time for church, we'd better get going!"

Robin looked at him searchingly. "Are you here for the rest of your vacation? You don't want to spend it in church...do you?" Her expression was skeptical.

"Why not?" he answered, meeting her gaze boldly. "Come on, let's get going." Her smile faded and he knew she was recalling that conversation about him attending church just to be with her. But in his secret heart, he was jubilant, awaiting just the right time to spring his surprise on her.

"Come along, boys," Robin directed as she smoothed her hand over Jason's hair, idly brushing it back into place. She was bursting with curiosity but Bryce's hand on her elbow was urging her forward along the side path to the street.

Jason's eyes darted up and down the street. "Where's your car, Bryce?"

"Right there," Bryce tipped his head towards a blue minivan, touching the remote to unlock the vehicle.

Robin stopped still. "A minivan? Why? What happened to your car? Did you have an accident?" Her worried gaze swung back to his.

He threw back his head and laughed. "Whoa, too many questions! No, I didn't wreck it. This van is mine."

"Why? What happened?" She scanned him anxiously, looking for tell-tale bruises.

He read her correctly. "No accident, I'm okay. Come on, get in, we can talk later." He slid open the back passenger door so the boys could get in. They climbed up, grinning, their eyes wide and wondering at sight of the plush seats and carpeting. They carefully settled into the seats while he showed them how to buckle the belts, then he stepped around and opened the front passenger door with a flourish.

"Your chariot awaits, m'lady," he bowed and gestured with his hand. Eyeing him warily, Robin let him take her hand and help her in, his fingers warm against hers. A jolt of awareness snaked up her arm and Bryce grinned as she jerked her hand away.

Slamming the door, he ran around the front and slid in behind the wheel. Looking in the rearview mirror, he delightedly watched the boys checking out all the gadgets while he turned the key in the ignition. He smoothly backed out, turning towards the church.

"Do Dorine and Dean know you're back? Or did you stay there last night?"

He nodded. "Yep, but I wanted to surprise you so I asked Dorine not to call you." Feeling Robin's gaze on him, he glanced over at her.

"Why?"

"Why what?" he asked innocently.

She opened her mouth to reply but they were at the church and his attention was focused on parking under a cottonwood on the side street. He turned off the key and pulled it out, looking over to see Robin still warily studying him.

He grinned. "All in good time, my dear, all in good time." He twirled an imaginary moustache as he got out and slammed the door.

Why was he being so secretive? Rounding the hood, he opened Robin's door to find her still staring at him. "Come on, we'll be late if you keep sitting there."

Robin shook her head and slid out to the ground. "I still don't underst—" Bryce took her elbow and his touch felt like a brand, warm and possessive. She stumbled and he tightened his grip, helping her step up on the sidewalk. She was kept from saying anything, as neighbors came along to greet Bryce, welcoming him back like a long-lost relative as he helped the boys out of the van.

She managed to get into the building and up the center aisle to the front pew. Bryce had trailed in after the boys, following them into the pew and settling himself next to the wall. Still perplexed, she gathered her music and went to the piano, glancing over the congregation as she seated herself.

She caught Dorine's eye and correctly interpreted her friend's shrug. She smiled in return and the interchange helped to ground her. Dorine didn't know what was going on either. Turning her attention to the opening prelude, she struggled to concentrate, but it was almost impossible. Good thing she knew the piece well, because she was so attuned to the man behind her that she didn't know a C chord from a sea shell!

Pastor Rick stepped up to the pulpit and began the service. Acutely aware of Bryce's eyes boring into her back, Robin fought to keep her focus on the order of worship. But when Bryce's rich tenor sang out during the first hymn, she almost stopped playing. *Where had he learned to sing like that?* He knew not only the words but the music as well. When she hit a wrong chord, she quickly yanked her mind back to the task at hand. It would never do to let him know how much he flustered her.

With the sermon about to begin, Robin discreetly slid off the piano bench and slipped into the space on the pew between the boys. It struck her that they probably looked like a family at worship. Her neck grew warm when she heard twittering directly behind her.

Oh boy. This would be all over Silverdale by tomorrow.

Not only that, but Bryce had the audacity to stretch his arm along the back of the pew to rest his fingers near her shoulder. She almost missed turning to the passage in the Bible when the reference was given. She chanced a glance at Bryce and caught his amused expression. But the next thing he did had her eyes widening incredulously—Bryce took a small New Testament out of his pocket! She watched in helpless intrigue as he opened it to the book of First Corinthians. He glanced at her again and winked, then turned his attention to the book held in his large hands.

No matter what life handed her after this, she would never have as monumental a shock as seeing Bryce holding the scriptures. She was still staring when without looking at her, he whispered, "Shut your pretty mouth, it's a fly trap."

Jeremy giggled and looked up at her, clearly content between the two adults. The giggle brought her back to reality and she dropped her gaze to her own Bible. Drawing in several shallow breaths, she allowed herself a small glimmer of hope. Surely Bryce wouldn't misuse God's Word to get close to her? Her mind full of questions, she hardly heard the sermon and was surprised when the closing hymn was announced.

After the benediction, she played the postlude, her fingers shaking. She heard the rustle of people rising from the pews, conscious that some had come forward to greet Bryce. The noise of chatter rose and fell as the church gradually emptied and she finished playing, hearing her children talking and giggling with Bryce. She closed the hymnbook and gathered her sheet music into a neat pile.

But the church wasn't entirely empty. Dorine walked up the aisle toward her. "Is it okay if the boys come home with me? It's supposed to be pretty warm this afternoon and it might be one of the last chances they have to swim in the pool." Something was up, and Robin glanced from her to Bryce and back. Dorine was the picture of innocence and Bryce looked as though butter wouldn't melt in his mouth.

He shifted his gaze from Dorine to Robin. The scent of his spicy cologne drifted over her. "Can the boys go with her? I need to talk to you."

"What about? Bryce, I—"

He put his finger over her lips. "I'll explain. It is okay for the boys to go with Dorine?"

Robin searched his eyes then turned to Dorine, who gave a slight nod of her head, a secretive smile adorning her face. "I suppose so…" her voice trailed off as her mind tried to sort through this situation. Dorine herded Robin's boys up the aisle ahead of her, their footsteps and chatter echoing in the empty building. A shiver went down Robin's spine as she realized she and Bryce were totally alone.

Chapter 14

Bryce took Robin's cold fingers in his warm hands and gently urged her to sit down in the nearest pew. "Your hands are cold," he observed. "Are you okay?" When she nodded, he breathed out a long sigh. "Well...*I'm* not." He didn't recall ever being so uncertain, not even when he asked the prom queen for a date in high school.

"Bryce, what is this all about? Has something happened?" Her heart was pounding so hard that she was sure he could hear it, but she put her other hand on top of his. He turned his palm up and threaded their fingers together. Her heart skipped a beat at his warm touch.

"Yes, something's happened." He paused. "I've been thinking about...spiritual matters."

The statement was so far from what she'd ever imagined, that shock rippled through her. *"What?!"* Then more calmly, she added, "I don't understand. What made you think about spiritual things?" The little flame of hope began to burn brighter.

"The sermon I heard that Sunday when I first got here was about the Roman Road to Salvation, do you remember?" She nodded, eyeing him warily. But he was encouraged that she didn't pulled her hands away from his. "I've never had much use for God or the Bible, but I just couldn't get it out of my head, it was like a replay that wouldn't quit. Even after I went back to St. Louis, God wouldn't leave me alone." He stopped and swallowed.

Robin couldn't believe what she was hearing, but the earnest look on his face and the serious way he spoke threw more fuel on the flame of hope. Her hands began to warm. "God is often referred to as 'The Hound of Heaven'," she replied simply.

"I talked a lot with Darrell and Dean while I was here, did you know that?"

"They mentioned it, yes."

"I figured I could disprove the claims of Christ, but you know," he looked directly in her eyes. "I couldn't. The more I read, the more I could see that the Bible is the Word of God, and that it is true." He took a deep breath, encouraged that the wariness was fading from Robin's face. "I started going to church." He swallowed and his eyes grew brighter. "I've accepted Christ as my Savior, Robin."

For a moment she sat still, her eyes searching his, then, with a glad cry, she threw herself into his arms, tears running down her cheeks. "Oh, Bryce!" He held her tightly, relief flooding through him. He hadn't completely blown his chances with her.

"Oh, I've prayed for you for so long," she exclaimed. The little flame of hope flared up into a blaze that threatened to overwhelm her. It suddenly all fell into place—his knowledge of the hymns, the Bible in his pocket.

"There's more," he replied.

"What could be more wonderful than surrendering your life to Christ?" she sniffed, drawing away and searching for a tissue.

"Nothing can compare to that, but it's a close second." She had his attention as she wiped her adorable little nose. "I've fallen in love with the woman of my dreams."

Robin froze, afraid to believe what she wanted her heart to tell her.

He took her hands again, tissue and all. "A spunky, adorable, aggravating, beautiful woman. I love you, Robin."

She closed her eyes then opened them, leaning back to search his face. The love she saw there made her catch her breath. "You only wanted a summer fling," she whispered.

His face colored. "I know. That's what it started out to be. I had no idea that you would come to mean so much to me." He hesitated. "Can you forgive me for being so shallow?"

"There's nothing to forgive, you didn't know Jesus then."

"You know, it takes a lot of guts for a guy to lay his heart out like this and he would hope to hear his feelings are returned." He looked anxious.

"Oh, Bryce, I was so sure you must have guessed how much I care about you, I was positive it was written all over me!" She chuckled with joy, sliding her hands up his chest and around his neck, bringing them close together. She looked into his eyes, noting little gold flecks in the brown. "I. Love. You."

Silently, he moved closer and when she closed her eyes, he gently touched her lips with his. A warmth flooded him and he deepened the kiss. Coming up for air, he nuzzled her ear and whispered, "Wow!"

"Double wow!" she added, snuggling close.

With his arms looped around her, he leaned back against the pew.

"There can never be anyone else but you," he admitted, looking speculative. "I was attracted to you, when we met several years ago. You were married then and I didn't mess with married women. But when I saw you again, I knew in my heart there was something special about you."

"I have to confess that you caused a stir for me too."

"But you never wavered in your convictions," he replied seriously. "I was so wrong to expect you to compromise your values. I really do need you to forgive me."

She smiled tenderly, dropping her head back to gaze up at him. "Of course I do, you were in darkness then. But," she paused, "I admit that I liked matching wits with you."

He chuckled, bringing her close again. "I haven't been on one single date since I left. You consumed my thoughts day and night."

"Blarney, all blarney. What about your little black book?" she teased.

Soberly, he continued his confession. "I've dated a lot of women and I'm not proud of my past, sweetheart. And I have never told any other woman that I loved them. It was as though I was waiting for the right woman." He beamed down at her. "And here you are. Now I know that it was God's timing, not mine. And, what better place to tell you that I love you, than right here in church before God?"

A sound at the door had them turning to find Pastor Rick walking up the aisle, his smile a benediction on them. "Did I stay away long enough?" He cleared his throat. "I assume that kiss meant something?"

Robin turned back to Bryce, a question in her eyes.

He smiled. "I asked him to give me a few minutes alone with you."

"So," her eyes darted between the men, "you've been talking to each other?"

"Quite a bit, in fact," Bryce admitted. He'd tell her some day of the long evening sessions he'd had with Pastor Rick via email and phone, why some evenings he hadn't called her because he was praying with Pastor Rick long distance. He stood and shook hands with the pastor. "Thank you, Rick. I believe we'll be on our way. We have lots to talk about." He pulled Robin up beside him.

Pastor Rick took Robin's hand, a gentle smile on his lips. "I hope your talk goes well. This is a fine young man here." He pressed her hand and winked.

She darted a look at Bryce but his expression was unreadable.

Taking their leave of the pastor, they walked out the door and down the steps.

"What did you do with your car? Do you still have it?" Robin asked as their footsteps crunched across the gravel.

He opened the door and helped her in. "No, I sold it. It's too small for a family car." He slammed the door and went around to slide in behind the wheel. At her perplexed expression, he leaned towards her and looked deep into her eyes. "When we go somewhere as a family, there has to be room for all of us." He paused, then added, "I want to marry you, Robin, have no doubt about that." He started the van.

"Wait just a minute, bub!" Robin gathered her wits and reached out to clutch his hand on the gearshift. "If that was a marriage proposal, it leaves a lot to be desired!"

He looked startled, then laughed, his eyes twinkling. "Oh, my little crackerjack!" The engine idled as he leaned over and pressed a hard kiss on her lips, then drew back to contemplate her seriously. "I do want to marry you, but," he held up his hand to stop anything she might have said, "we're going to start over. I'm going to date you the way Christian couples should date."

"But...but you live in St. Louis, how are we going to manage that?" she sputtered.

"I don't live in St. Louis anymore." Her eyes widened in surprise, her lips parting. "I moved to Rapid City last week. The manager in our branch office there has wanted to retire for the past year so I put in for a transfer and as of Monday, I'm the new manager."

Her eyes softened. "You did that for me? Moved your whole life?"

"Yes," he stated simply and gently took her hand from the gearshift.

Warmth spread through her and she raised her hand to touch the side of his face. "That means the world to me, Bryce. If you're here, that means we *can* date."

"Umhumm," he murmured, eating her up with his eyes.

"Bryce. What about the boys? You know I come as a package deal."

He grinned. "I love those two little guys. It's funny, I never thought much about having children until I met Jason and Jeremy. But then," he smiled wickedly, "I never thought I wanted a wife either, but it looks like I got three for one!"

She gazed at him, loving shining out of her eyes as a slow smile spread over her face. "I should be offended that I sound like a Saturday Special."

"Oh, you're special alright!" He suddenly leaned back. "We can find someplace better to be romantic," he muttered in frustration. "Dorine packed a picnic lunch for us," he jerked his thumb over the backseat.

She turned to see a cooler and hamper on the back floor. "So you had this all planned." Her eyes narrowed. "That's why your calls have sounded so mysterious lately."

"Didn't want to let the cat out of the bag," he agreed. "Buckle up and let's go," he shifted the van into gear.

They drove out in the country, while Robin silently contemplated this turn of events. Bryce told her about his new apartment and the on-the-job training in Rapid City. He eventually pulled off the road into a grove of trees where a thoughtful rancher had placed a picnic table. Bryce carried the food and Robin spread the picnic table with the cloth that she found tucked into the hamper. Dorine had thought of everything, it seemed. But Robin wasn't hungry for food, she was hungry to hear more about Bryce's plans, and she said as much, adding that she wasn't that hungry.

A rich, blue autumn sky stretched from horizon to horizon like a giant bowl above them, and only a slight breath of wind passed by instead of the strong Dakota breezes that usually bent the trees. Birds flitted through the warm fall air, and a pleasant drone of insects provided harmony for background music. It was a perfect Indian summer day.

Bryce took a container of fried chicken legs out of the hamper, another container of potato salad and one of baked beans. He hummed as he went about his task. Robin found a small jar of Dorine's homemade pickles, an opened can of drained olives, plastic cups and cans of soda nestled alongside napkins folded next to a mouth-watering chocolate cake frosted in thick chocolate icing. Bryce set out the plastic forks and sat down across from her. He gave her a slow smile, then reached across the table to take her hands. "Let's ask a blessing."

She closed her eyes and listened to his earnest, prayerful voice. Then he picked up a fork. "Whoever eats the fastest gets the mostest."

She gave him a half-hearted smile and it melted his resolve to keep her guessing about his intentions. He laid down his fork and cleared his throat. Robin gazed expectantly at him. "I don't really feel like eating now either," he began. "You don't know how much this means, to have you here alone with me at last." He slipped his hand over hers on the table and gave her a tender smile. "I never thought it would happen, considering how I've acted over the summer." He hesitated. Robin wisely kept silent, sensing he was gathering his courage. "I need to tell you some things before we go any farther in our relationship. I haven't led a very chaste life, Robin, and I am sorrier than I can ever say." His voice caught and he swallowed before continuing. "But I can't change it. I've asked forgiveness from some of the women I dated, the ones I could find, and those whom I've defrauded in sexual ways. Jesus has forgiven my sins, but...can you?" His eyes were filled with sorrow and hope as he raised them, pleading silently with her.

He sounded like Little Boy Lost and her heart expanded with love for this man who was so willing to open his soul to her. "In the Book of Malachi in the Bible, God says He throws our sins into the deepest sea and puts out a 'No Fishing' sign."

"Does that mean you forgive me?"

"It means I don't have a fishing pole," she nodded. "Besides,

Jesus meets us where we are, right at this point in our lives. God has forgiven you and...so do I."

"I've never cared about anyone's feelings but my own, until now. Knowing Christ has changed that. You *are* special, and I want to put you first after God. Do you think you can consider a future with me? I mean...considering you loved someone else first?"

Her gaze left his to study the rolling prairie beyond their sheltered table. "I loved Randy and our marriage was good," she replied earnestly, returning her gaze to him. "But he's gone and...I had started to let go of him even before you came into my life. There will always be a part of my heart that treasures what we had. Just like you can't redo your past, neither can I. Randy was a part of it, and I thought life was over for me when he died. But then...you came along and showed me that my emotions didn't die with him. However," she hesitated and glanced away, then up at him again. "I'll always want the boys to remember him. Will that be too difficult for you?"

"No." He answered quickly. "He's their father and will always be their father. Without him, they wouldn't be here. I'm grateful to him and I would never take away their memories of him. I will always honor him for their sakes. They had a father but they need a Dad now, and I want to be that Dad."

Her eyes filled with tears. "I think they already love you that way."

"What are we doing with the table between us?" he asked wryly. Standing, he stepped around the end and straddled the bench, taking her in his arms.

Her heart began a rapid pitterpat and her chest felt heavy as she watched his face come nearer. Her eyelids fluttered shut as his mouth settled on hers in a gentle, tender kiss. She kissed him back with such ardor that he groaned and gathered her closer.

In a moment, he groaned again and loosened his hold on her. "I love you, so much, Robin," he breathed against her lips.

"I love you too, Bryce," she murmured, her eyes still closed, a rapt expression on her face.

He gazed down at her and chuckled. Her eyes popped open and she gave him a quizzical look. "You are so adorable, I could just eat you up." At that moment, her stomach loudly growled and they both erupted in laughter. "And on that note, I better feed you."

Which he did. He picked meat off the chicken bone and fed it to her, while she dutifully opened her mouth like a bird. In between bites, they sweetened the food with kisses. He helped himself to chicken and potato salad, continuing to feed Robin little bites.

The sun was still overhead when they finished. They packed away the food, then Bryce spread a blanket under a tree for Robin to sit on. He dropped down beside her, taking her hand and gazing at her. "I could look at you all day."

She leaned forward and gave him a gentle kiss, then turned serious. "We have to talk about our future, Bryce. How this will affect the boys, my business, everything." She searched his eyes. "I know it isn't easy for a man to accept another man's children, and you've said you already love Jason and Jeremy, but are you really ready to be a father to them?"

He pondered her question. "I don't know a whole lot about raising kids, especially since I didn't have any brothers and sisters. I guess I'll have to rely on your guidance at first."

"What I mean, Bryce, is this—are you going to be able to hang in there for the long haul? Kids aren't just something you play with, then set them on the shelf and go off to do your own thing. They need a lot of attention. And discipline. Are you willing to invest yourself in their lives?" He listened patiently as she outlined the future that he would be embracing. "Will you be able to practice tough love? Especially when they're teenagers?"

He shifted. "I'm going to be the best goshdarn dad I can be," he promised. Robin arched her brow at his language.

"Scratch the goshdarn," he grinned at her, drawing her close again.

She snuggled into his embrace, leaning against his chest, loving the sound of his rapidly-beating heart. "I know you'll learn, just like I've had to do. Kids don't come with an instruction manual, you know. It's a lot of trial and error."

He frowned. "I thought they were born with instructions tattooed on their tush," then, not able to keep a straight face, he laughed at her comical look. She snuggled closer, feeling that she couldn't ever get enough of this wonderful man.

He took a deep breath and looked down at her. "I'm trying to keep my mind above board here, honey, but if you keep that up, I don't know how much longer I can behave."

She blushed prettily as she hastily moved back. "I'm sorry…it's just that I love you so much and missed you like crazy!"

He smiled knowlingly and linked his hands loosely behind her back. "There's something else I have to do—I need to ask permission from the men in your life, to date you."

"My father?!!"

He roared with laughter. "I'll do that too, but I was thinking of Jason and Jeremy."

Chapter 15

Following their picnic and a long talk about their future, Robin and Bryce settled into a routine as he went about courting her. The boys had responded to Bryce's request to date their mother with unabashed glee, and hugs of joy were passed around in abundance. Bryce lived in Rapid City during the week, coming to Silverdale on weekends where he stayed overnight at the DeFoe Ranch. It was a big change in all their lives and they grew to know each other's personalities, likes, and dislikes, which sometimes sparked animated discussions. But right from the start, they were a team, and when Bryce hesitantly made his first decision as a fledgling father, Robin backed him up.

One weekday afternoon, Robin left the café in Marietta's care, and slipped away to the cemetery by herself. Standing by Randy's grave on the sloping hillside above town, she told him about Bryce, knowing he wasn't there but it helped to focus her thoughts as she gazed at his headstone. Tears flowed freely as she knelt in the grass, the sun hot on her head. Placing her fingertips over Randy's engraved name, she bade a tearful goodbye to her teenage love. She stood, wiped her cheeks and with a lighter heart, made the return trip down the hill.

When Robin learned that Bryce was the silent partner in his friend Mark's restaurant business, she forgave his omission and was thankful that he *was* so at home in the kitchen. She treasured the Saturdays when he worked alongside her at the café. He learned the recipes for many German foods and became an expert candymaker. But not without many an energetic sparring as their ideas clashed and they learned how to compromise, followed up with kisses that curled Robin's toes.

Sundays, Bryce came to escort her and the boys to church, then planned fun excursions for the afternoons. She refused his offer to buy her a car, saying she could wait until after marriage to accept his gifts. It was an exercise in self-control for Bryce, who was learning the give and take of a committed relationship, instead of imposing his will on others.

But the biggest change was the spiritual one. Bryce devoted himself to the study of God's word with the same enthusiasm he applied to his investigative skills—gone were the flirty side-glances at other women, the double entendres that formerly dominated his language. He had solemnly declared that he would be getting married only once, and he intended to do it right—God's way.

They both had a lot of adjusting to do, but were pleasantly surprised to discover they had many things in common in their tastes for movies, books and music. Bryce sealed his commitment to Robin by reading books on marriage, and shared his thoughts in a way that she and Randy had taken for granted. She was deeply touched by Bryce's eagerness to be a spiritual husband while at the same time to be a role model for the boys.

One of their first business decisions was for Bryce to buy into the Sweet Schoppe, thus infusing it with much-needed capital. Robin demurely stated that she doubted many business agreements were sealed with all those kisses, making Bryce shout with laughter. Espresso was now available at the Sweet Schoppe, and townspeople quickly embraced her new venture.

Two of the biggest decisions involved marketing her *kucken*, and leasing the two-story brick building next door, with the intent of enlarging the café. Bryce had a head for finances and had made good investments, assuring a comfortable future. He wanted Robin to be in no doubt that he would provide for her no matter what was ahead.

One evening after Bryce had gone, Robin checked on the boys before going to her bedroom. She crossed to the dresser to pull out her pajamas, her eyes coming to rest on her wedding picture.

Randy still smiled up at her, his features so much younger than even a few months ago. She studied the photograph tenderly, then picked it up and slid it into the drawer.

Weeks turned into months but the time seemed to fly for Robin. The boys were doing well in school, and she hosted pizza parties at the café after home football games. Having had almost no vacations to speak of, she consented to a week away when Bryce took her to St. Louis to meet his mother and step-dad. With Marietta's help running the espresso, Dean's mother and the DeFoe's housekeeper, Mrs. Mac, took over the Sweet Schoppe for the week, and later had hilarious stories to tell about their adventure.

Dorine and Dean accompanied Robin and Bryce, going sightseeing while Robin nervously accompanied Bryce to the sedate mansion in an exclusive part of the city. Her heart sorrowed for the cold reception he got, and while the Armstrongs were polite, they clearly could have cared less about knowing their future daughter in law. How could such a warm, caring man have such a standoffish mother?

Later, Bryce shrugged and assured her that he couldn't remember his mother being any other way. Robin suggested that it could have been his father's death that made his mother close off her affections, even to her own son. Bryce conceded Robin could be right but his mind was obviously relieved the "duty call" was over.

"We'll pray for them to have their eyes and hearts opened, but the Lord has to do the work in their hearts," he told her. Her heart swelled with pride at how far he had come.

On Christmas Day, Bryce officially proposed to Robin in front of her parents and sisters' families who had come for the holidays. Amid much hooting and encouragement, Robin teased him by adopting a thoughtful attitude as she tilted her head and looked up at the ceiling before singing out a resounding "Yes!"

The one thing she'd always remember about that day, was Jeremy whispering to her, "I've got two daddies now. One in heaven and one here!" Neither he nor Jason could understand why their new "daddy" couldn't live with them yet, even when Robin explained.

"But you like each other real well, you're always kissing, I don't see any difference," Jason grumbled. She laughed and explained that God wanted them to make promises in church in front of God before she and Bryce could live together, and the boys had to be satisfied, if not happy, about that arrangement.

The brick building next door gradually underwent a transformation—remodeling that included enlarging Robin's house. A second story was added, and her new office space over the restaurant fronted the street where she had a bird's eye view of the whole town. She enjoyed the spacious family room that now ran the width across the back of both buildings, with ceiling to floor windows and solar heating.

In January, they opened the "Schnitzlehaus" for Friday and Saturday night dinners. Surprisingly, in spite of snowy weather, they were booked solid for the rest of the month. Word had spread about the German cuisine, and many folks, having already sampled Robin's *kucken*, wanted to have an authentic German meal. Bryce even went so far as to dress in Alpine costume with walking shorts and a jaunty green hat sporting a long feather. Robin fell more and more in love with him, and was warmed through by his seriousness in taking the lead as the future spiritual head of his new family.

To that end, Bryce had been training an assistant manager to take over at the insurance office in Rapid City on days when Bryce stayed in Silverdale. He planned to spend no more than two days a week at the office, and in time, hoped to ease out of that altogether, becoming a consultant and private investigator. That, along with his share in Mark's restaurants, would ensure a comfortable living for his family. He was thankful that even with all his riotous living, he'd still had the foresight to plan ahead. Part of those plans now included adopting Jason and Jeremy, paperwork already in the hands of an attorney.

In late spring, Bryce and Robin repeated their wedding vows in the community church in front of the congregation and their families who had traveled to Silverdale for the joyous event. Dorine and Dean were their only attendants, with Robin in a long flowing pale green gown that floated in organdy wisps around her legs as she walked beside her father down the aisle. She carried a simple nosegay of spring flowers and wore a wreath of the same flowers in her hair.

Bryce was more nervous that he could ever remember, and couldn't keep his eyes off his bride as she came toward him, her love for him shining out of her beautiful hazel eyes. He swallowed and clenched his hands. Jason and Jeremy looked cuter than h—heck as they stood beside him watching their mother take her place. All Bryce wanted was for the ceremony to be over so he could whisk Robin away on a Caribbean honeymoon to be alone with her. She had learned that the Sweet Schoppe could get along without her for a short while, and even her boys did too—all she had to do was let Bryce share the load.

After the couple said their vows and exchanged rings, Jason and Jeremy sidled in between Robin and Bryce to face the minister.

Pastor Rick grinned down at them. "Boys, do you take Bryce to be your daddy? To honor him and obey him as your father for all your days? If so, answer 'I do.'"

"We do!" they both shouted at once.

"Not so loud," Robin admonished softly, an indulgent smile on her lips. She glanced nervously out at the onlookers where there was a smattering of twitters and whispers.

Pastor Rick turned to Bryce. "And do you, Bryce Martin, take Jason and Jeremy to be your sons? To respect them, to teach them, to love them and to be their spiritual father?"

Bryce kneeled down and said with conviction. "You bet I do!" Both boys lunged for him, wrapping their arms around his neck. Robin's eyes grew misty and Pastor Rick cleared his throat while Bryce disentangled himself from his new sons and stood up.

"Then, according to the statutes and laws of the state of South Dakota, I pronounce you husband and wife, and parents of this fine family. You may kiss the bride," he said, turning to Bryce.

"Yes! Yes!" the boys chorused, jumping up and down. Robin and Bryce both blushed but leaned towards each other over the boys' heads, brushing their lips together with promises for more later.

As they turned towards their future, Bryce took his new wife's arm and grinned down at his instant sons. "Lead the way, my Dakota boys!"

And to Robin's everlasting embarrassment, the "Dakota boys" whooped and laughed as they boisterously rushed down the aisle.